MW00876554

SEDUCING
CHARLOTTE

AN ACCIDENTAL PEERS NOVEL

Other books by Diana Quincy

SEDUCING CHARLOTTE

AN ACCIDENTAL PEERS NOVEL

DIANA QUINCY

Entangled Publishing, LLC
2614 South Timberline Road
Suite 109
Fort Collins, CO 80525
Visit our website at www.entangledpublishing.com.

Edited by Alethea Spiridon Hopson
Cover design by Libby Murphy

Ebook ISBN 978-1-62266-103-9

Print ISBN 978-1493708208

Manufactured in the United States of America

First Edition April 2013

This book is dedicated to my father, Hasan A. Hasan,
with love and gratitude.

.

Chapter One

Sweet angels in heaven. Where ever did she learn to do that?

The Marquess of Camryn lost his line of thought as Maria Fitzharding's expert ministrations began to have an impact on him. One hand resting atop her head, he fell back against the tree, oblivious to the evening chill, and looked down at the woman kneeling before him. The full moon cast a blue glow over her form, treating Cam to glimpses of an impressive décolletage. He'd met Maria a time or two at one of the few social affairs he'd attended this Season. The lady had been the one to seek him out this evening and now, well, he discovered she had her charms.

Turning his head to the side, he glanced up at the baroque manor glittering in the velvet darkness, its imposing stone belvederes standing rooftop sentry against the night sky. Muted sounds of music and laughter wafted into the boundless gardens where the pungent aroma of cultivated blooms engulfed them. Fruity fragrances and darker, somber aromas intermingled with the sweet and sharp.

His body tensed as pleasurable sensations shot up the back of his legs. Closing his eyes, he tilted his head back against the rough bark, shuddering when physical release came to him.

"I suppose we shouldn't dawdle, my dear," he said sometime afterward, offering a hand to help her up. "Someone is bound to notice our mutual absence."

Coming to her feet, she cast a satisfied look in his direction. "No need to worry on that account," she said. "My husband is no doubt paying court to his mistress this evening."

Husband? A dull pain throbbed at the nape of his neck, threatening a headache. He helped brush leaves from the lady's skirt, her heavy perfume, a mixture of cloves and rosemary, stung his nostrils. "Allow me to escort you back."

"Lud." She laughed, patting her coiffed golden curls into place. "Let's not make more of this than it is. I shall return first so we are not seen together." Maria turned to go. "Oh, and Camryn?"

"Yes?"

Her eyes glimmered in the darkness. "I look forward to our next meeting."

Cam bowed, his polite smile fixed, knowing he would not pursue a liaison with a married woman. "You honor me with your attentions." As she faded into the shadows, he finished fastening his breeches, still somehow unsatisfied.

Hollowness stretched inside his chest. The physical exhilaration of sexual release had never seemed so fleeting. The empty sensation reminded him of why he hadn't been with a woman in months. He pressed the palms of his hands against his eyes to counter the pounding in his head. Such associations had once been vastly entertaining.

The sound of a tiny hiccup punctured the air. Stilling, he cocked his head. It happened again, only this time it was the muffled squeak of someone trying to contain a sneeze. Someone in close proximity.

His skin prickled. "Who's there?" The words, low and unfriendly, were met with silence, except for the strains of music and conversation floating through the darkness from the main house.

"Ah choo!" There it came again, this time louder and unrestrained. "Ah, choo! *Ah choo!*" Distinctly feminine sneezes. A guest? The brisk evening air kept most people from strolling this deep into the garden. And no innocent maiden would venture this far alone. Perhaps it was a servant out for a liaison of her own.

Cam released the breath he'd been holding. "Come now, you've already been detected." He eased his tone, injecting his usual amiability into it. "You may as well show yourself."

The bushes rustled, followed by sounds of swishing skirts and skittish footsteps bounding away. Shrugging, he turned to stride onto the path toward the manor, ignoring the delicate blooms he trampled underfoot until their heady perfume enveloped him, chastising him for his indifference. He rubbed his throbbing temples and thought again of the mystery girl somewhere out there in the dark. Whoever the chit was, he regretted she'd witnessed such a show.

Muffled sounds drew his attention once he neared the manor. He strained to see two people struggling by the white marble fountain just below the terrace. A tall, lanky man in uniform clutched a much smaller, slender female form in plain servants' clothing.

"No, please, sir," she pleaded in a wobbly voice.

A gruff laugh followed. "You've got lovely bubbies, my dear. I'll wager no one else has had a look at them yet." The man wrestled with the girl's arms, causing the gold spangles and tassels on his uniform to dance in the glimmering torchlight.

Cam blinked hard and focused; his flesh crawled when he recognized the military officer in the crimson coat. He'd never had much use for Titus Boyle, one of the Earl of Townsend's many sons. They'd been together at Eton, but Cam hadn't seen the man since he'd joined the fight on the continent. From the looks of things, Boyle hadn't changed much.

The girl fought to free herself, but Boyle wrenched her against him, his free hand yanking up her skirts to expose slender, waiflike limbs. "Let's see what delights you have hidden under here."

Cam stepped out of the shadows. "Boyle."

The man jerked in Cam's direction. Disheveled, dark curls fell onto a flushed face drawn with refined features. He dropped the girl's skirt, his wary, bloodshot eyes homing in on Cam. "Arthur Stanhope? Is that you?"

"In the flesh."

"I say, you shouldn't sneak up on a gentleman like that." His voice grew louder. "I hear you've come into your title."

"Yes, I'm Camryn now."

"Some culls have all the luck." The words had a bitter edge. "Bloody fortunate thing for you that your uncle could only spawn wenches."

Cam recalled hearing rumors of Boyle's preference for

innocents. "Allow the girl to return to her post."

Boyle yanked the girl hard against him. She shrieked and jerked. The despair in her eyes reminded Cam of an animal caught in a trap, one who knew the fight was futile.

"No, please!" She appeared no older than fourteen, perhaps younger.

"Mind your own affairs, Camryn. This fresh one is mine." Scorn twisted Boyle's smile. "You're welcome to the chit once I'm done tupping her."

He wanted to shove that smirk down Boyle's throat. "I strongly suggest you release her."

"Bugger off. This is none of your concern." Boyle rubbed the girl's bottom. She squeezed her eyes shut, her chest heaving. "This one should count herself lucky one of her betters is willing to give her a tumble."

"The chit is young and appears unwilling." The pain drumming inside his head sharpened. "You will let her go."

"Or what?"

Boyle's sneer snapped what little was left of Cam's patience. He smashed his fist into the man's face, his knuckles screaming in protest when they made contact with Boyle's nose. The man teetered for a moment, his arms swinging about in a futile effort to keep his balance. His eyes rolled back in his head, and he crashed to the floor with a heavy *thud*.

Cam shook his head. Boyle must be foxed out of his mind to go down cold after one chop. Cradling his throbbing fist, he turned to the girl. "Are you injured?"

She shook her head, her gaze fixed on the heap of man lying inert on the floor.

Cam suppressed the urge to give the scum at his feet one

last swift kick. Instead, he gentled his voice. "Go on then. And don't wander alone when your master is entertaining."

With a shaky smile, the girl curtsied before scurrying away. Cam watched her for a moment before trotting up the terrace stairs and slipping inside through an arched door.

"There you are, Cam." His cousin Willa, Duchess of Hartwell, narrowed in on him the moment he reentered the ballroom. No small feat given the crush of dancing and chattering guests in the immense columned chamber. "Where have you been? What use is it to have London's most eligible bachelor in attendance if he will not take to the dance floor?"

"My apologies." Trying to ignore his smarting knuckles, Cam bowed over her hand. "I promise to locate the nearest wallflower and take her for a turn."

Her husband, the duke, lifted a dark eyebrow. "I suppose we should feel honored by your attendance," said Gray Preston. "You've been conspicuously absent from social gatherings of late."

Cam took a glass of champagne from a passing footman. "There are several matters involving the Luddites in the Lords that require my attention."

"Is there someone on the terrace who requires your undivided attention as well?" Hart asked with a sardonic twist of his lips.

"One Titus Boyle." Cam sipped champagne to wash the sour taste out of his mouth. "He might require assistance to reach his coach."

"Boyle?" Hart grimaced. "I won't even ask what that jackanapes did this time to draw your ire." Turning to a nearby footman who stood at the ready, he murmured a few quiet instructions.

Willa's mind seemed to be on other matters. "You look fatigued, Cam. You mustn't work so much."

"I was loath to leave work for several days in the country. But as I'm never able to deny you, here I am."

"Imagine all of the hearts that would break if you neglected to attend," she teased. Marriage to the duke agreed with Wilhelmina. With her chestnut curls and alabaster skin, she had an innate grace befitting a duchess.

Sipping his drink, Cam surveyed the crowded ballroom. The orchestra played on a balcony mezzanine which overlooked the crush of dancers below. Clinking glasses and the loud murmuring of dozens of conversations filled the air which, despite the open terrace doors, grew warm and humid.

"What you require is a wife," his cousin said. "I shall make it my mission this season to find one."

"Count on trouble now, my friend," the duke said, dismissing the footman and returning his attention to them. "My duchess is unshakable once she sets her mind to something."

"Willa is determined to fell me with the same marital bliss from which you are unable to recover."

"Quite right." The harsh angles of the duke's face softened into a contented smile. "There is no hope of a cure for my affliction."

Willa's ears turned red as they always did when she was embarrassed. Her gaze swept beyond them. "Splendid. Charlotte has arrived. Cam, you must take a turn with her."

"Must I?" He couldn't see why. The humorless bluestocking likely had as little interest in dancing with him as he had in engaging with her. He drained his glass as Miss Livingston approached. The smooth liquid slid down his throat, its warmth radiating into his chest.

She wore a plain, dark-colored frock, which did nothing for her tall, shapeless frame. Their eyes met for a brief moment before both hurriedly looked away, but he caught the way her disdainful little nose wrinkled at the sight of him standing next to the duchess.

Careful to maintain a neutral expression, he said to Willa, "Perhaps Hart would care to dance with her."

The duke chuckled. "I wouldn't dream of denying you the pleasure. Besides, I shall be taking a turn with my lovely duchess." He inclined his head at the approaching lady. "Miss Livingston."

"Your Grace." She curtsied. Willa barely gave the woman time to exchange the usual pleasantries before pulling her aside for an animated conversation. He wondered what his cousin saw in the cold, strident Miss Livingston.

Admittedly, the lady's looks improved a bit upon closer inspection. Some might even consider her handsome in a lackluster sort of way. Tall for a female, she had the bluest eyes he'd ever seen. Definitely her best feature, they were like an island sky, clear and cloudless against her fair skin and firm patrician nose. Her unremarkable brown hair parted down the middle and was pulled into an austere bun at the nape of her neck. His gaze dropped to the modest neckline of her simple gown, which suggested little in the way of curves. She wasn't to his tastes at all, which ran to buxom females with ample hips and an abundance of feminine slopes and valleys.

"You do remember meeting my cousin in town," Willa said to Charlotte, drawing the gentlemen back into the conversation. Cam certainly recalled meeting the baron's daughter once, several months ago at one of Willa's salons, where the lady's ardent diatribe on the importance of public education for the masses had been difficult to forget.

What he recalled most about Miss Livingston was her utter lack of feminine interest in him. Not that it mattered to him, of course. But if there was one thing to which he was unaccustomed, it was being ignored by the opposite sex. He knew he had a certain appeal to women and, except for the strange sexual doldrums he'd experienced of late, had been more than happy to return their attentions.

"My lord." Miss Livingston regarded him with a courteous expression, but Cam detected a flash of discomfort in those soft blue depths.

"Miss Livingston, what a pleasure it is to see you again," he lied, bowing over her hand.

Hartwell took his wife's elbow. "Darling, let's dance, shall we?" He glanced back over his shoulder as he ushered his wife toward the dance floor. "Cam, perhaps Miss Livingston will honor you with a turn as well."

Left on their own, they faced each other in silence for an awkward moment. Then he donned a cool and polite smile since anything more would no doubt be wasted on this particular female. "Miss Livingston, will you do me the honor of standing up with me?"

She pursed her lips. "I suppose there's nothing to be done for it. After all, the duke has practically commanded it."

"Indeed." He suppressed a sigh of irritation. Normally, his dutiful attentions toward wallflowers, spinsters, and bluestockings met with blushing, delighted gratitude.

Proceeding to a spot among the humid, perfumed throng of dancing couples, he placed his hand at the lady's lithe waist and led her into a waltz. At least her height complemented his, and she moved across the floor with graceful ease. Surprising. Her subtle floral scent teased his nostrils, triggering an unexpected urge to lean forward to inhale it more fully. "You are quite an accomplished dancer, Miss Livingston."

Extraordinary azure eyes considered him. "It is hardly gentlemanly of you to appear so thoroughly surprised."

He was though. She didn't seem the type to spend an abundance of time in ballrooms. He assumed she devoted most of her days to her causes. "Not at all," he said with practiced gallantry. "No doubt your dance card is always full to bursting."

Her even forehead rose in obvious amusement. "Hardly. You would not have asked me to dance had His Grace not badgered you into it." Her voice did not match that prim exterior. It was smooth and rich, with just a touch of spice, a resonant sound that satisfied the senses like a fine, warmed liqueur on a lonely winter evening.

"Do you always speak so plainly, Miss Livingston?"

Her answering laugh was that of a woman, ripe and throaty, not the girlish tittering cultivated by most gently bred maidens. "Much to my mother's chagrin. Unfortunately, there are times I simply cannot stop the words from slipping out."

"Imagine that." Plain as she was, upon closer inspection and acquaintance, Miss Livingston exuded an elusive allure, an indescribable something he couldn't quite identify. Perhaps it was the translucent nature of her eyes that made them appear endless. It was almost startling to gaze into those plunging depths.

"Yes, indeed," she said agreeably, inclining her head toward the blank-faced misses floating around them. "I look at the expression on their faces and wonder how they manage it." She cocked her head, as if considering the thought. "Why do they insult themselves by pretending they haven't a brain in their heads? Most women of my acquaintance are quite intelligent."

"I believe they cultivate it quite purposefully." He led her through another smooth turn, which she deftly followed. "A shy and gentle countenance is considered desirable for a young maiden of a certain station."

"Hmm, then I am afraid Mother has the right of it. My cause is lost." Mirth tinged her sparkling eyes. "I'm certain I couldn't master that vacant stare, even if so desired. And holding my tongue might be a challenge."

This time he was the one to laugh. "I'm beginning to see that." She certainly was direct. Perhaps he'd been too rash in judging Miss Livingston's appeal, having never engaged her in conversation before this evening. While her published essays on social reform hit a stentorian note, the lady herself apparently had a sense of humor. And she looked a little less plain floating in his arms, her cheeks flushed, those mesmerizing eyes shimmering with intelligence.

"I doubt you could look empty-headed, Miss Livingston. And even if you managed to pull off such a deception, your rather impressive writings would give you away."

She crooked her lips, drawing his attention to her mouth. Unlike the lean, spare lines of her body, her lips were plump and succulently rounded. A sudden, unexpected urge to taste them assailed him. Startled, he shoved it away.

"As if you have read my essays."

It took him a moment to refocus on their conversation. Ah yes, her essays. "Indeed I have. And I have enjoyed them." Her obvious surprise amused him. They took another lavish twirl. "Even if your point is somewhat misguided."

She stiffened, indignation shining in those brilliant eyes. "I beg your pardon?"

"Your essays on the Luddites are brilliantly written, of course. However, I find the sentiment in them to be rather naive." He smiled to realize he was enjoying the conversation. "You have an unfortunate tendency to romanticize the machine wreckers. There can be no legitimate excuse for behaving in an unlawful manner."

Her nostrils flared. "Machinery is driving down their wages at a time when food prices have never been higher," she said heatedly. "The fires have died in their hearths, and their children are starving. I think you, sir, are the one who is naive."

Her eyes were even lovelier when lit with passion. Desire warmed his groin. Devil take it. What was the matter with him? "The life of the operative class has never been ideal," he responded, trying to ignore his twitching prick. "Machinery could ultimately be advantageous for everyone, including our working people."

She wrinkled her nose. "It is certainly so for the factory owners who achieve higher profits by decreasing wages and reducing the number of hours worked."

She was no empty-headed chit. Refreshing. The throbbing in his head began to ease. Eager to engage Miss Livingston in an animated debate on the subject, Cam began to respond, but the swelling music cut him short. The movement reached a crescendo making it difficult to converse at all.

. . .

As she danced with the Marquess of Camryn, Charlotte became acutely aware of the envious gazes burning into her back by the marriage-minded maidens in attendance. They needn't worry. Camryn only danced with her out of courtesy, which suited her perfectly. She much preferred the forward thinkers in her circles, intellectuals who concerned themselves with pressing social problems. Even if they weren't particularly exciting.

Unlike the Marquess of Camryn. With his gilded looks and lithely muscled form, he exuded a blatant physicality that made a girl's insides quiver. Even when she should know better.

"Well, Miss Livingston," he said when the music softened, the candlelight shimmering through the rumpled waves of his amber hair. "Clearly I have been negligent in not asking for a spot on your dance card. You must promise me a waltz each time we meet."

She smiled with genuine amusement. "Are you taking pity on a wallflower, my lord?"

"Hardly." Camryn regarded her through lowered lashes, drawing her attention to the tiny specks of gold glittering in his sea-green eyes. They were laughing eyes, which crinkled at the corners even when he wasn't smiling, giving the impression of perpetual amusement. "Surely you are aware that you are the last woman deserving of pity." He spoke softly as if his own words surprised him. "Rather, it is the gentleman who falls under your spell who deserves sympathy."

"Oh?" To her annoyance, her heart fluttered. "Do tell, why is that?"

"I sense there are very few men who would be a match for you." He answered in measured tones, as though the thought had just occurred to him. "Most would be helpless to resist your charms."

This time, her heart didn't merely flutter; it thumped so hard she feared he'd notice it knocking beneath her gown. "I'm afraid I've never been accused of possessing charms before."

"That's just it. They are well hidden, but those fortunate enough to glimpse them would be utterly defeated long before they comprehended what was occurring."

Irritated at herself for allowing him to fluster her, she forced a stilted laugh. "You have a very talented tongue, my lord."

"I do give it my best effort," he answered in a velvety tone.

Heat flooded her body. It didn't seem like they were talking about the same thing anymore. Lord, it was better when he ignored her. The way Camryn regarded her now prompted a curious warmth to ooze through her.

"Goodness, it's close in here," she said, eager to be away from him. The man emanated an energy that made her nervous, which was absolutely ridiculous. She, of all people, knew what a rakehell he could be. Lawks, the images were branded on her brain.

Camryn's bronze face creased into a frown. "Are you

unwell? You do appear flushed." He waltzed her toward the open terrace doors, coming to a stop in front of them. Releasing her, he offered his arm. "Perhaps some fresh air will do you good."

Drat. Charlotte could think of no graceful way to disoblige him. Resigned, she took his arm, strolling across the terrace where other guests also mingled, their light chatter filling the night. She sucked the brisk air deep into her lungs, its cool sharpness filled her chest, contrasting with the warm, muscled arm beneath her hand.

He examined her face. "Better?"

No. "Yes, thank you. I am well. Truly." She smoothed her free hand over front bodice of her dress. "I am not much for large routs. To be truthful, I avoid them whenever possible."

He nodded in agreement. "As do I."

"I came for Willa as she is my dearest friend. Is that the reason you are in attendance?"

"In part. I also have business to attend to."

"Business? Cheshire is a long way from Town."

"Not the lords. I have a factory near here."

The brisk air turned icy sharp in her lungs. Halting, she pulled her hand from his arm. "A factory?"

He placed a hand against his chest. "Surely, you don't hold to the Ton notion that engaging in enterprise is beneath a gentleman?"

Tension strained the muscles across the back of her shoulders. "What kind of factory?"

"I have a textile mill."

"I should have known." Her chest burned at the realization the Marquess of Camryn was far worse than a mere rakehell. "You are an industrialist."

"You take offense because I dabble in enterprise?"

"Dabble?" Her voice rose. "Your so-called dabbling leaves textile artisans with no way to provide for their families."

"Mechanized looms are the way of the future, as we've just discussed." He spoke in a calm, almost offhand, manner, as if wrecking people's lives came as naturally to him as strolling on the terrace. "Perhaps you'd care to visit one of my factories to investigate for yourself."

"I know all about how workers are treated in those places, my lord." It wasn't as though she hadn't visited factories before. She'd seen people working in filthy, overheated buildings with no ventilation. Dust choked the air, and floating fibers crept into the workers' lungs, stealing their breath. The child laborers often fell ill from moving between the sweltering heat of the workroom and the cold, damp outdoor air. Many of the youngest gasped and wheezed, their lungs inflamed. He dropped his proffered arm. "You know nothing of *my* factories."

Factories. As in, more than one. "I fully comprehend starving weavers are cheated out of their livelihoods by your mechanized looms. All so men like you can fatten their already considerable purses." Charlotte's entire body quivered. "And the deplorable working conditions in factories such as yours are well known." She strode away, unable to bear being in the presence of a man responsible for devastating so many lives. She realized they'd walked well beyond the other guests and were quite alone on the section of terrace that hugged the side of the manor.

Long, implacable fingers closed around her upper arm, a vise impeding her departure. "How dare you presume to touch me." She spun around, indignation swelling in her chest. "Unhand me this instant."

Camryn leaned closer, until his flushed face was inches from hers. "What gives you leave to make ignorant assumptions about my character?" Although the words were low and contained, they simmered with power and aggression.

"I make no presumptions about the quality of your character. Your actions speak for themselves."

"Do they now?" His musky, masculine scent blanketed her, making Charlotte aware of just how close he stood. She could smell the flinty, fruity aroma of champagne on his breath. Waves of tension vibrated off his body, rolling over onto hers. Something shifted in her belly.

Camryn's consuming gaze held her captive, as surely as if her feet were rooted into the stone terrace. The air around them crackled, charged with something more than anger. Charlotte inhaled and tried to fill her lungs. Just before Camryn's lips came crashing down on hers.

Chapter Two

Charlotte's first instinct was to shove him away. Only her thoughts scattered like birds responding to the crack of a gunshot the instant Camryn's mouth touched hers.

Hard and pressing at first, his lips demanded a response. Then she felt his sharp intake of breath, and his mouth gentled. Lips that were both firm and soft slid against hers, taking thoughtful, entrancing nips. He even tasted good, a mix of crisply sweet champagne and something uniquely, ardently male. If passion had a taste, this must be it.

She glowed with delicious heat, from her heart to her stomach, and to other places she usually didn't give much thought to.

He gave a throaty murmur, as though he'd sampled something delectable. Strong, sure hands slipped around her waist, drawing her closer. His tongue, wet and warm, flickered against the seam of her lips. The movement shocked her back to her sensible self, and she pulled away, her heart clamoring so hard she thought it might burst out of her chest.

Camryn's face was flushed. His eyes lit with surprise and something much more elemental, almost savage. He stepped closer.

She drew back. "Don't," she whispered shakily. "I wonder, my lord, have you no shame?"

To her horror, she realized she was in danger of swooning. She turned away, hoping he wouldn't notice, praying her tottering limbs wouldn't fail her before she stumbled back to the safety of the ballroom.

• • •

When Miss Livingston pulled away from his kiss, the astonishment and haze of desire in her endless eyes sent unfettered lust rocketing straight to Cam's prick. Her high, angled cheeks were flushed with the rush of passion, her plush lips pink and swollen. She'd looked considerably less plain. In fact, she'd looked almost…appealing.

Struggling to calm his raging body, he locked his gaze on her long, lithe form as she made her retreat. He paid scant attention to the single leaf that broke free of her indignantly swishing skirts and fluttered quietly away.

• • •

That evening he slept fitfully, jolting awake just after dawn in an agitated state. After throwing on some clothes, he headed for the stables, anxious for a solitary ride before the rest of the guests stirred. Restless clouds loomed overhead, casting a gray pall over the rolling landscape. As he stalked through the grass, the morning dew left damp speckles on his worn leather riding boots.

He barely noted his surroundings, for his thoughts were full of last evening and the source of his discomposure. He hadn't meant to kiss Miss Livingston. Charlotte. And he wasn't quite sure why he had. One minute he'd been furious at her presumption to judge him. She had no business casting aspersions on his factories and the treatment of his workers, which she knew nothing about. The next thing he knew, his lips were consuming hers, devouring the nectar he found there, as if he couldn't get enough.

Cam plowed both hands through his hair. His reaction perplexed him. With her slender form and serious nature, Charlotte wasn't the type of female who normally attracted him. She couldn't be more different from the voluptuous, flamboyant females with whom he usually consorted. And, yet, kissing her, holding her willowy softness in his arms, had set his blood rushing and his heart pumping as though he'd run the race of his life.

All in all, it had been anything but mundane.

The realization that he'd taken liberties with a gently bred lady, an innocent, also plagued him. It was a line he'd never crossed before. Perhaps he'd overstepped because Charlotte didn't seem innocent. She wasn't young and foolish like most coquettes on the marriage mart.

His unfathomable attraction to her might also stem from the challenge she presented. Up until last night, she'd barely acknowledged his existence. Then again, maybe he just itched to wipe the look of disdain off her face. Or silence the insults that flew out of her mouth. Whatever his motivation, an apology was owed and he intended to deliver it.

As he approached the stables, an appealing sprinkling of female laughter cut into his thoughts. She appeared, and his chest felt lighter. Partially visible inside the stable door, Charlotte conversed with someone Cam couldn't see from his vantage point. Leaning forward, she laughed openly, with warmth and affection, her incomparable blue eyes glittering while she replied to something her companion said. The movement took her out of his line of sight until she pulled back again with an unguarded expression on her face. She reached out to touch her companion's arm with shocking intimacy. Irritation stabbed Cam's gut.

"Good day, Miss Livingston," he called out. "I see I am not the only early riser at Fairview Manor this week." She looked in his direction and her eyes widened once she registered his presence.

When she took a smooth step away from whoever she'd been talking to, Cam quickened his step, eager to see whose company she so enjoyed. Rounding the door to the cavernous stable, he saw no one at first, except for a groom walking away. Cam glanced around. Surely she wouldn't allow such familiarity with a stable boy. He looked back at Charlotte and any questions or gentlemanly intentions he might have had flew right out of his head.

She wasn't wearing a riding costume. No, she'd clad herself in riding breeches just like any buck. His cousin, Addie, a first-rate hoyden of whom he was very fond, had been known to do so on occasion, but never in front of polite company. And certainly never to this effect.

The way the fawn-colored fabric caressed Charlotte's subtle curves looked anything but masculine. Cam's eyes widened while another part of his anatomy stirred with interest.

"What a surprise to find you up so early, my lord."

"Are you going riding, Miss Livingston?"

She stretched her arms out at her sides as though showing off her clothing. "It would seem so, yes."

The movement drew Cam's eyes to her breeches again and the entrancing way the clinging material swept over the delicate turn of her hips, down a length of leg that seemed to go on and on. "If that is an example of your usual riding attire, I can see why poor Mrs. Livingston is often scandalized."

She glanced down at her breeches, her eyes widening as though she'd quite forgotten them. "Oh," she said. "I never encounter other guests this early. I'm usually safely back in my chamber before anyone awakes." Her gaze flickered over him. "I must confess I am shocked to see you awake before noon. One would think last night's activities should have quite worn you out."

Did she refer to their argument? Or the kiss? "I am especially glad to have awakened early this morning." He gave his smile a roguish slant. "Nothing in my bedchamber is as entrancing as the sight of you in those breeches."

She flushed, vibrant slashes of pink against her pale complexion. Funny, today he found her to be far less commonplace. Those extraordinary azure eyes, set off by a straight nose and plump, pink lips, shone brightly against smooth skin. She was refreshingly free of artifice. What might have struck him as plain yesterday seemed appealing in a natural way this morning. Especially since she wasn't looking at him with outright derision.

"Nathan is saddling a mount for me." Her casual use of the groom's Christian name distracted him from the curve of her hips. So she knew the groom's name. Unusual for a visiting guest.

The groom she called Nathan, a slim, tall, dark-haired cull, walked her horse forward. "There you go, miss. Have a care while you are out this morning. The gamekeeper is having trouble with poachers again." He patted the horse's flanks. "And Flame here can be skittish around sudden noises." He glanced at Cam. "Good morning, my lord." Cam noted the groom's tone stopped just short of insolence.

Cam inclined his head, motioning for one of the other stable boys to saddle his stallion. Turning his attention back to Charlotte, he said, "Perhaps you'll permit me to join you."

"Lud, Camryn, you needn't be polite on my account. After all, His Grace isn't here to mandate it. If you slipped out early to enjoy a solitary ride, I won't encumber you with my company."

"It's no encumbrance unless you are a novice rider." He baited her on purpose in hopes of seeing her eyes flash again as they had last evening. "I do like to give my steed a good run."

Her crystal-blue eyes lit up just as he'd hoped. "As do I," she said, bristling at having her riding prowess called into question.

"Besides, if there are poachers afoot you shouldn't be riding alone."

"Very well, let us ride together." She stroked the horse's neck with a smooth, pale hand. The tapered line of her slender fingers struck him as surprisingly feminine and delicate for such a capable female. "Flame and I shall get on splendidly, shan't we, girl?"

A slight, young groom brought Cam's powerful black

stallion forward, keeping a tight grip on the bridle as the massive animal snorted and pranced with anticipation.

"That's quite a beast you have there." Charlotte ran an admiring gaze over Hercules' elegant, arched neck, down to the pronounced musculature rippling under the animal's glistening midnight coat. "He must be quite the challenge."

Cam took the ribbons from the relieved groom, gripping them with a firm hand. "I find I am drawn to magnificent creatures who appear untamable."

He thought he heard her snort, but couldn't say for certain because she turned from him and hopped onto the mounting block. Hoisting herself into the saddle, she swung one of those cascading legs over the side of her mare. So she planned to ride astride. That explained the breeches.

She caught his look and raised her brows. "I warned you. I can be most unladylike."

He swung up onto Hercules, allowing his gaze to slide over the breeches. She really did have far more in the way of curves than he'd presumed. "Rest assured, no gentleman who has the pleasure of seeing you thus would ever forget you are female."

The groom coughed, his posture rigid. He planted himself beside Charlotte's mount, clutching the horse's bridle in a way that appeared almost territorial. The man barely had time to jump out of the way before Charlotte urged her mare onward, taking off at a gallop.

Cam shook his head and grinned before sending Hercules flying after her. He couldn't resist holding back a bit to admire the view those breeches afforded him. She bent low over her mare's neck as the animal accelerated into an all-out run, her slim round hips thrusting back in a slight up-and-down rhythm. Cam's mouth went dry. Lord, but she sat her mount well.

Forcing his attention away from Charlotte's delectable bottom, he gave his powerful stallion its head to catch up with her. The endless green spaces surrounding Fairview Manor were made for such a ride, with long, smooth expanses of grassland, dotted with trees, which went as far as the eye could see. Great swathes of wildflowers carpeted the landscape in vibrant hues of yellow, violet, and lavender. Cam inhaled the morning air, savoring the crisp scent of a new day and an unexpected sense of well-being.

Both he and Charlotte were accomplished riders, and before long they were goading each other into taking small jumps. But he balked when Charlotte wanted to move onto more challenging ones. "I am afraid that would not be wise," he insisted. "The higher jumps are too dangerous."

She cast him a skeptical glance. "And here I thought you were a gentleman who enjoys living dangerously."

Cam frowned. She must now be referring to the kiss. He took a deep breath. Time to deliver the overdue apology. The sight of her in those damn breeches had quite distracted him. "Miss Livingston—"

But she'd already taken off again, barreling toward the daunting jump. He followed, admiring the fearless and determined way she soared through the air, coming down easily on the far side of the low hedges. Obviously the breeches helped her perform at a skill level rivaling any gentleman.

He took his turn, coming across to join her. "I see now why you choose not to don appropriate riding clothes."

Her exquisite eyes moved over him. "It appears you also

aren't overly concerned with your riding apparel."

"You are quite right, of course." He glanced down at his wrinkled white shirt and dusty, well-worn brown Hessians. He never bothered to wake his valet for his early morning rides. "I shall have to relieve my man of his duties as soon as we return."

Her head snapped around to look at him. "You cannot be serious."

"Indeed." Cam shrugged his shoulders to hide his irritation that she so easily believed the worst about him. "I shall cast him out just as soon as I allow him out of Hartwell's dungeon."

The tiny frown lines between her brows vanished. "You are toying with me," she said turning her mare in the direction of the manor.

"Why would you think that?" His mount fell in step beside hers. "After all, as my valet, Onslow is accustomed to the most degrading working conditions."

"You may think the hardships endured by the operative class are a matter for mirth, but I assure you, my lord, that I do not."

Frustrated, he rubbed the back of his head. "Having never visited any of my factories, you are in no position to pass judgment on them."

"I know they are putting weavers out of work. I don't know why I should be surprised at your involvement. You are clearly a man who takes what he wants."

She must be referring again to the kiss. He cleared his throat. "Miss Livingston, I feel I must apologize for last evening."

Her face squinted. "I beg your pardon?"

"I took liberties with your person. I do hope you will accept my most sincere apology."

Comprehension and something akin to disappointment crossed her face. "Ever the gentleman." She regarded him with those indecipherable eyes of hers. "No need to apologize for a trivial kiss. But, of course, I accept your apology if it relieves your mind." She shook the reins, urging her mare into a trot, leaving him behind.

Trivial kiss? He frowned. His amorous efforts had never been labeled as such before. And Charlotte seemed affronted by his apology.

"Have I insulted you?" he asked, catching up to her. A gunshot sounded in the distance, the loud popping noise close enough to make Charlotte's mare fidgety.

"Whoa, there." She firmed her hold on the ribbons and patted Flame's neck.

"It must be the poachers the groom warned of." Tension fired through the muscles in his arms and legs as he scanned the wood line. "Let's get you back."

She nodded, still stroking the mare's neck as they moved into a trot. After several minutes, when they had neared the manor, Cam peered over at Charlotte. "You neglected to answer my question. Did my apology insult you?"

"No." She shook her head. "Of course not."

"Then what was that look you gave me?"

"It is of no consequence."

"Please do tell me."

"I simply don't understand men like you. You feel worse about a simple kiss that injures no one, than about putting so many people out of work."

Her words were swallowed by an ominous cracking

sound that echoed through the air. Another gunshot. This one so close Flame shied away, spooked. She reared, the abrupt movement taking Charlotte by surprise. She slid off backwards, the back of her head slamming the ground. Flame circled then broke off into a skittering run.

"Charlotte!" His heart pounding, he leapt from his horse and ran to her. She lay motionless with her eyes closed, her face pale and still. He bent over to cradle her upper body in his arms, alarm blasting through him.

"Miss Livingston. Charlotte, can you hear me? Are you all right?" Her translucent blue eyes blinked open, peering up at him with a blank look. "Charlotte, can you hear me? Charlotte?"

"You called me Charlotte. I have not given you leave to do that."

He let out the breath he didn't realize he'd been holding. "Yes, I hope I did not offend. Do you think you can sit up?" He helped her into an upright position, his concern spiking when she seemed to waver.

"Easy now." He put an arm around Charlotte to keep her steady and bent his knee, bracing it behind her for support. She leaned against his knee and dropped her head into her hands. Stroking her hair with his free hand, an unexpected tenderness welled up in Cam. "There now, just rest for a moment until you regain your bearings."

She made a murmur of contentment as her entire body sank against his chest, all warmth and suppleness, her gentle scent embracing him. Cam tensed at the unexpectedly provocative feel of her. His prick perked up, too, stirring with interest. Cursing to himself, he shifted to lessen the physical contact between them.

Opening her eyes, she smiled weakly. "Don't worry, I shan't take advantage of you."

Ah, but was she safe from him? He allowed his lips to brush the softness of her hair; its silken length smelled of lavender. He wondered how long it fell. Did it reach the small of her back? If he pulled it loose now, would its glistening strands brush over the gentle curve of her hip?

The sounds of shouting in the distance distracted him from such fanciful thoughts. A man on horseback charged their way, his mount's beating hooves kicking up grass. As he neared, Cam recognized the groom from the stable riding Charlotte's errant horse. Nearing them, the man leapt down before his animal had time to come to a complete stop.

"Char…Miss Livingston, are you hurt?" The urgent words throbbed with concern, his eyes wild with anxiety.

"Yes, yes, please don't worry on my account." She managed a smile, although it looked more like a grimace, and made an effort to pull away from Cam. "I took a spill."

The groom ran his gaze over the length of her body. Cam wanted to slap him for his impudence. The stable boy seemed not to notice because his intense focus remained fastened on Charlotte.

"Are you certain no bones are broken?" The groom reached for Charlotte, but stopped himself before touching her. "When your mount came back to the stables without you, I feared the worst."

"Oh, Nathan, I am sorry to have worried you."

Oh, Nathan? Cam examined the groom, taking in the tall, lanky form, brown hair, and quiet determined way he carried himself.

"Come now, let's see if you can stand," he said, feeling

a need to take command of the situation. Holding on to Charlotte's arm, he helped her up. Nathan shot to his feet and moved toward her.

Cam stopped him with a territorial gaze and a crisp, brusque tone. "That will be all, Nathan, is it?"

Nathan stepped back, bowing his head in acquiescence, but not before Cam saw anger flash in the man's soft blue eyes.

Charlotte rose a little unsteadily. "I was knocked about a bit, but nothing seems to be broken." She gave Nathan that grimacing smile again, one that was meant to be reassuring but instead had the opposite effect.

Cam frowned at her ginger movements. "I think perhaps you should ride back to the manor with me, on my steed."

"My lord," the groom interjected. "Miss Livingston can ride back on her mount. I will walk."

"Miss Livingston is in no condition to ride alone. She is still quite unsteady. I will accompany her." He guided Charlotte over to his horse. "You may go. Take her mount with you."

Climbing into the saddle, Cam ignored the departing groom. Once seated, he took hold of Charlotte's hand while she placed her foot on top of his boot so he could hoist her up. Settling Charlotte sideways in front of him, he wrapped his arms around her delicate waist to keep her steady and set the stallion in motion at a slow pace. He tried to maintain focus on the path ahead, and not the scented feminine softness pressing up against his chest and stomach. And other regions he had no business thinking about at the moment.

"Just a little bit farther, sweet," he said. Although he

couldn't see her face, he felt it the moment Charlotte lost consciousness. Panic flashed through him when her body went limp and lifeless just as Fairview Manor came into view. Some of that tension released when he caught sight of Hartwell outside the stables with several guests, preparing to lead a riding party. "I need your assistance," he called out.

The duke came forward, and alarm stamped his dark face once he took in Charlotte's still figure. "What the devil?"

"She took a fall. Help me take her down. Slowly." Cam eased off the horse with Charlotte still in his arms. Hartwell provided a stabilizing hand until Cam touched the ground. Cradling her long, slender form in his embrace, Cam's strides ate up the ground as he closed the distance to the house. Every muscle in his body had gone taut and his heartbeat drummed in his ears. A murmur moved through the gathered guests who watched with open curiosity at the sight of Charlotte in the marquess's arms.

Hartwell turned to the nearest groom. "Go to the village and summon the doctor."

Reaching the manor, Cam glanced back in time to see Nathan mount almost before the command left Hartwell's lips. Kicking up a cloud of dust, the groom spurred the mare onward, the thumping sounds of galloping hooves quickly fading into the distance.

Chapter Three

"You've suffered a brain commotion," Doctor Guelph said to Charlotte. She lay in bed battling another wave of nausea, one arm draped over her eyes to block out the painful light.

"How serious is it?" asked her brother, Hugh.

"Miss Livingston will be right as rain provided she follows my orders." The doctor turned back to Charlotte. "You must remain abed for a fortnight. Rest and sleep as much as possible to allow your brain to recover from the trauma it has suffered."

"Two weeks?" she whispered, trying to still the clanging in her head. "That sounds interminable. And the house party ends well before that."

"Nonsense," she heard Willa say. "You'll stay until Doctor Guelph says you are completely recovered. You cannot travel all the way back to Leicestershire in this condition. Besides, I shall delight in your company."

"What is that racket?" Charlotte groaned. "Who is

ringing that infernal bell?"

"The ringing in your ears is quite normal and will clear up with time," Doctor Guelph assured her. After giving her maid a few more instructions in regards to her care, the doctor announced he'd return in a sennight to check on the patient. Willa and Hugh saw the doctor out, leaving Charlotte alone in the darkened room.

Her head drummed as though a hundred people rioted inside of it, but thoughts of Camryn helped distract her from the pain. Her belly twinged at the memory of those golden-green eyes crinkling with concern for her. Even the scent of him lingered in her senses, that purely masculine combination of musk, leather, and sweat. She'd felt the marquess's heart clamoring beneath his chest when she'd laid her head against him. Despite her fog, she'd been aware of Camryn's embrace and the feel of his taut body against hers.

She twisted in the bed trying to ease her discomfort. Her thoughts became a confusing jumble as the laudanum took effect. The medicine lulled her into a fitful sleep where impressions of Camryn floated among the edges of her consciousness until everything finally went black.

• • •

Anxious for word of Charlotte's condition, Cam paced in one of public reception rooms. His brothers, Sebastian and Basil, looked up from their chess game.

"It's hard to concentrate with you moving about like that," complained Basil. "What's got you looking like you're ready to tap the claret?" At two-and-twenty, Cam's youngest brother was a hellion who did well with the ladies. He had his older brother's lean build and golden coloring, but Basil could easily be considered the most classically handsome of his brothers. Cam had often heard ladies ramble on about his brother's large blue eyes, perfectly structured nose, and chiseled jawline.

"Miss Livingston has taken a fall from her mount," Cam mumbled. "I'm awaiting word of her condition."

"Miss Livingston?" One side of Basil's mouth shot up in confusion. "Oh, Shellborne's sister," he said with obvious disinterest.

Sebastian moved his queen. "Check."

"Bollocks!" Basil turned his attention back to the board looking for a way to save his king from his brother's predatory advance.

"Was it a serious fall?" Sebastian asked.

"I cannot say. She hit her head while we were out riding this morning."

"While you were out riding?" Sebastian steepled his fingers beneath his chin. His dusky good looks were a marked contrast to his sun-sprinkled brothers, his powerful build unlike their lean, lithe forms. "Alone."

"Leave off," Cam retorted sharply, reacting to the unspoken censure in his brother's question. "We met quite by accident and proceeded to ride together."

Basil tapped his knight as he studied the chessboard. "Besides, isn't Miss Livingston as good as on the shelf?" he asked without looking up. "She's a little long in the tooth to worry about such proprieties."

Cam quashed an immediate urge to defend Charlotte's feminine appeal. "Any discussion of Miss Livingston's age is highly inappropriate."

"Highly inappropriate," echoed Sebastian, "as is riding without a groom."

Basil chuckled and moved his knight. "There, I've stopped you." He twisted around in his seat to look at Cam. "You rode alone with a lady. Of course, Saint Sebastian does not approve. He can do no wrong."

Sebastian's hooded gaze moved back to the chessboard, a victor's smile curving his lip. "Certainly not today. Check and mate," he said moving his queen in for the kill.

"Damnation, there is no beating you," Basil said good-naturedly.

Willa appeared on the threshold. "Charlotte has suffered a commotion of the brain," she announced. "The doctor says she is to remain abed for a fortnight."

Relief loosened Cam's muscles. "Will she be all right then?"

"Yes, provided she rests and sleeps." Willa went toward him. "She'll remain here under Hartwell's protection until she is recovered."

"I suppose I cannot see her."

"Why would you want to?" asked Basil.

Ignoring Basil, Willa gave Cam a reproving tap on the arm. "Charlotte is confined to the sickroom. She can hardly accept gentleman callers."

"I am hardly a gentleman caller."

"What were the two of you doing out riding together?" she asked.

"I found Miss Livingston having a mount readied for her. Since there are poachers afoot, I offered to accompany her. There was nothing inappropriate or untoward about it."

"Nor did I say there was, cousin," she said, examining his face. "I was simply curious."

"My brother seems to have forgotten to take a groom with them." Sebastian reached for the newspaper on a nearby side table. "Whether you intended it or not, you have helped make Miss Livingston the subject of unsavory gossip."

Willa regarded her dark cousin with fondness. "Oh, Sebastian, I fear none of your brothers can live up to your impeccable standards."

Cam snorted. "Yes, thank goodness we have the moral compass that is Sebastian Stanhope to make certain we are not led astray."

"It is only when compared to my wayward brothers that I appear virtuous. I assure you, I am but an ordinary gentleman." Sebastian regarded his brother with cool green eyes. "One, for example, who would never forget Miss Livingston is a lady who should be treated in a most honorable way."

"I went riding with the lady." Cam scowled at his brother. "I didn't ravish her."

Chuckling, Basil bottomed out his glass. "Besides, if Cam was of the mind to ravish someone, I doubt it would be Miss Livingston, of all people."

"I'm of the mind to thrash you." Grinding his teeth, Cam resisted the urge to pummel his youngest brother. "We are speaking of a lady. I'll remind you to keep a civil tongue."

Sebastian's mouth quirked. "*Now* you worry about protecting Miss Livingston's reputation?"

"What do you know about anything? I don't believe I've ever seen you so much as look at a lady."

Even though Sebastian's inscrutable expression didn't alter, Cam regretted the words as soon as he uttered them. Everyone present knew precisely why his brother showed no overt interest in females.

"That is outside of enough." Willa tilted a stern look at him. "What in the world is wrong with you?"

Basil nodded. "You are behaving most unusually."

"Perhaps my brother's intentions toward Miss Livingston are not as honorable as they should be," Sebastian said, with only his dark curls visible from behind the newspaper.

Blatant disbelief stamped Basil's face. "Surely not."

"I don't think Cam has any intentions, honorable or otherwise, towards her," Willa said. "He seems to find Charlotte rather uninteresting."

"To the contrary." Sebastian's dark-lashed gaze peered at her from above the top of the newspaper. "His actions suggest my brother finds Miss Livingston far more intriguing than he cares to admit."

An odd emotion tugged at Cam's gut. "Leave off," he growled, his face burning as he stormed from the room.

• • •

The remaining days of the house party passed in a sleepy haze for Charlotte, who spent most of that time resting and occasionally dreaming of a certain amber-haired gentleman in snug breeches. Gradually, her confusion cleared and the only ringing she heard came from church bells in the nearby village.

On the final night of the house party, the Duke and Duchess of Hartwell hosted a farewell dinner and dance for their guests. Still confined to the sickroom, Charlotte didn't attend even though her headaches had receded and she grew more restless with each passing day. Thinking of the lively activities from which she was excluded highlighted her boredom.

Music drifting from below stairs, she plopped down into a chair with a book, but it was hopeless because she couldn't concentrate. Thoughts of Camryn intruded.

Her mind kept returning to the memory of that kiss, to the potent press of his lips against hers. Even now, just replaying it in her mind sent bright sparks of pleasure raining down her spine.

Although she'd always held herself aloof, Charlotte had felt a powerful attraction to the marquess from the moment she'd first set eyes on him months ago in town. But she hadn't expected to take pleasure in Camryn's company, which she had, even when they were sparring. And he'd shown such tenderness after she'd been thrown from her mount. She'd felt safe in his arms and in his fierce concern for her.

The very idea that she could actually be drawn to the entire man, and not just to his obvious physical attributes, unnerved her. The Marquess of Camryn was a rakehell and an industrialist. He exploited people. Camryn stood for everything she disdained in a man.

Sighing, she pushed to her feet and walked over to crack the door open. Leaning her forehead against the cool wood, she listened to the strains of music and chatter emanating from the farewell dance. On the morrow, he would be gone and in all likelihood, it would be months before they crossed paths again. Which was just as well, she tried to tell herself, because Camryn clearly saw the world through different eyes.

What was he doing at this precise moment? Perhaps he stood in the garden receiving a special farewell from Mr. Fitzharding's lady wife. She flushed at the memory. She'd been returning from a walk with Nathan when the strange murmurs and muted groans drew her attention. The carnal nature of what she'd chanced upon still shocked her, even now. It wasn't as if she was completely ignorant of the intimacies between a man and a woman, but seeing Mrs. Fitzharding perform such an unthinkable act on Camryn stunned her.

It had also done strange things to her body. At first, the mechanics of it held her spellbound. The moonlight had cast a glow on the lady's back-and-forth movements, highlighting the startlingly expert actions of her mouth and tongue, as well as the knowing, satisfied expression on her face when the marquess undulated against her.

Then there was the kingly way Camryn had stood against the tree, the noble majesty with which he accepted the pleasure she offered, as though it was his right. He'd looked arrogant and graceful even then, his imperious hand resting atop the head of the woman who pleasured him, his green eyes reflecting the moonlight, infusing them with an otherworldly glow.

She'd never seen a grown man's private bits before. Camryn had been clothed but his breeches were open, allowing his prodigious male appendage to jut out from a thicket of tawny curls. Illuminated by the moonlight, it had been proud and hard, thick and long, much more substantial than she would ever have imagined could fit in a man's snug breeches. Or in any feminine orifice.

When Camryn had closed his eyes and shuddered, her own heart had convulsed, the heat in her body surging. Afterward, she'd been startled to witness his bored satisfaction and bland politeness. The lack of intimacy between two people who'd just engaged in a deeply sensual act had baffled her. It still did.

She'd been undeniably mesmerized once his lover left him, unable to tear her eyes away as the sublime creature tidied himself, deftly recreating the illusion of gentlemanly civility he usually showed the world. It did no good where she was concerned. The image of Camryn preening lazily up against the tree flaunting his virility with a careless confidence, branded itself upon her mind.

The memory had a hot impact on her as she leaned up against the open door and listened to the strains of music. Her cheeks warmed and the lowest part of her belly twitched with anticipation. She groaned. How in the world could she react to Camryn in this way? Smart, sensible Charlotte Livingston mooning over a man who appeared to have little respect for females and even less for the common man. She forced a deep breath and shook out her shoulders, determined to put him out of her mind.

"Miss Livingston?"

Startled, Charlotte peered around the open door to find the flesh-and-blood object of her musings standing outside her bedchamber. "Oh, Lord Camryn!" she said, the heat rising in her cheeks again.

"I'm sorry to intrude." He was dressed in dinner attire, his deep blue, superfine tailcoat, and underlying dark paisley waistcoat, hugged the clean, taut lines of his body. Pale grey breeches clung to the defined curves of his strong thighs like a besotted lover. The clothing's formal, restrictive elegance somehow enhanced the untamed, earthy quality that radiated from the marquess.

Tugging at his snowy cravat, he said, "I, well, ah, take my leave tomorrow and wished to ascertain for myself that you are recovering."

"I am quite well, thank you." She tried to ignore the thrill that shivered through her. "Except for the interminable boredom that comes with being in the sickroom, but there it is."

Camryn grinned in a radiant, full-toothed way which made her heart stumble. "I am so relieved to hear it." He fell silent and she couldn't think of a thing to say. All she knew was that she didn't want him to leave. He turned to go. "Very well then."

"I could use a walk in the garden." The words tumbled out in the rush to stay his departure. "If you would be kind enough to escort me."

"Of course." His face brightened. "It would be my pleasure. I shall await you at the end of the corridor."

Spinning around, Charlotte grabbed her shawl and dashed over to check her reflection in the mirror. She pinched her cheeks before grabbing a bonnet and rushing to the door. Halting, she forced herself to step out of her chamber in a graceful manner, attempting a ladylike glide toward Camryn, instead of galloping down the corridor like a thoroughbred at Newmarket. Reaching the marquess, she took the arm he extended. "Thank you for taking pity on an invalid."

"Are you certain it is wise to move about? Willa said the doctor ordered complete bed rest."

"A serene walk about the garden will not jangle my brain." She quickened her step, urging him along before he changed his mind. "And the invigorating fresh air will no doubt speed my recovery."

"As you wish." The lines of concern on his forehead eased. They walked in silence, making their way through the cavernous house toward the garden. The cool night air and pungent scent of blooming flowers greeted them as soon as they stepped outside.

"These gardens go on forever," she said, breathing in the crisp air.

"Hart says there are seven acres of garden. One could get lost."

"Then I am fortunate to have you as my guide. Are you very familiar with the paths?" Her cheeks flamed as soon as she asked the question, suddenly remembering the last time she'd seen him in the garden.

He appeared not to notice. "My brothers and I have spent some time here visiting Willa since she married. Hart and I were old friends at Cambridge, so the visits are quite amiable." They were silent for just a moment, strolling at an easy pace.

"How many brothers do you have?"

"Sometimes I think too many," he said with an easy laugh. "Four. I am the eldest of five."

She recalled meeting two of them before her fall. "Willa mentioned having a cousin at war. I understand he serves with great distinction."

"That would be Edward." Camryn's eyes seemed to darken, even in the moonlight.

"You were against his choice to fight?"

"His reasons for doing so concern me. Edward became enamored with the daughter of an earl. As my brother was a second son with no grand prospects, her father rejected his offer. Not long after, Edward went off to join the fight." He stared out into the darkness. "My brother has fought with great valor and is a brilliant strategist. He's even been knighted for his services. He's Sir Edward Stanhope now."

"You must be very proud."

"Indeed, I am. Enormously so. It's just that it is so unlike him. Edward is a talented musician, an artist. I would never have guessed he would excel in military endeavors."

Charlotte answered with a sneeze. It must be something in this garden, she thought, sneezing again.

Camryn froze beside her. Sensing the change in his demeanor, she peered up at him, dread rippling through her. His face flushed and tightened, a look of shocked comprehension washing over it. She went very still when that hardened leonine face stared down on her, his round pupils reflecting the moonlight much as they had that night.

"It was you," he said.

Chapter Four

Cam's head pounded with disbelief. *It couldn't be.* He searched Charlotte's face and, even in the torch-lit garden, could discern the deep crimson staining her cheeks. The crisp garden air suddenly felt thick and oppressive. Finally, she raised her eyes and met his gaze. "Yes."

Something in his chest jerked. A jumble of emotions tumbled through him as he fully realized Charlotte had witnessed the coarse act. He was ashamed she'd seen him participating in it. Yet he admired the way she'd answered him. Not in a simmering, silly, or bashful way, but with shocking honesty.

"I see." He looked away from her, his face and chest burned with mortification. "Are you always so truthful?"

She resumed walking. "I'm afraid so. Be careful of what you ask me. You might hear something you'd rather not."

He already had. "Thank you for your candor." Cam fell in step beside her, still pulsing with disbelief.

No gentlewoman should be subjected to such vulgarity. But more than that, it distressed him that the episode had no doubt caused him to plummet even further in her esteem. Now she probably saw him as both an uncaring tyrant *and* a depraved degenerate.

"I apologize for the insult to your sensibilities." The muscles in his face were so taut with strain he thought they might snap. "I am beyond chagrined that a gently raised lady should witness such a disgusting display. It astonishes me you would deign to be in the same company as me."

"I did not think it disgusting." Charlotte's eyes popped wide open. Her hand flew to cover her mouth as if the words had slipped out on their own accord.

"I beg your pardon?"

"I did not think it was disgusting," she whispered, taking a sudden interest in staring at her silk slippers.

"I see." In reality he didn't. Not at all. Cam was at a loss for words. This frank talk was most inappropriate, but he felt compelled to know more. "Whatever to do you mean?"

Her head jerked up. "Beg pardon?"

His question seemed to shock her as much as it did him. So she wasn't as unflappable as she'd have him believe. He halted, compelling her to stop as well. "I know it is beyond the pale. But there is something about you, Miss Livingston, that compels me to dispense with propriety and speak quite plainly." His gaze held hers. "You have said you never lie."

Admiration rushed through him when she turned to face him, cool and unafraid, allowing her frank gaze to remain steady with his. "You should not ask me such a thing."

"You would be well within your rights to slap me for my impudence." His heart thumped in his head. "However, I find I cannot help myself."

She held his gaze as rising tension tightened the air between them. "I would rather not say." She finally mustered the words. "As a gentleman, you should accept my response."

He looked at her for a moment, then smiled with reluctant resignation, allowing the pressure of the moment to ease. "When you put it that way, you leave me no choice. I can only hope the unfortunate incident has not lowered me too greatly in your esteem."

She remained silent and walked on ahead, clearly signaling her desire to end the conversation. There was nothing to be done for it. Holding his tongue, he followed, wondering how he'd managed to botch things so completely with the first woman to rouse his interest in a very long time.

• • •

"Charlotte! You look wonderful." Willa embraced her friend. "I'm so pleased you are finally returned to town. These last two weeks have been dreadfully dull without you."

Handing her wrap to the waiting footman, Charlotte returned Willa's embrace, her mood buoyed by the chattering sounds streaming down the corridor, emanating from Hartwell House's salon.

"It is so good to be in London again. I came as soon as Mother allowed me to make my escape." Charlotte hadn't seen Willa since leaving Fairview Manor to recuperate at home in Leicestershire under her mother's watchful eye. "I dread the thought of the Season ending and retiring to the country again."

"Perhaps she will allow you to spend the summer at

Fairview." Willa's soft, dreamy smile held a sharp, secretive edge. "Although I can't promise the usual coterie of interesting guests."

She eyed her beautiful friend. "You look lovely as usual. One could even say you are glowing." Her gaze moved down to her friend's midriff. "Willa, are you—"

"We are not announcing it as of yet, but yes, I am increasing." The duchess's enormous, velvety-brown eyes shone with happiness. "Hartwell is thrilled. We both are."

"Willa, how wonderful."

"I'll enter my confinement once the season ends. Please say you'll consider spending my lying in with me at Fairview." She looped her arm through Charlotte's. "I won't press you for an immediate answer. Come, the guests are already gathered."

They entered the large parlor where the guests had gathered. Disappointment flashed through Charlotte to see no sign of Willa's cousin. She'd not seen Camryn since their walk in the garden almost three weeks ago. Shaking off the feeling, she tried to remember she had no business being interested in the marquess. She forced herself to picture him at one of his dingy factories driving the downtrodden workers with impossible demands.

The Duke of Hartwell approached and Charlotte felt a twinge near her heart at the loving look the two exchanged before the duke's sharp-cut features focused on her.

"Miss Livingston. I am gratified to see you have recovered fully."

"Yes, Your Grace, I have. Thank you." She never felt at ease with Willa's dark, enigmatic husband. Already an imposingly tall man, he wore unrelenting black except for the bright white of his cravat. She wondered why he still wore his hair long, tied back in a queue. It was quite out of fashion and made his bold features appear all the more severe.

After exchanging a few pleasantries, she moved about the room, soon settling into a conversation with Jonathan Martin, a wealthy man of business and Robert Gibbon, who shared Charlotte's interest in social reform.

"Miss Livingston, have you heard the dreadful news from Crosland Moor?" Gibbon inquired.

"I'm afraid not," said Charlotte. "I have been at home in Leicestershire quite removed from the news."

Martin, the man of business shook his head. "It's most distasteful, but not unexpected. It seems the Luddites have struck there again."

"Only this time, they've really done it," interjected a crisp, resonant voice that made Charlotte's heart jump. "They ambushed and murdered a mill owner in Marsden."

She turned to see the Marquess of Camryn approaching them, his gilded presence as radiant as the candles illuminating the room around him. Dark, formfitting evening clothes showed his lithe, lightly muscled form to extreme advantage. Her stomach tightened at the way his sculpted thighs flexed and slid beneath snug breeches.

"Ah, Camryn, do join us," said Gibbon. "We could use your noble outlook."

"As cousin to an earl, you're hardly part of the working class," he said in wry tones.

"Sadly, blue blood alone does not put food on one's table."

Camryn snorted before settling a mesmerizing amber

gaze on Charlotte. "Miss Livingston, forgive my lack of manners." He bowed, his rumpled tawny hair in pointed contrast with his impeccably tied cravat. "I trust you are recovered from your fall?"

Charlotte's pulse somersaulted under his keen gaze. He had a way of looking at a female that made her feel like the only person in the world. "Yes, my lord, thank you for your concern."

"So, what say you about the happenings at Marsden, Camryn?" asked Gibbon.

The marquess settled into a chair. "The perpetrators are no better than footpads who must be dealt with swiftly and severely."

"The risings are a reaction to the loss of wages," Charlotte said heatedly.

"Miss Livingston, surely you comprehend these acts are primitive responses to progress. Machinery is here to stay and more will inevitably follow. The operative class must change with the times. There is no alternative."

"Easily said by a man who stands to gain significantly from the advance of machinery," Gibbon scoffed. "Your factories can now produce large quantities more cheaply and quickly, boosting your profits considerably."

"Despite producing inferior articles," Charlotte muttered.

"All of the workers must learn a new skill." Crossing an ankle over the opposite knee, Camryn drank from his brandy. "Progress is not an easy journey, but it must be undertaken nonetheless."

"That same progress threatens the very hierarchy that places you at the top of society," Charlotte said. "One day soon wealthy merchants could be on an even footing with a peer of the realm."

The way Cam's provocative amber-green eyes seemed to continually assess her warmed Charlotte's cheeks. "As I said, Miss Livingston, no one can stop progress, not even the peerage. We must all adapt, including the machine wreckers."

Hartwell appeared. "Forgive me for stealing Camryn for a moment. There is an urgent matter we must discuss before supper."

Camryn rose. "Of course, if you will excuse me."

Gibbon watched them go. "I wonder what urgent matters Camryn has with His Grace," he mused to no one in particular.

Martin relaxed back into his chair. "It is my understanding Hartwell is joining Camryn in the textile business. I hear they have recently acquired another cotton mill." The tradesman gave a cynical smile. "I never thought to see the day when the loftiest members of the peerage would dirty their white gloves by dabbling in trade."

"Not only lords of the realm but cotton lords as well," Gibbon said. "It appears even the most esteemed members of the peerage are anxious to be on the profitable side of progress."

• • •

Throughout supper and afterward, Cam was surprised at the significant masculine attention directed at Charlotte. Gibbon sat to her right side while Martin claimed the left. Another gentleman Cam wasn't acquainted with sat across from her, listening to Charlotte discuss her latest writings on the advantages of educating all children no matter what their station in life.

He had no explanation for his attraction to her. Since Willa's house party, he'd danced with some of the Ton's most sought-after lovelies at the few social events he'd forced himself to attend, mostly for political reasons. Yet his thoughts kept returning to Charlotte.

Fashionable society's incomparables, with their fancy dresses, opulent jewelry, and ornate hairstyles, suddenly struck him as garish and overwrought in comparison to Charlotte's natural simplicity. Their coy behavior and flirtatious laughter left him longing for a certain bluestocking's plainspoken manner. Even though the lady in question had shown she could be too forthright. And maddeningly wrong in her assumptions, especially about him.

The men surrounding her this evening paid rapt attention when she spoke. He appreciated their interest. His blood warmed at the way those lucent azure eyes sparkled with intelligence, her lithe body vibrating with energy and intent.

"The American Thomas Jefferson has long argued for a public education system," she said to the men around her.

"The Americans?" The man Cam didn't know scoffed. "Surely you're not suggesting we follow their lead. Theirs can hardly be deemed an orderly society. There is no peerage there. Really," he sniffed, "they are practically savages."

The corners of Charlotte's plump mouth lifted. "Savages who could soon have a better educated and more informed citizenry than we have here."

Cam didn't notice Willa slip beside him until she spoke.

"They seem quite enthralled by her."

"Apparently."

Willa crossed her arms. "She's quite sought after, you know, by a certain type of gentleman."

"And what sort of gentleman might that be?" Cam asked in a flat tone that invited no follow-up conversation.

Not that that would dissuade his cousin from making her point. "A learned sort. A gentleman who appreciates her intellectual pursuits."

"Just as I appreciate yours?" Hartwell asked, sidling up next to his wife and slipping his arm around her waist. Beaming, she relaxed her body into his.

Cam looked to the ceiling. "Really, Hart, the last thing I need to witness is you pawing my cousin in polite company."

Hartwell's answering laugh was soft and low. "Oh, Cam, you've no idea."

"Do behave yourself." Willa's ears blushed as she pulled away to go and join a group of ladies seated near the window.

Reluctantly releasing her, the duke turned to Cam. "Miss Livingston certainly commands attention, wouldn't you say, Cam?"

"I suppose."

"She appears to be drawing your interest."

There was no use denying it. "I'm not quite sure why." He exhaled through his nostrils, still mystified by his attraction to her. "She's hardly my type. I normally shag girls who are a bit more fleshy, shall we say."

"Yes, but what one seeks out for a little slap and tickle is far different from what you desire in a life's companion."

Life's companion? "Why do you presume I seek a wife?"

"Oh, you don't have to be looking," the duke said in

mild tones. "When your time comes, fate manages to find you all the same."

Cam's gaze ran over Charlotte's willowy form. "And does this fate also alter one's tastes in females?"

"Who can say? Perhaps a man doesn't truly know what his type is until he meets the right woman."

"Interesting theory."

"Thus far, you've purposely consorted with certain females who only serve to fulfill your physical needs."

Who now bored him senseless. Unlike Charlotte, who intrigued him for some unaccountable reason. "Are you suggesting I now need more than just a good shagging?"

"A meeting of the minds can be as seductive as a mingling of the flesh." Hartwell shrugged as if it were all the same to him. "Perhaps she appeals to all of your senses, not just the physical."

"When did you become so wise?"

"Around the time I married your cousin," the duke said as he drifted away to mingle with his other guests.

Cam continued to observe Charlotte from a safe distance while nursing his brandy. He'd always assumed a lack of eligible suitors accounted for her spinster status. In the glittering atmosphere of the Ton, he'd mistaken her clean simplicity for plainness, but others had not made the same error. This evening, she shined, appearing to be in her element as she commanded attention and interest. Charlotte Livingston was a diamond who could easily be mistaken for plain glass if one didn't look carefully enough to appreciate all of her brilliant facets.

Before long, the object of his admiration artfully detached herself from her circle of admirers. She mingled a bit before discreetly slipping out of the room. No one else appeared to notice. Eager to get her alone, Cam saw his chance. He stole away a few minutes after Charlotte so as not to draw attention to their mutual absence. Looking around the small garden, he saw no sign of her. The only activity seemed to come from the direction of the mews where the horseflesh was kept. The sound of her voice, along with the pungent, grainy odor of hay and horses, drifted out to greet him.

"Willa has asked me to spend her confinement with her at Fairview Manor," she said. "So I shall be able to see you all summer." A man responded in a low murmur that was impossible to decipher. He approached quietly, already quite certain of whom he would find Charlotte speaking with.

He peered in undetected from among the shadows just in time to see Charlotte embrace Nathan. The stable boy again. A territorial flash of anger swamped him, leaving a hollow feeling in his chest. He fought the urge to pounce on the servant and thrash him for touching a lady in such a familiar way. Not just any lady. Charlotte.

What the devil was going on? Would the sister and daughter of a baron actually dally with a servant? Cam withdrew as quickly and quietly as he had come, slipping back into the townhouse to rejoin the other guests. He busied himself chatting with a small group that included Willa and Hartwell, and pretended not to notice when Charlotte reappeared a short time later.

She smiled, approaching their group. "Willa, it's a most lovely evening." A blind, jealous fury took hold of Cam. He rose without speaking and gave Charlotte his back, turning to leave the room. He heard her sharp intake of breath at being given the cut direct.

Willa gasped at the obvious slight. The chatter in the room quieted. Hartwell's somber voice followed Cam's retreating form. "Miss Livingston, perhaps you'd care to take a turn about the room with me." The Duke of Hartwell offered the power of his rank to protect Charlotte's reputation in front of guests who witnessed Cam's deliberate insult.

He didn't bother to wait for Hartwell's Indian butler to fetch his greatcoat. After murmuring a few words to the man, he bounded down the front steps just as Willa appeared on the threshold.

"Your Grace, the Marquess of Camryn has been called away," the butler said to Willa.

"Indeed?" muttered Willa. She raised her voice calling out into the night. "He is not going to evade me that easily."

· · ·

"More coffee if you please," Cam grunted to a footman the next morning as his cousin strode in unannounced.

"What in heaven's name was that all about?" Willa asked without preamble. She slid into a seat at the breakfast table next to Sebastian, which prompted him to look up from his newspaper.

"Why do I even have a butler?" Cam grumbled to no one in particular. "By all means, do join us, cousin."

"Smythe knows he doesn't have to announce me," she said, referring to his butler. "Why would you embarrass Charlotte in that manner?"

"I must remember to have a word with my butler." Leaning back in his chair, he closed his eyes and pinched the bridge of his nose. The image of Charlotte embracing the stable boy sloshed around in his mind. "I'm afraid I can offer no excuse. I will, of course, apologize to Miss Livingston at the earliest opportunity."

"Which will be next week at the Fulsome-Thrusby ball."

Sebastian's astute emerald gaze flickered between the two of them. "And what precisely is Cam apologizing for?"

"I hardly know myself," said Willa with obvious exasperation. "He gave Charlotte the cut direct last evening."

"I see."

"You don't see anything," Cam said curtly. "And don't give me that look. Why are you here anyway? Why do you have bachelor's quarters if you are never there?"

"You invited me. We have a standing weekly breakfast appointment and have for some time." Sebastian disappeared behind the newspaper. "As I recall, it was your idea."

"You haven't explained your behavior," Willa said.

"Nor do I intend to." Still leaning back in his chair, Cam clasped his hands behind his head. "Suffice it to say that I will offer the necessary apology."

The footman entered with a cup of steaming chocolate for Willa. Cam waited for him to withdraw before speaking. "I see your stable boy, Nathan, is in town with you."

Willa's brows drew together. "What has he to do with anything? And he is the coachman."

"From stable boy to coachman in the space of one month?" Cam's mood blackened. "That's laudable progress."

"Hart is impressed with his command of the horses. And Nathan is very good with numbers and calculations as well."

Irritation flared in his chest. "Is he new to Hartwell's employ?"

"Why is Hartwell's coachman of sudden interest to you?"

"Why indeed," echoed Sebastian from behind his newspaper.

"No reason in particular." Ignoring Sebastian, he injected the words with casual interest. "I suppose it is because he seems a cut above the usual servant. His manner of speaking is almost like a gentleman's."

Willa reached for a sweet bun. "Oh, that's because he was educated by a governess with Charlotte and her brother, the baron."

Cam leaned forward. "How did that come about?"

"You should ask Charlotte about Nathan if you can manage to be civil to her." Willa chewed her roll with robust appreciation. "She is well acquainted with him. They grew up together."

"How so?"

"I believe I heard he was the son of a footman at Shellborne Manor. Apparently, Charlotte's father appreciated his keen mind and grew fond of him." She sipped her chocolate. "He allowed Nathan to join in on the children's lessons with their governess."

"Interesting," said Sebastian from behind the newspaper.

"So Miss Livingston received her empathy for the plight of the working man from her father. How did he come to be in your employ?"

"Nathan? It was at Charlotte's request." Willa finished her chocolate and leaned back. "Oh no, now I feel impossibly full."

"Miss Livingston asked Hartwell to hire Nathan?"

"Why? Are you thinking of trying to steal him

away?" Willa eyed him suspiciously. "Are you in need of a coachman?"

"Perhaps," he lied.

"Yes, I am certain that is what motivates his interest," said the wry voice behind the newspaper.

Willa stood up, bringing both men to their feet. "I must go. I have an appointment at my modiste. Absolutely nothing fits anymore now that I am increasing."

"And yet you remain the most beautiful woman in London," Sebastian assured her.

"Such a liar. You truly are a saint." She gave him a peck on the cheek before taking Cam's arm so he could escort her out.

She rattled off final instructions as they walked through the foyer and stepped out into the cool air. "Now remember, you should dance with Charlotte at the Fulsome-Thrusby's next week."

Cam lifted a brow. "I recall agreeing to apologize. However, I don't recall agreeing to dance with Miss Livingston."

"Nonetheless, your gaffe was a large one," she said in a clipped tone that brooked no nonsense. "Dancing publicly with Charlotte will lay to rest any gossip about the cut you gave her last night. It is the least you can do."

Chapter Five

"There, this ice blue is the perfect complement to your eyes," Willa said to Charlotte. "You must stop dressing as if you are in mourning."

"Really, Willa, this sort of elegant creation suits you. It is too much for me." Struggling not to fidget while Willa's maid fussed with her hair, Charlotte tugged her new gown upward in a futile attempt to cover the top surges of her breasts. "This neckline is scandalous. I look like a courtesan."

"Nonsense, it is far more modest than most gowns, mine included," Willa said. "You'll look perfect at the Fulsome-Thrusby's ball. And you hair is most becoming in that fashion."

"Not that I can tell since you won't allow me to look in mirror."

"Be patient. Clara is almost finished. I want you to get the full effect." Charlotte answered with a scowl, wondering how she'd ever allowed Willa to talk her into all these fripperies. Earlier in the week, the duchess had dragged her to the modiste, convincing Charlotte to order several gowns and day dresses in vibrant fabrics and flattering styles. It was all far different from Charlotte's usual sensible attire. Although she cared not at all about being in the first stare of fashion, Charlotte had gone along, mostly because it was far easier to agree with Willa than to naysay her.

"You certainly are taking a great interest in my appearance for the ball," she said. "Might I ask if there is a reason?"

"You hide your loveliness behind those sad colors," Willa said. "I have a strong desire to see you in shades that are more becoming to you."

Clara finished her ministrations and nodded to the duchess.

"There, it is done," Willa said with a bright smile. "Now you can look."

Turning to assess herself in the duchess's dressing room mirror, Charlotte froze, at first not recognizing the attractive woman staring back at her.

Small strings of pearls were woven into her hair and the high-waisted gown Willa selected for her shimmered when she moved. Her usually lifeless skin looked almost luminous. Who knew the color of one's gown could make such a difference? With her loosely upswept locks and artfully styled gown, she almost looked pretty. "Oh my."

"You look so handsome." Willa clapped her hands together with exuberant delight. "Your dance card will be full once all of the gentlemen see you looking so lovely."

"You are far too optimistic." She eyed her friend with skepticism. "If I didn't know better, I would think you are trying to see me wed at this very late date."

"Don't be ridiculous." Willa fussed with her gown, avoiding eye contact. She wore a dramatic red dress that artfully hid her expanding belly while highlighting her glowing alabaster skin and shining chestnut curls.

"If I have any hope of being noticed, I would be wise to stand as far away from you as possible," Charlotte said. "You are so impossibly lovely that everyone pales in comparison."

"Nonsense, I'm growing as big as a carriage." She paused. "Charlotte, what happened with Cam the other evening?"

Heat stung Charlotte's cheeks at the memory of Camryn's public cut. "I've no idea. We only spoke briefly before dinner. I have not and will not give it another thought." But she had of course. She'd been terribly wounded and confused by his public slight, and coming from Camryn, it had been that much more painful.

"It is so unlike Cam," said Willa. "He is usually all that is agreeable. I've never seen him treat a lady in such a manner."

"Apparently, I rouse his disagreeable side," she said tartly, reaching for her wrap. "At least I am unlikely to see him this evening."

Willa coughed delicately. "Why ever would you presume that?"

"He rarely comes out in Society. I see no reason for him to attend this evening's crush."

"Perhaps." She surveyed Charlotte's appearance again. "You truly look wonderful. Let us go then, shall we? Hart is waiting."

The Fulsome-Thrusby ball, an annual event that took place in the waning weeks of the season, traditionally drew the highest-caliber crowds. This evening was no exception,

Charlotte could see as soon as they arrived. A throng of people filled the vast ballroom and adjoining public rooms. Opulent flower arrangements adorned side tables and hundreds of candles shimmered throughout the spaces.

Hugh emerged from the crush, his girth making him look a bit sausage-like in his close-fitting formal clothes. "There you are, sister dear." He brushed a light kiss on her cheek before turning to Willa and Hart. "Your Graces. My thanks for allowing my sister to accompany you."

"The pleasure is ours. Miss Livingston is delightful company," Hartwell said as he guided Willa away. "Come dear. I think I see Mother."

"Bravo," Hugh said, watching them go. "A public show of ducal support will no doubt raise the Shellborne name immeasurably in Society."

Charlotte rolled her eyes. "Yes, that is precisely why I am friends with Willa."

"My, but don't you look pretty." He ran an interested gaze over her gown. Although Hugh kept a tight hold of his purse strings, he'd happily agreed to fund the enhancement of Charlotte's wardrobe once he'd learned of the duchess's involvement. "I trust this is one of the creations Her Grace selected for you."

"Gad, Hughie, I cannot fathom why I allowed Willa to talk me into wearing this." She tugged the low neckline of her dress upward, fearful that her breasts would spring free at any moment.

"I'm certain that if the Duchess of Hartwell chose your gown, it must be all the crack." He nudged her back. "And don't call me Hughie. We are not in the schoolroom any longer. I'm Shellborne, if you please."

She shook her head in fond exasperation. She loved her brother, but he really took himself far too seriously. Moving her gaze back to the crush, she spotted Camryn making his way toward them. She froze. Surely, he wouldn't dare approach them.

The marquess seemed to have made an attempt to tame his hair, but the wiry, amber mane was already appealingly tousled. Beige breeches gloved his strong thighs, and his striped, silk waistcoat caught the candlelight. The tails of his double-breasted, deep purple tailcoat flapped as he strode toward them. He moved with the perfect-postured assuredness of a commander leading his troops into battle, who had no doubt victory would be his.

"Good evening, Shellborne." Even his tone was imperious as he shone those penetrating eyes on her. "Miss Livingston." Her stomach flip-flopped and she averted her eyes, focusing her attention on the violet gemstone of his cravat pin glittering against the bright white neck cloth.

Hugh beamed. "Camryn, well met." After an awkward pause, Hugh glanced at his sister, clearly wondering why she hadn't returned Camryn's greeting.

"I was hoping Miss Livingston would honor me with a dance." The words were bold, fearless. "If you will recall, after our last waltz we agreed you would save a spot on your dance card for me."

Charlotte's temper flared. It was all she could do not to slap Camryn across his smug face. How dare he approach her as though nothing had happened? After the way he'd embarrassed her, did he truly expect a calm return to civility?

Hugh's round face flushed with delight. "Of course, my sister will be delighted to stand up with you, Camryn."

"Excellent." Camryn turned to leave. "I shall return for the next set, a waltz I believe."

Charlotte's hands fisted at her sides. "Why that arrogant — "

Hugh watched Camryn vanish into the throng before turning to give her a meaningful look. "A marquess, Charlotte. Consider the possibilities."

"I will not dance with him."

"Why ever not?" Hugh's brow furrowed. "You are aware he is a marquess, are you not?"

"Save your breath, Hughie. I would not dance with the Marquess of Camryn even if he were the King of England." The words vibrated with indignation. "And no one and nothing will ever make me change my mind."

"You are only in town because I am acting as your chaperone."

"I have an abigail who accompanies me," Charlotte said sharply, seeing the direction of his thoughts. Of course her brother wouldn't let the opportunity Cam presented pass them by.

"All the same, since Mother does not like town life, you are here under my direction and guidance. If you cannot act in a manner which does credit to the Livingston name, then you should return to Leicestershire without delay."

"Don't be intolerable, Hughie." She gritted her teeth. "I do not respond well to threats."

"You have already given the marquess a cut by not speaking when he addressed you. If you don't have a sound reason for not dancing with him, I must insist that you do."

"I do have a sound reason."

Hugh's eyes rounded. "Lottie, has the Marquess of

Camryn insulted you? Or something worse?" He drew up his chest. "If he has, he will answer to me, by God."

Charlotte's irritation gave way to a rush of amused warmth for her brother. The stout, pompous baron would be no match in any area for the formidable Marquess of Camryn. She squeezed his arm. "I am fortunate to have a brother who would go to any lengths to protect my good name, even if it meant upsetting a peer."

"In all seriousness, Charlotte, has he trespassed?"

"No, of course not," she lied. "I'll dance with Camryn. He's harmless enough."

. . .

Desire bolted through Cam the minute he spotted Charlotte at the ball. She'd obviously put some effort into her appearance this evening. The sky-colored gown flattered her complexion, its cut favoring the slender lines of her body far more than the drab sacks in which she normally enshrouded herself. Her translucent eyes appeared even more brilliant than usual, mesmerizing really.

Taking her into his arms for a waltz, he couldn't stop noticing the lower cut of her neckline. Still modest by Ton standards, her décolletage nonetheless offered a tantalizing view of Charlotte's womanly assets. What a pleasant surprise to discover she possessed more curves than her severe dresses suggested. Her breasts were not large, but they were creamy, pert, and softly rounded. Very appealing. He wondered what it would be like to take one of those sweet, perfect mounds into his mouth. Heat blasted through his body at the thought of suckling her woman's flesh.

"Why have you asked me to dance?" Charlotte's curt tone sliced into his wayward thoughts.

"In order to apologize for my behavior the other evening." He struggled to ignore her enticingly subtle floral scent. The last thing he needed was to come to an embarrassing point right here on the dance floor like some untried swell. "It was not my place to cut you in that way. Please accept my apology."

"Why did you do it?"

He should have guessed she wouldn't let him off so easily. Most other females would have. They were happy to flirt and fawn over him, but this tempting chit was decidedly unlike most females.

"I would rather not go into that," he finally said, sounding high-handed, even to himself. "Suffice it to say that I very much regret causing you any pain or embarrassment."

"No."

He raised his forehead. "No?"

Charlotte cut him a defiant look, pressing her lush lips into a tight line he had the mad urge to kiss away. "No." She emphasized each word as if he were deaf, daft, or both. "I. Will. Not. Accept. Your. Apology."

"I beg your pardon?" he said, startled to be confronted so directly. Most maidens hung on to his every word, laughed at witticisms even he knew weren't particularly amusing.

"You, my lord, are a rag-mannered coxcomb and I will not accept an apology without a full explanation for your behavior."

"A rag-mannered coxcomb?" He could hardly believe his ears. "Now see here, Miss Livingston—"

She sighed, her exasperation plain. "No, you see here,

my lord. I tire of your strange temperament, your arrogant manner, and most of all, I tire of dancing with you. Please excuse me."

She was halfway off the dance floor before Cam recovered himself and strode after her. He caught her gloved hand and placed it on his arm. "Tsk-tsk, Miss Livingston, tantrums do not become you. You risk causing quite the commotion."

Small round spots of color stamped her angled cheeks. "Please unhand me," she said through clenched teeth.

"Unfortunately, I cannot oblige you." Cam held on to her hand, pasting a polite smile on his face. "Willa will have my head if we cause another scene. And, at the moment, I am more wary of her wrath than yours. She'll put it all on me. Even though this outburst is your doing." He kept his free hand clamped over hers to prevent any escape. "However, since you demand an explanation, I will oblige you. But not here."

"Don't tell me you have the perfect secluded corner of the terrace to take me to."

Cam barked an amused laugh. "Touché, Miss Livingston. Alas, no. Everyone rants about the Fulsome-Thrusby portrait gallery. It is both private and public enough for the discussion you insist on pursuing."

He escorted her toward the gallery, a long wood-paneled hallway adorned with paintings of the Fulsome-Thrusby ancestors, who appeared to be a rather humorless lot.

Charlotte halted, pulling her hand away. "Well?"

He fought to keep his eyes politely level with hers and well away from that intriguing curve of bosom she displayed this evening. "Well, Miss Livingston, it likely comes as no surprise that I have developed something of a *tendre* for you."

If the way her mouth fell open was any indication, it did surprise her. In fact, Charlotte looked downright shocked. Surely she could not be that unaware? The lady blushed, a delightful shade of pink, all the way from her face, through the turn of her neck, and down to that unexpectedly lovely bosom.

Warmth glowed in her crystalline eyes, causing his own heart to tighten with an unfamiliar emotion. "If this is how you show affection, my lord—"

"Pray allow me to finish, Miss Livingston," he said trying to get a hold of himself. "I have had the occasion to come upon you twice in what could be construed as an inappropriate situation with a male."

She stiffened. Any warmth she'd exhibited just a moment ago turned to frost. "I beg your pardon, Camryn, but the only gentleman who has made inappropriate advances toward me of late is you."

Her recall of their terrace kiss brought back the memory of the sensuous sweetness of her startled lips. "Oh, he is not gentleman. The very idea that you would dally with a groom in the stable —"

"Dally with the groom?" she sputtered. "Are you referring to Nathan?"

"Yes."

"Lord Camryn—" She drew herself up. "While it is none of your affair, I must tell you that you are gravely mistaken about Mister Fuller. He and I are longtime acquaintances and nothing more."

Mister Fuller. It almost sounded respectable. "Mister

Fuller is the stable boy known as Nathan, I presume?"

"One and the same. And I assure you that he is a longtime family friend and nothing more."

"I see."

"Although, I must say, I find your code of conduct to be most fascinating," she said in a tart tone. "It is not my perceived dalliance with a gentleman that offends you, but rather the fact that I would allow a man who is socially beneath me to take certain liberties, is that it?"

A pang of jealousy quickened in Cam at the memory of Charlotte in Nathan's embrace. "You play a dangerous game, Miss Livingston. You risk shredding your reputation by having a blatant dalliance with a groom."

Her eyes flashed. She tugged the neckline of her dress upward, the movement drawing Cam's attention to her décolletage, which heaved with delightful indignation. He pictured those enticing white orbs bouncing out of her gown so he could cup each soft, warm handful.

"Hardly a stable boy. Nathan is a grown man who also happens to be Hartwell's coachman. He is coachman to a duke and is entrusted with many responsibilities, including the oversight of all of the other grooms and stable boys."

Cam's thoughts left her bosom. "How enlightening. I am quite aware of the duties of a coachman. After all, I do employ one myself." His mouth twisted. "Hartwell's esteemed coachman clearly has a fondness for you. Perhaps you've given him cause to hope a baron's daughter would welcome the advances of a coachman."

"So it is Nathan's low birth which offends your gentlemanly sensibilities." Ice formed over Charlotte's vibrant eyes. "Perhaps you would find it more acceptable for me to dally with, say, a marquess?"

He stiffened at the implication. Looking into her endless eyes, he realized Charlotte Livingston had the amazing capacity to both annoy and arouse him at the same time. "There is no need for vulgarity, Miss Livingston."

"I see. Nathan's fondness for me is vulgar, while your propensity toward garden activities with married ladies is what, exactly?"

"There you are, Lord Camryn." A honeyed voice interrupted. Cam suppressed a groan as Maria Fitzharding swept towards them, pausing to give Charlotte a quick, dismissive glance before focusing her full attention on him. "My lord, I understand Lord Fulsome-Thrusby's portrait gallery is simply not to be missed."

Charlotte stiffened. Her cool gaze rolled over Maria's full curves and overly generous breasts, which lurched in his direction. Her perusal swept upwards to Maria's full mouth before she flushed and diverted her eyes.

Maria fluttered her dark lashes. "Perhaps you would care to escort me. I understand a stroll through Fulsome-Thrusby's gallery can be most stimulating." The obvious implication of her invitation hung in the air.

Cam sketched a bow. "Of course, my dear. I would be delighted." He turned to Charlotte. "Perhaps Miss Livingston would care to join us?"

Maria, who seemed to have forgotten Charlotte's presence, glanced over at her. "Oh, yes, yes of course," she said with an obvious lack of enthusiasm. "Do join us Miss Livingston."

To his satisfaction, something akin to jealously flared in Charlotte's eyes. "I've seen quite enough...of the gallery.

But by all means, please do go and enjoy yourselves."

Chapter Six

It finally felt like summer in London. The days grew warm and sunny, and were sometimes punctuated by light rain showers. With the season all but ended, the most prominent families had already made the annual exodus to the country.

Charlotte had decided to accept Willa's invitation to spend the remainder of the summer at Fairview Manor. The duke and duchess had already removed to the country, having left the city early to accommodate Willa's fast-approaching period of confinement. Hugh planned to escort Charlotte to Fairview in a few days' time.

She was sitting in the upstairs family room at Shellborne House on one of those last lazy days in London when a footman knocked to inform her that Hugh requested her presence in the drawing room. Making her way there, she wondered why she'd been summoned.

Her brother's florid, beaming face greeted her when she entered the chamber. "Ah, here she is now," he said to a figure seated by the window.

Camryn stood, his gleaming presence dominating the room. "Miss Livingston," he said. "I hope you don't mind that I have taken the liberty of calling upon you and Shellborne."

He was dressed for riding in a close-fitting, black, cropped riding coat. His athletic thighs were snugly encased in tan leather riding breeches that buttoned and tied at the sides of his knees. His brown riding boots had a slightly worn look to them, but his linen shirt, waistcoat, and cravat were all a crisp white. As usual, his tawny hair was in a state of controlled disarray.

She hadn't seen the marquess since the Fulsome-Thrusby ball almost a fortnight ago. Angry jealousy flared in her chest at the memory of him slipping off with the very eager Mrs. Fitzharding. What a strumpet. Not to mention Camryn, whose behavior had been no better. She didn't have to imagine what they'd done after she left them. The vivid images of their previous encounter at Fairview were still emblazoned in her mind.

With Willa gone and the season's grand routs at an end, she hadn't expected to see the marquess again so soon. But here he was, calling on her and despite all reason, her heart glowed with happiness. "Lord Camryn."

"Camryn has requested permission to call upon you," Hugh said with barely contained excitement.

Charlotte's surprised gaze flew to Cam. Her mouth went dry. The marquess had just formally declared his intention to court her. She forced herself to remember the man stood for things she despised. It didn't help. She still felt positively giddy.

"I was hoping perhaps you would favor me with a

ride along the Row," he said. "I seem to recall you favor a vigorous ride."

"That sounds agreeable." She struggled to sound calm. "With your leave, I will go and change."

He favored her with a devastating pearly smile that made her toes curl in her slippers.

"Of course."

"Do enjoy yourselves," said Hugh. "Charlotte, do not forget to take your maid."

About an hour later, they were riding along Rotten Row. It was not a fashionable time of day to be seen there. Except for the occasional rider, the trail appeared deserted since almost everyone of consequence had left town. It gave them a chance to gallop freely, which they both preferred.

Charlotte laughed as she finally pulled her horse to a stop. "What an excellent time to ride," she said, her cheeks warm from their exertions. "It is my first time back in the saddle since my fall."

His golden-green eyes crinkled. "I am grateful there are no high jumps to tempt you into losing your seat again."

"You are a cad to mention that." She tossed her head. "As you will recall, I did not take a fall from the rigors of the jumps. My horse was startled, and since I was distracted by you, one could argue the fault lays with you."

He threw his head back and laughed, the sun skimming the admirable cut of his profile, a sculpted masculine nose and firm chin. His laugh was so like him, full and unbridled, rumbling deep in his chest. "Well then, allow me to apologize by treating you to a picnic," he said, his eyes twinkling. "My cook has prepared a veritable feast for us."

Glancing at the satchel attached to his saddle, she said,

"You were confident I would accompany you?"

He slid effortlessly off his horse and came over to help her down. "I know the powerful hold the promise of a rigorous ride has on you, Miss Livingston. I was just clever enough to insert myself into that appealing picture."

His large, warm hands wrapped around her waist, helping her dismount, unsettling her insides. She glanced down the path from where they had just come. She could not see Violet.

"I seem to have lost my abigail," she said once her feet touched the ground.

He gazed down the path. "Your maid will catch up with us in good time." He moved to spread a blanket for their picnic. "We aren't far off the path. She cannot miss us."

She decided he had the right of it. They were close enough to the row to be noticed, so Violet would likely see them. He'd selected a scenic spot near the Serpentine. She walked over to stand by the water's edge, pulling off her bonnet and snug red riding jacket. Underneath her jacket, Charlotte's white blouse tucked into a brown riding skirt held up by suspenders.

"What are you thinking?" he asked.

"That it is presumptuous of you to call upon me after our last encounter."

"But, Miss Livingston," he said, "as I recall, I issued an apology at our last meeting."

"It was what occurred after the apology." She faced him. "Do you truly wish to court me?"

"Indeed, Miss Livingston, I do. Since you appreciate honesty and directness, I felt this was the clearest way to demonstrate my intentions."

She flushed with pleasure. *He meant to court her.* "It is insulting that you presume to court me after that crude scene with Mrs. Fitzharding."

His golden eyes darkened. "I have already apologized that you had to witness that unfortunate encounter."

"No, not at Fairview. I am referring to the rout at the Fulsome-Thrusby's when you stole away with that woman." Her insides burning, she walked back to their picnic area and threw her riding jacket and bonnet onto the blanket. "When you knew I was completely aware of what was to follow once I left you."

His eyes twinkled as he strode over to her. Overwhelmed by his closeness, she backed up against the tree. He placed his hands on either side of her head, his palms flat against the thick trunk, effectively boxing her in. "Is this jealousy I detect?"

"Hardly." The beat of her heart accelerated. "It is difficult to put aside your blatant insult."

He leaned a little closer, his musky scent surrounding her. "Would it comfort you to know that nothing happened beyond a companionable stroll through the portrait gallery?"

She swallowed. "I find that difficult to believe."

He leaned in just a little more. His gaze raked over her face, seeming to take in each curve and every line. "I have enjoyed a, shall we say, friendship with Mrs. Fitzharding." His provocative voice caressed her. "It would be rude and hurtful of me to cut her off completely simply because I no longer desire a physical relationship with her."

"Is that so?" The bottom of her womb pulsed as he ran his intent gaze down the length of her body. He reached out to lift a suspender strap away from her body, his long, tapered fingers stroking it inches from where it had just rested over her breast. Her body tingled all the way down to her toes. To her mortification, her breasts awakened fully, their crests straining against her white shirt.

The darkening of Cam's eyes suggested he noticed. His breathing changed, becoming shallow in a way that spurred her blood. He leaned toward her, placing warm lips on the pulse point at the side of her neck. "Yes," he murmured against her sensitive skin, "that is so."

She trembled at the featherlight flirtation of his mouth at her throat. "How gallant of you," she said, breathless. "And do you take liberties with me now because you assume a lady who dallies with a stable boy would surely grant favors to all others who ask?"

He chuckled against her neck, the puff of warm breath tickling her skin. "No," he said, straightening up to replace her suspender strap over her breast. "I no longer believe that to be the case."

"And why is that?"

He watched his fingers brush over her hardened nipple, moving with a slow deliberateness that provoked soft waves of painful pleasure within her. Shocked and aroused, she looked up into his heated eyes.

"You have described yourself as a woman who never lies, and I believe you. I have your word that nothing untoward has occurred between you and the stable boy." He moved his lips back to her neck.

"Coachman," she said with a sigh closing her eyes, lifting her chin to receive the delicious kisses he peppered along the side of her neck.

"My apologies," he murmured, undeterred from his task.

"*Coachman.* Unforgiveable of me to forget."

"Why, then, did you give me the cut direct at Willa's party?"

"Because I didn't care for the thought of any other man touching you." His lips moved languidly up her neck and over to her mouth in one fluid movement and took hers with a soft insistence, nipping and tasting in a teasing way that left her senseless with need. "Do say you'll forgive me."

When his tongue flicked against the seam of her mouth, she couldn't remember what there was to forgive him for. She parted her lips, eager to taste him. He swept in at once, exploring the slickness he found there with deep, soulful strokes. She kissed him back, sliding her tongue against his. Forgetting all propriety, she embraced him, letting her hands run over the extraordinary blend of smooth muscle and bone in his back. He felt solid and pliant, and she wanted more. So much more.

The movement seemed to embolden Cam. He pushed up against her, his unrelenting body flat against hers, kissing her more deeply. She moaned at the feel of his aroused male flesh pressing against her belly. Her mind remembered the sight of it unleashed, large and proud. Cam moved his warm hands down the sides of her body to cup her bottom, pulling her tight against his hips.

She rubbed her body against the hot, hard length of his, trying to ease a hunger growing inside of her, vaguely wondering how she could be so intoxicated by a man whose goals in life were so contrary to hers.

Breaking the kiss, Cam rested his forehead against hers. "Charlotte, love," he rasped. "Tell me to stop."

Exhilaration surged through her to think she could

drive this magnificent creature to the edge of his control. "Don't you dare stop," she panted. Putting her hand behind his head, she pulled his mouth back to hers. Her tongue reached out to taste his again, sucking lightly, wanting this feeling to never end.

An elemental sound came from somewhere deep in Cam's chest. Giving up all pretense of restraint, he ravished her mouth, grinding his manhood into her. Charlotte gasped at the wondrous feel of him. Pushed up against the rough bark of the tree, she opened her eyes to see Cam fully, eager to take in every nuance.

Instead, her heart dropped. Violet's horse appeared in the distance coming along the path. She pushed Cam away in something of a panic. Dropping down on the blanket in one swift movement, she busied herself with unpacking their picnic.

"We have been caught up to, just as you surmised," she said, making a show of setting the food out. Cam pivoted, striding over to the water's edge, keeping his back to both Charlotte and the path. Violet approached, bobbing haphazardly on her mount, out of breath, and flushed.

Charlotte greeted her maidservant as if nothing was amiss, grateful her abigail couldn't detect the way her body still pulsated from Cam's caresses. Calling out to the marquess, she pulled out the roast chicken and they all began to eat.

• • •

Cam called upon Charlotte again the next day and the one after that. The more he saw of her, the more he wanted to see her. Both times they went for a ride, always with Violet in tow. To Cam's frustration, they had not managed to lose the abigail again. After her initial lapse, Charlotte's faithful maid seemed determined in her duty to safeguard her mistress's virtue.

They weren't able to steal time alone together again until the following week, when Cam escorted Charlotte to the Ellerbee's picnic luncheon held at their estate just outside of London. The elegant outdoor affair featured an elaborate feast laid out in the back lawn where manicured gardens eventually gave way to untamed grass and wooded areas. The gathering was not overly large since most of the Ton had already retired to the country for the summer.

Cam watched Charlotte mingle among some of the season's most desirable young maidens, most of whom wore elaborate day gowns that somehow seemed too fussy. The gauzy fabric of Charlotte's simple peach gown had the perfect light touch for a summer's day. Her maid had put her brown hair up, with ringlets cascading down, highlighting her long, pale neck, and the soft swell of her round breasts. Desire swirled in his gut. What a handsome woman. *Handsome*? It startled him to realize just how attractive she'd become to him.

After filling their plates, he escorted Charlotte to a shaded area a bit removed from the other picnickers, happy to have her to himself again.

She looked around, sipping her lemonade. "This is a secluded spot."

He took her food from her and placed it on the ground. "Yes, I selected it quite on purpose." He took the glass from her as well, carefully placing it on a level spot so it wouldn't topple.

"And why is that?"

He marveled at the way the sun illuminated the clear blue in her eyes. "I won't bother to dissemble, Miss Livingston." Taking hold of her hand, he pulled Charlotte around the massive tree trunk, out of the sight of the rest of the guests.

"I hope to steal another kiss. Actually, I have thought of little else since our last one. Will you allow it?"

She flushed, her gaze floating beyond him. "Really, Camryn, if you ask for permission, it hardly qualifies as *stealing* a kiss."

Blood raced to his vitals when it registered she'd just told him to take what he wanted. Shaking his head, he wondered what is was about this woman that made him desperate to touch her again. It had been an agonizing week since he'd last felt her lips beneath his. Now, finally offered the opportunity, he greedily grasped it.

Cupping Charlotte's cheeks, he marveled at their satiny softness before lowering his face to hers, kissing one side of her succulent mouth and then the other. Then he intensified his actions, pressing down on her lips, bidding her to open them to him as she had once before. When she did, he kissed her as deeply as he had ever kissed a woman. He licked and plunged his tongue deeper, greedy to taste more, losing himself in her subtle floral scent. She tasted of lemonade, a woman's softness, and unlimited possibility. Her untutored tongue ventured to taste him as well, provoking a delighted sound of surprise from him. The wondering hum that sounded from the back of her throat made his body quicken in a rush of heat.

Awareness gradually filtered back to him, reminding

Cam of their surroundings. He pulled away with great reluctance, his blood at a boil, and forced himself to take a step back lest he pull Charlotte to the grass and make love to her right there with other guests nearby.

She stood frozen in place with her eyes still closed, red circles burned into the high arches of her cheeks. After a moment, as if in a daze, her lids fluttered open. He easily recognized the hazy arousal in those unfocused blue depths for they mirrored his own.

They stood facing one another for a moment, bodies apart, but gazes interlocked. She blinked. "When I said you had a clever tongue, I really had no idea."

"I say, Camryn, is that you?"

He looked blindly toward the voice, grateful an outsider would only see two people standing an appropriate distance from each other and not the firestorm of passion arcing between them. As the man drew nearer, he recognized his old friend from Cambridge.

"Selwyn, as usual, your timing is impeccable."

David Selwyn grinned, bowing toward Charlotte. "Miss Livingston, I'm delighted that not all that is lovely and gracious has deserted town as of yet."

She returned his smile, managing to appear remarkably calm despite her flushed cheeks. "I hope you will join us, Mister Selwyn."

Cam walked over to settle himself on the blanket. "Yes, by all means, do."

Along with the Duke of Hartwell, Cam and Selwyn had led a raucous group at university that excelled equally at sport, women, and their studies. Selwyn's wealth and rank did not match that of his friends, but he made up for it with an obvious intelligence, agreeability, and quiet flare. Not a particularly handsome man, Selwyn had a pleasant demeanor and took a great deal of care with his appearance and manners.

"Thank you." With a quick, appraising gaze of his companions, he settled on the grass.

Cam's body still hummed from his encounter with Charlotte. "I, for one, am starved," he said reaching for his plate.

As they ate, the two men fell into an easy banter born of longtime friendship and familiarity. Once they'd had their fill, they settled back with a fresh glass of lemonade brought over by a footman, enjoying the partial shade the tree offered on the pleasantly warm summer day. Charlotte rested her back up against the tree while Cam stretched out on his side, propping himself up on one elbow.

Unfurling his legs and crossing them at the ankle, Selwyn planted his hands on the ground behind him to support his weight. "Have you heard about the latest Luddite disturbances in Lancashire?"

"Yes." Turning his face upward, Cam basked in a warm sliver of sun that had broken through the tree's branches. He yawned as lazy contentment spread through him. "One would think the Crown would have quelled that by now."

"The only way to stop the risings is to offer workers an alternative means of providing for their families," Charlotte said.

Selwyn looked over at Cam. "Did I hear that you are dabbling in the loom business, Camryn?"

Cam lay down flat on his back with his hands behind his head, enjoying the lulling warmth of the sun's rays, yet fully aware that Charlotte had stiffened beside him. "Yes, Hartwell and I recently acquired a new factory not far from Fairview Manor."

"So the two of you see a future in these machines?" Willa's husband had proven himself an astute businessman, making most of his fortune through Indian sugar exports.

"The machines work much more quickly than people." Cam slid a sidelong glance at Charlotte, noting how she'd pressed her swollen lips into a tight line as he answered. "And ultimately produce more at a lesser cost."

Selwyn shook his head. "Yet the machine wreckers make it a perilous venture."

Cam nodded his agreement. "Now that machine breaking is a capital crime, some of them need to swing."

"It's that Ned Ludd," said Selwyn, of the agitators' enigmatic leader. "If he does indeed exist."

"I'm certain he's just a myth." Charlotte's blue eyes darkened. "It's said the real Ned Ludd was a simpleton who broke a stocking frame by accident, not this charismatic General Ludd people speak of, who leads the rebellion."

"If he does exist, he should be hunted down mercilessly." Cam stretched out with a contented sigh, enjoying the feel of his full stomach, the mild weather, and the surprisingly warm satisfaction of having Charlotte by his side. "I would be happy to lead the charge. If you hang their leader, you cut the head off the snake."

Darkness had begun to fall by the time Cam escorted Charlotte home. Sitting across from her in the backward facing seat, he examined the details of her face — the high-cut cheekbones and smooth turn of her jaw, those vibrant eyes, and below them, pink, plump lips. Sitting ramrod straight, she didn't seem aware of his inspection. Pale and drawn, she appeared lost in thought. Perhaps talk of his factories had upset her again.

Or maybe today's kiss had embarrassed her. He hoped not. After all, he'd announced his intention to court her and his mind was rapidly embracing the idea of marriage. The more he thought about it, the more he came to believe Hart might be correct about Cam's attraction to Charlotte. Perhaps she was the one.

He'd thought of her often since their first ride together at Fairview. Today's embrace had been a revelation, demonstrating the depth of the physical attraction raging between them. Along with her sharp mind and tart tongue, life with Charlotte as his marchioness would never be dull.

Of course, he longed to bed her, to see that lithesome softness stripped bare of all clothing. He wondered what it would be like to stroke in and out of her, to hear her cry out with pleasure. The thought of exploring how her honesty would play out between the bed linens made his body stir below the waist.

Would she bring that same level of directness and lack of artifice to the marital bed? Not everyone did, but he suspected she would. The corners of his mouth tilted upward. Yes, this had the makings of a good match. Yet he was unsure of her thoughts and feelings on the subject of matrimony. No matter. If she proved to be reluctant, he'd employ a bit of seduction. Putting a little effort into seducing Charlotte would be well worth the outcome.

At three-and-thirty, he was past the age most men married and set up their nursery. He'd never really given the concept of children much thought before. Of course, he'd always known an heir would be necessary. But now the idea of a little girl with Charlotte's incomparable blue eyes made his throat feel as though someone had lodged a fist in it. Having a family with her seemed like a natural progression toward the future.

When they arrived at Shellborne House, he helped Charlotte from the carriage and escorted her to the door. "Thank you for a most lovely day, Miss Livingston," he said warmly. "I hope you will allow me to call upon you tomorrow."

A shadow crossed those azure eyes, dimming the light in them, making her seem strangely cool and closed off. Foreboding shivered through him.

"Thank you, my lord," she said. "But I don't think that would be wise."

"Oh?" he pressed, his mind unwilling to grasp what instinct already told him. "Do you have a previous engagement?"

Her face shuttered. "No, but I prefer that you no longer call upon me. Ever. We do not suit."

He jerked his head back, certain he hadn't heard her correctly. "You cannot be serious." Granted the time they'd spent together had been brief, but it had also been as close to idyllic as he'd ever experienced. She couldn't possibly believe they didn't suit.

He frowned. "Surely, what today has demonstrated is that we suit each other in many ways." He moved closer to her, speaking in a rapid, urgent tone. "Is it this business with my factories? Once you visit them, you will change your opinion."

She stepped back, her cold blue eyes meeting his. "I

doubt that. Anyhow, it is of no account. It's only right that I acknowledge there is another with a claim on my affections."

Another man? The ground shifted beneath his feet. "May I inquire as to who this gentleman is?"

Scratching behind one ear, her eyes slid away. "It is as you suspected. I have an attachment to Mister Fuller." She turned to go inside. "There is absolutely no point in furthering our friendship."

The stable boy? He didn't believe it. Before he could say anything further, she stepped into the house and slammed the door shut behind her, leaving Cam on the doorstep, dumbstruck and alone.

Chapter Seven

"Ugh," Willa said, as she and Charlotte strolled through Fairview's meticulously maintained gardens. "I know this is meant to be blissful, but I am so uncomfortable."

They stepped along a gravel walkway lined with vibrant blooms, the yellow, violet, and lavender shades crowding each other as though competing for attention. The mixture of fragrances shifted as the women moved, the sweet potency of some flowers intermingling with the light, almost ephemeral, scents of others.

Since arriving four days ago, Charlotte had joined the duchess' daily exercise ritual. "It would be easier to sympathize if you didn't still look so comely," she said, strolling at an easy pace. "Gad, Willa, if anything I think being with child makes you even more beautiful."

Like most people, Charlotte remained in awe of her friend's dark, earthy beauty. Willa's large, velvet-brown eyes and delicate porcelain complexion were topped by a luxurious mane of unruly chestnut curls. Charlotte felt tall and shapeless next to the duchess's pleasing curves, which were remarkably enhanced by her current condition. Glancing at Willa's full chest, she said, "I'd wager the duke is appreciative of some of those changes."

Willa's eyes widened. "You are so wicked." She laughed and looped her arm through Charlotte's. In the year since they'd met, the two women had forged a deep bond. Both read widely, enjoying the challenge of new ideas. And while they appreciated serious discourse, the women also indulged in the frivolous side of friendship, mixing gossip with an abundance of silliness and laughter.

"I understand you spent time with my dashing cousin before joining us here," Willa said.

"How in the world would you know that?" Pain twisted deep in her chest at the unexpected mention of Camryn. It had taken all of her strength to turn him away in London. The misery of it still lingered.

"Mister Selwyn came to call last week." Coming to a bench, Willa sank down to rest. "I gather he had some business matters to discuss with Hartwell. He mentioned an afternoon picnic with the two of you."

"Yes." Trying to affect an indifferent tone, Charlotte plucked a primrose and brought it up to her nose to inhale its spicy scent. "We rode a few times in Hyde Park as well. It was pleasant enough, but I have not seen the marquess since." She gave her friend a pointed look. "And I do not expect him to call again."

Willa's mouth curved downward. "Well, that's distressing. I've always thought you two would suit each other."

"How could you possibly think that?" She studied the

primrose, methodically plucking its deep violet petals. "My published writings rail against industrialists of his sort. We are as suited as a feline is to a hound."

"Nonsense, you just don't know Cam well enough yet. He engages in serious social pursuits and even has political ambitions."

She looked up from the half-naked flower. "Political ambitions?"

"He doesn't speak of it, but Hart says Cam is fast becoming one of the more influential members of the House of Lords. He believes Cam's potential to be unlimited."

She threw the flower down. "Do you think he will pursue higher office?"

"Hart thinks Cam could very well be a minister one day if he so chooses." Willa pushed heavily to her feet to resume walking. "And if you were to marry him, think of how you could influence him to support your causes."

"Marry him?" Her heart ached with the knowledge it would never come to pass. "Please Willa, put such nonsense out of your mind. Camryn has made his disdain for my causes quite clear. I could never hope to influence him in any meaningful way." She looped her arm through Willa's, tugging her along. "Enough of this talk. Let us turn back while you tell me whether you've decided on a name for the babe."

They returned to the manor to find the duke had been called away on urgent business. Shellborne, who'd escorted Charlotte to Fairview and planned to depart the following day, had accompanied him, along with Hart's valet and a few grooms. However, Digby, the butler, didn't know the exact nature of the matter.

Willa frowned as the two women proceeded into luncheon alone. "Where could he have gone? And why did he take so many people with him?"

"Perhaps it's an emergency with one of his tenants," Charlotte said.

Willa's perfectly arched brow furrowed. "Hart planned to stay in and work with his steward today. And if it involved the tenants, his steward would have gone with him."

The afternoon dragged into evening, leaving them to take their supper alone before retiring to their chambers near midnight, still with no word of the gentlemen. It wasn't until morning that Charlotte had news of them.

"His Grace and the others are returned." It was Molly, the maid who brought Charlotte her chocolate, who relayed the welcome information.

Relief loosened her muscles. "They are safe and all is well?"

"Appears so, ma'am." Molly knelt to clean the fireplace grates. "'Tis a relief because we all think highly of His Grace." She wiped the hearth down with water, drying it with a linen cloth. "I don't mind telling you I was afraid to leave Lord Camryn's employ, but all turned out well, it did."

Charlotte''s heart squeezed at the unexpected mention of Cam. Swinging her legs over the edge of the bed, she reached for her dressing gown. "You were in service at Camryn Hall?"

"Yes, miss. Her Grace wanted me and Clara, that's her lady's maid, to accompany her when she wed, so here we are." The girl used a tinderbox to light the fire.

"And how was your time at Camryn Hall?"

"'Twas very fine, miss. The old marquess, Her Grace's

sainted father, was kind enough. But Lord Camryn made some changes, he did." Molly stood up to assess the fire before deciding to throw more wood on it. "In town, he bettered the servants' sleeping quarters. Me being an upstairs maid, I had me an attic room. But the below stairs servants—" She shook her head.

"Go on," she urged, desperate for any small sliver of information about the marquess.

"Their basement quarters was bad, if you excuse my saying so, miss. 'Twas dark and you couldna even see where you was going." Molly moved to open the curtains. "And the smoke, bless the Lord, it was so smoky from the candles and oil lamps. Hard to breathe, it was."

Sipping the warm chocolate, Charlotte took a chair by the kindling fire and folded her legs beneath her. The conditions Molly described were not unusual for servants in town, whose basement quarters were known for their darkness and lack of ventilation. Many had rounded corners so servants wouldn't injure themselves as they rushed to serve their masters.

"And Lord Camryn rectified the situation?" Charlotte prompted over the rim of her cup.

"Yes, miss. Shocked he was to see how things was down below." Molly moved about the room, straightening up. "Most masters don't bother to visit the servants' quarters, but my lord did. He made a special place over the mews so the below stairs could sleep with the grooms. Now they have fresh air to breathe."

"Commendable," she murmured, sipping her drink, its sweet heat sliding down her throat and warming her insides. So Camryn was not quite the autocrat he appeared to be.

"And the wages, miss, he said we was past time for an increase."

"Did he?"

"Yes, miss. We all of us got an increase and not just the senior servants. Raised me pay a good ten pounds per annum. And even the junior housemaids got an extra five pounds."

"How generous." A smile tugged at her lips. "Are you just as well taken care of here?"

"Oh yes, miss, Lady Willa…begging your pardon…I mean Her Grace…promised me wages and bonus would keep to the same here at Fairview. And I don't have me any family in the village at Camryn Hall, so here I am."

Later, Charlotte found herself humming as she dressed, buoyed by Molly's revelations about Cam's quiet generosity to his servants. However, her high spirits were dampened at breakfast once she learned why the men had been called away.

"Machine wreckers attacked the mill," the duke told them as they ate. "Some of the looms are badly damaged."

"Pardon me for saying, ladies, but it's those deuced Luddites." Hugh swallowed a bite of kidney pie. "The crown must send more troops to quell the risings before it's too late."

A chill ran through her. A clandestine evening raid to attack and destroy looms had all of the earmarks of the Luddites.

"Will it prove costly to repair the damage?" asked Willa.

"I'm afraid so." Movement at the threshold of the breakfast room distracted the duke. "Ah, here's Cam."

Entering the chamber, the Marquess of Camryn inclined

his ruffled, amber mane at the assembled group. "I give you good morning." Dressed in a country style, his skin was bronzed and fawn breeches hugged his trim hips while his white shirt opened at the throat to reveal a flash of golden-brown skin dusted with tawny hairs.

Charlotte's lungs felt sore. What was he doing here?

"Willa dear." He flashed that heart-stopping, wide grin at his cousin, before acknowledging Hugh and Charlotte, his golden-green eyes brushing over her. "Shellborne. Miss Livingston."

Willa's face brightened. "Cam, what a lovely surprise. When did you arrive?"

"Just a few hours ago. I set out as soon as Hart sent word of trouble at the mill." He went to the sideboard to fill a plate, his snug breeches offering an excellent view of a firm, well-shaped backside. A frisson of longing moved through Charlotte when she realized he wore the same slightly tattered brown Hessians from their afternoon rides in town.

"How bad is the damage?" he asked, seating himself across from Charlotte.

"Rather extensive, I'm afraid." Hart spoke from his seat at the head of the table. "A few of the looms sustained serious damage. I am told most are repairable but just barely."

Cam frowned. "What occurred exactly?"

"They took sledgehammers to the factory door. From what was left behind, it appears they employed pieces of cast iron and wood to do their machine breaking."

"How long will it take to repair the looms?" asked Charlotte. As she spoke, Cam focused on eating his breakfast.

"It could be a few days before we can resume full production." Hartwell looked at Cam. "I suppose we should ride out again on the morrow to have a look."

"What happens to the workers while the mill is closed?" asked Charlotte. "Can they survive without a week's wages?"

For the first time since arriving, Cam gave her his full attention, pinning her with a cool green gaze. "Contrary to your belief, we won't allow our workers to suffer through no fault of their own. They'll continue receiving full wages until we are back in full production."

Heat licked her cheeks at his chastisement. Stung, she pretended to busy herself with a mouthful of eggs which, unfortunately, now tasted like foolscap.

Hartwell shot Cam a reproving look before turning to Charlotte. "They will of course be working on the cleanup and to restore order."

Eager to be as far away from Camryn as possible, Charlotte rose and turned to Willa. "Shall we leave the gentlemen to their business and take our walk?"

• • •

After finishing breakfast and consulting further with Hart about the factory, Cam headed to the stables to check on Hercules. He'd ridden the stallion hard in his rush to get to Fairview Park. He also hoped the fresh air would clear his head. Seeing Charlotte again had his mind churning. Back in town, when she'd told him the truth about the coachman, he'd resolved to put her out of his thoughts, but it hadn't been easy.

His mind kept returning to that last kiss. He believed Charlotte to be an honorable woman. If she had a significant attachment to the stable boy, why would she have accepted the idea of his courting her? Why had she not only allowed a kiss, but also responded to it? Her body had undoubtedly enjoyed his touch. Kissing her had not only been pleasurable, it had had an element of truth to it. Their last afternoon together, in particular, had left him with a strong feeling of contentment, a sense that he and Charlotte were a good fit.

With her, things seemed to fall into place. Charlotte's presence in his life eased the malaise he'd been experiencing of late. Their fiery intellectual connection, coupled with an astounding physical attraction, left him feeling keenly aware of what had been missing in his life.

As he approached the stable, Shellborne's indignant voice rang out from around the corner of the structure. "What the devil is he doing here?"

"He is the Duke of Hartwell's coachman," came Charlotte's calm reply.

So, it appeared he wasn't alone in his dislike of Fuller's presence at Fairview. Cam stopped short behind the stables, out of view, and cocked his head.

"Do you expect me to believe his appearance here is a coincidence?" Shellborne's voice shook with fury. "Have you been struck senseless?"

"You have no call to speak with me in that manner." The words were calm. "I'll do as I please."

Cam smiled despite himself. He admired her feistiness.

"The devil you will. I am the head of this family and you have defied me."

Cam peered around the corner to see Shellborne pacing in a small circle, hands on his portly hips as he stared at the ground.

"Blast it all. I sent him away to protect you." The man's

voice rose. "To save our family from scandal and ruin. And you bring him here, to the *Duke of Hartwell*?"

"I love him," she retorted. "I won't let him starve or go without. Nathan is willing to work hard. He deserves a chance to better himself."

She loves Fuller. Cam's heart seemed to shrink and harden in his chest.

Shellborne's face reddened. "He's a servant, a by-blow. You are the daughter of a gentleman. For God's sake, Charlotte, at least pretend to know your place!"

"Stop acting so high in the instep. Either one of us could easily be in his place." Charlotte's tone softened. "It's the luck of fate that you are a baron and he a coachman."

"Balderdash!" Shellborne's voice went higher. "It was no luck of fate. You and I are the result of generations of good breeding. He's nothing but a low class side-slip and you are making a cake of yourself. Think Charlotte, *think*, before you ruin us all."

She turned to go. "I *think* I've heard quite enough."

He grabbed her arm. "Don't you dare think of going to him. I won't allow it."

"Hugh, you're hurting me." She tried to pull away. "Unhand me."

Cam's temper flared. He started forward, but halted at the sound of a third voice.

"Unhand her, Shellborne." Fuller's voice.

"Do not presume to tell me what to do." Unbridled contempt contorted Shellborne's face. "You are nothing but a by-blow. I am *Shellborne* and she is under my care."

"That may be." The calm tone held a hard note of warning. "However, I won't allow any harm to come to her."

Fuller moved into Cam's line of vision, allowing him to take a full measure of the man. He stood a full head above Charlotte's rotund brother, with soft blue eyes blazing in the sunlight. A cold, barely leashed rage seemed to simmer along the surface of his skin. The man exuded danger. Yet Fuller's menacing presence didn't seem to cow Shellborne in the least. "If you would know your place, Charlotte wouldn't be in any trouble. By God, I will see you dismissed."

"Perhaps you will succeed. That will be up to His Grace." Fuller started toward Shellborne. "But you will unhand her. *Now*."

Cam stepped into view. "There you are, Miss Livingston. I was hoping you would favor me with a walk. With your leave, of course, Shellborne."

The baron dropped Charlotte's arm. "Of course, Camryn." He pasted an expression of placid courtesy on his flushed face. "By all means, it's a lovely day for a stroll."

Out of the corner of his eye, Cam noticed Fuller fade back into the stables. The man was like a shadow. He offered Charlotte his arm. "Shall we?"

• • •

As they strolled away from the stables in silence, Charlotte was acutely aware of the warm, lightly muscled arm beneath her fingers.

"I gather your brother doesn't approve of your interest in grooms," he said once they were well away from Shellborne.

She focused on her feet, picking her way over some uneven swells on the ground. "What Hugh thinks is of no concern." She looked up to find that keen golden-green gaze searching her face, as if he might find answers there if he looked hard enough. Tensing, she asked, "Why are you regarding me in that manner?"

"I'm wondering what it is that motivates you."

"That's a large, unanswerable question, don't you think? It is rather like asking one what the meaning of life is."

"I was thinking of your attraction to Mr. Fuller."

"Oh."

"Is he what motivates your fierce passion for the lower classes?" he asked. "Willa tells me Fuller grew up alongside you and Shellborne. Your father allowed the child of a servant to be educated with his own children? It's quite unusual."

The thought of Cam inquiring about Nathan made her uneasy. "Yes."

"Is your father's generosity to the lower classes what informs your interest in helping them?"

"My father was no advocate of the operative class." Bitterness swelled in Charlotte's chest. "In some ways, he was every bit the pompous peer that Hugh is."

"And yet he allowed Fuller—"

"Papa had a special affection for Nathan, so he extended him the privilege of working with our governess." She waved a buzzing insect away. "If he'd been a real advocate of the lower orders, he would have sent Nathan away to school as he did with Hugh."

Cam's tawny brows drew together. "Surely, you're not suggesting your father should have provided the same education for the child of a servant as he would for his own heir?"

"Nathan has a keen mind. If he'd attended Eton or

Cambridge, he could have become a solicitor or a barrister, someone of consequence and not just a coachman." She gestured into the unknown. "How many other Nathans do you think are out there?"

His eyes softened in a way that made her throat ache. "I am sure there are many, Charlotte."

"Should they all be condemned to a life of poverty and stench because they weren't born into privilege as we were?"

"So you think to save Fuller?" His eyes locked with hers. "Perhaps by wedding him?"

She looked away. Her ears started to itch. "I cannot say."

"Has he declared himself?" His voice tightened. Halting, she gazed up to see determination glinting in his fierce eyes.

"No." A hot wave of yearning rippled through her. "He has not. Nor do I expect it of him. Still, we have an attachment that precludes me from accepting the attentions of another gentleman."

His large hand cupped her jaw, the pad of his thumb caressing of her cheek. "Is that so?"

She closed her eyes and inhaled the masculine scent of his hands, momentarily giving in to the sensation of his roughened skin touching hers. Before she could open her eyes again, Cam's soft, warm lips brushed against hers.

At first, he gave her sweet, small kisses, which offered the promise of so much more. He kissed her top lip. He nipped and then sucked lightly on her plump bottom one. Moving at a languid pace, he seemed to luxuriate in the taste and feel of her. His gently insistent tongue touched the seam of her mouth.

Leg-melting pleasure washed through her. Warning bells clanged somewhere in her head, but she barely heard them amidst the sweet assault of Cam's kisses. She opened her mouth and took him in. He tasted sublime. His tongue stroked hers, exploring with soft, flickering licks before suckling it. The part of her that knew she should stop moved her tongue away from his. He chuckled against her mouth before his tongue went after hers, wrestling playfully with it. Arousal curled hot and deep in her belly.

She surrendered, kissing Cam back with pressing need. Making an approving sound at the back of his throat, he deepened the kiss, plunging farther into her mouth, tickling and titillating the roof of her mouth.

Nerve endings she didn't know she possessed thundered to life. Sighing into Cam's mouth, she wanted to protest when he slowly withdrew his tongue, giving her another smattering of light, gentle kisses before pulling away. Still cupping her jaw, he looked down at her with glittering eyes, the sunlight glinting off his carved features.

"This might be an opportune time to mention," he said hoarsely, "that I fully intend to seduce you over to my way of thinking."

"Hmmm?" she asked, still dazed by the sensations shimmering through her. "How so?"

"I fear you are stealing my heart. Consequently, I plan to employ every weapon in my arsenal to win you."

The ground jerked beneath her. "Stealing your heart?" She reared back. "You shouldn't say such things."

"Why ever not?" He touched his forehead to hers. "You value forthrightness. I am being so now." He kissed her once again, more sweetly this time, pressing softly firm lips against hers, treating her with a tenderness which made her heart swell.

"I have an attachment elsewhere." She forced out the words. "As you well know."

"What I know, Miss Livingston" —he planted a small kiss at the side of her mouth that almost made her swoon— "is that you are a liar."

"Are you wooing and insulting me at the same time?" She couldn't resist pressing a light kiss along the strong cords of his neck.

He groaned with pleasure. "Absolutely. Only you do not possess what it takes to lie convincingly."

"I'm sure I don't know what you mean." She nipped his neck, tasting the salty sweetness of his warm skin.

"You're an honorable woman who wouldn't allow me such liberties if your heart lay elsewhere."

She pulled back, warily taking hold of her senses. "Is that so?"

"Yes, it is and that is why I have decided that you are indeed a liar." He spoke somewhat absentmindedly, watching the movement of his thumb stroking her cheek with a feathery touch.

Unable to stop herself, Charlotte tilted her cheek more fully into the caress of his hand. Although a million responses went through her head, she gave voice to none on account of being too distracted by the way his other hand traced her hairline.

"I'm certain that whatever is between you and the coachman, it is not what you pretend." He smiled with satisfaction. "I wonder, are you lying to me, or are you deceiving yourself as well?"

Panic bubbled up in her. How could she have let down her guard when so much was at stake, when her carelessness threatened to place someone she loved at risk? She pulled away, her pulse thumping, her ears itching. "My lord, you do not know what manner of woman I am." She called back over her shoulder so he would not see her face. "I have allowed you favors on more than one occasion. Do you flatter yourself to think you are the only one?"

Chapter Eight

The next morning Charlotte found herself on the way to the cotton mill. Molly accompanied her in the carriage while Cam and Hartwell rode on horseback. Hugh had departed and Willa was too round with child to make the trip, but she'd strongly encouraged Charlotte to go and see the factory for herself.

She thought of the factories she'd visited in the past. With strikes and unions forbidden by law, workers were left at the mercy of their employers, often made to work eighteen-hour days at starvation wages. She found it difficult to reconcile the two conflicting images of Cam. How could the man who ordered his servants moved to better quarters also preside over shameful factory conditions?

They made excellent time, reaching the mill by noon. Loud clattering reached Charlotte's ears long before the factory came into view. The power looms were obviously in working order. As they drew near the building, she studied the large stone edifice with interest. It contained a number of windows that were propped open, and the extensive lawn surrounding the structure appeared neat and well maintained.

Hartwell dismounted to speak with a man who hurried from the building to greet them. Intrigued by the sounds coming from the mill, Charlotte alighted from the coach. Taking the arm Cam offered, she let him lead her inside, with Molly trailing behind.

There were two long rows of power looms at work side by side in the clean, well-lit room. Despite the heat, the air was clear and the temperature far from unbearable.

She pulled away from Cam, curiosity compelling her to step closer for a better look. She watched as a flat, narrow, sticklike tool, which was wrapped with yarn, accelerated back and forth across the frame. It shuttled between the lengthwise set of threads, weaving them into a parallel set of strands. Many more were drawn under and over the analogous set of lengthwise fibers in a continuous harmony of motion.

Cam stepped behind her as she watched, mesmerized. He pointed to the flat, sticklike tool sweeping across the length of the shed.

"That's a shuttle. It threads those two sets of heddles together," he said speaking loudly. He pointed to a line of cords suspended on a shaft of the loom. "Each one has an eye where the thread is pulled through." The precise, melodic motions yielded finished cloth that corded neatly around a thick spool.

"It's all powered by steam?" Charlotte practically had to shout to be heard over the cantankerous sounds of the noisy machines.

"Yes, the steam comes through the line shafts." He pointed to a rod suspended above the looms. The pipe ran the full length of the forty-foot factory floor, running down between the two rows of frames. Large barrel-like pulleys ran along the line, each suspended above two of the machines.

"Those are pulleys. They distribute enough power for two machines." Cam pointed to the overhead barrel-like contraptions. The thick leather belts rotating around them were also affixed to a spur wheel on the side of the looms each powered. "The frames are all driven by the belts from the pulleys on the overhead shafts."

Charlotte's breath caught. "It is so quick and precise."

"Yes. It makes cloth from thread faster than any weaver could," Cam said in a raised voice, trying to be heard above the clanging. The machines turned out cloth at an amazing clip. She wandered around, watching the rattling machines follow the same rhythmic patterns. Molly stayed where she was, wide-eyed.

Charlotte stopped next to the last power loom at the end of the floor. Cam followed, coming to stand beside her, his face glistening from the heat despite the open windows.

Her own face moist from the humid air, heaviness settled in Charlotte's chest, her sense of wonderment etched with sadness. Seeming to sense her unspoken dilemma, Cam's strong hand clasped hers and their fingers intertwined. From where they stood behind the last loom, their laced hands remained hidden from view. She exhaled, grateful for the comforting strength he offered, a lone, solid anchor in the world of change laid out before her.

Despite the warmth on the stuffy factory floor, she

shivered. The glancing pain of profound awareness slashed through her. Now that she saw it for herself, it all became clear. The clamorous machines were the harbinger of a new reality. The old way of life for the villages dotting the English countryside would soon be gone forever. What would become of the people? It was clear that nothing—not the desperate weavers whose generations of skill were being rendered useless, nor their hungry children, nor the marauding Luddites—were a match for this marvelous and frightening truth.

"So, now you see. We cannot stop progress. It was never in our hands to begin with." Cam's mouth came close to her ear, his hand still clasping hers as they watched the machine's parts march in rapid precise movements no human could ever hope to match. "It is nothing short of a revolution."

A short time later, Cam reluctantly released Charlotte's hand and went in search of Hartwell to discuss mill business. She used that time to wander around the factory floor on her own. It surprised her that many of the workers were women. And there were no children.

"Females are known to have more nimble fingers," the floor overseer said. "They are quicker and more meticulous."

"And the men," she asked. "What do they do?"

"Tasks that require physical skill. They move and load the bolts of fabric. The men also fix the machinery when there is a problem."

She moved around, engaging some of the female workers in conversation, learning they each worked two looms, which produced twenty-five meters of cloth a day. Charlotte noted many seemed to have at least a rudimentary education. Clean and neatly attired, they did not appear miserable.

She asked Cam and Hartwell about the female workers later as they finished the picnic lunch they'd brought from Fairview. Molly had set up the meal under the shade of a tree to the side of the mill.

"Many of our workers are young, unmarried girls from respectable village families," Cam said. "We have a boarding house for them."

Charlotte raised an eyebrow. "That hardly seems respectable."

Hartwell laughed. "I assure you it is, Miss Livingston." He turned to Cam. "You should take her and show her your project."

"His project?" Charlotte looked from Hartwell to Cam, intrigued.

Grinning, Cam rose and offered his arm. "Allow me to show you the future, Miss Livingston."

Eager to see more, she stood and took his arm. She looked back at Molly, who appeared uncertain of whether to follow.

"No need for a chaperone," Cam told Charlotte, gesturing toward Molly. "It's just a walk out in the open among the people who work the mill. It's all quite appropriate."

As they strolled away, she noted the walkways around the factory were clean and well trimmed.

"I must confess. The grounds are much more inviting than I expected."

"It's all part of our plan." His pride was evident. "I believe if you respect the workers and provide decent surroundings for them to live and work in, they will be motivated to make the mill productive and successful." They rounded a thicket of trees, bringing a charming little village into view.

He pointed to a row of neat, sand-colored cottages. "Those are for our workers with families." Each of the stone-and-thatched dwellings appeared to have its own garden containing flowers and vegetables. A few were obviously still in the process of being constructed.

"We use the local people to build them. They also built the mill."

When they came to a stop in front of a well-maintained larger building, Cam guided her inside. A kindly-looking, middle-aged woman met them at the door.

"Good day, Mrs. Mallory," he said to her. "My apologies for the intrusion. I wanted to show your finely run boarding establishment to my friend, Miss Livingston."

Clearly happy to see him, the heavyset woman smiled broadly. "Of course, my lord. But rules are rules. Gentlemen can go no further than the parlor, even fine gentlemen such as yourself."

He threw back his messy mane, laughter rumbling through his chest. "As you can see, Miss Livingston, the young, single ladies are well protected by this fierce matron. No randy scoundrels will get past Mrs. Mallory."

"No, indeed," the woman said to Charlotte. "This is a strict boarding house. No men upstairs and only the highest standard of behavior for my girls. I keep a respectable place here."

Charlotte looked around, impressed by the clean, inviting atmosphere. The parlor was a large room, clearly intended for visiting. There were three separate sitting areas, each with its own sofa and several comfortable chairs. After a few more minutes of exchanging pleasantries with Mrs. Mallory, they took their leave, pausing to admire a tidy church that appeared to have been built recently.

Excitement bubbled up in Charlotte. "Oh, Cam, this is staggering. I cannot believe you have done all of this for your workers."

"It is not for just for them. It is good business for us as well. When we first began building the mill, I kept thinking there must be a way for machines and workers to be compatible. Unlike what people like the Luddites believe, one does not have to mean the annihilation of the other." Looking upward, he surveyed the pale honey church with obvious pride. The sun illuminated the noble lines of his face, bringing to mind a master surveying his domain. "We can help them make a good life for themselves. We need a content, motivated work force."

They resumed walking. "You have created an entire community here for them," she said with wonderment. "It is far beyond simply offering them work."

"That was our intent. They now have a very real stake in the success of the mill. Their entire life is literally wrapped up in it." He offered her his arm again. "And our productivity and profits give credence to my supposition."

Her heart fluttered as she took in the sleek cut of his profile, a firm nose and strong chin topped by that unruly tawny hair. Warmth burgeoned in her chest, billowing downward to the bottom of her stomach. "I have done you such a disservice. Presuming the worst about you."

Cam chuckled. "Don't tell me you've decided I am not quite the ruthless industrialist you pictured?"

"You are so much more."

He raised a questioning eyebrow.

"Much more thoughtful and forward thinking," she said,

eyeing her surroundings.

"Perhaps I've realized seducing you is as much an endeavor of the mind as it is of the body. Ah, here we are." They came to a stop in front of a new structure that appeared too large to be a cottage. "This should be of special interest to you." They entered the empty building, which smelled of new construction. "It is not quite ready yet, but I hope to have it well in hand soon."

The entire bottom floor was one large bright room. Generous windows ran along both sides, allowing sunlight to stream inside.

"What is this?" Charlotte asked as she slipped her hand away from Cam's arm to walk around and get a better look.

"It's a schoolhouse," Cam said.

Charlotte's eyebrows lifted in surprise. "For whom?"

"The workers' children." He adjusted a bench near a table. "We also hope to eventually offer evening lessons for the workers themselves who cannot read."

"How much will you charge them?"

"For the adults to learn, nothing. For their children, five pence for each day they miss." He smiled at the confused look that came over Charlotte's face. "All mill workers will be required to send their children to this school."

"Who will pay for it?"

"The mill is covering the costs. We have engaged two teachers. They will live in comfortable quarters above stairs."

Her mouth fell open. Cam was offering a free, compulsory education to working-class children, the very thing she'd championed in her writings for years.

Tears blurred her eyes, closing her throat. "Oh, Cam, it's beyond wonderful." She ran her hands over the new wooden shelving, taking in its rich aroma. She pictured the books that would soon fill the shelves and the students whose imaginations would flourish here. Her heart felt ready to burst. "How did you come up with his concept?"

"The homes, the church, the town was from my own imaginings, but a mandatory education, free of cost for the working class?" A fierce look of soft emotion passed over Cam's face. "Why, Charlotte, isn't it obvious? That portion was all from you and your lofty ideas."

Her heart felt light in her chest. "My ideas?"

He laughed flashing his white teeth, the rich, rumbling sound echoing deep into her core. "From that first night at Willa's in town when you talked of free education for all. It didn't take at first, but as my town project developed what you had to say began to make sense to me. And then, when I read your essay — "

Her eyes rounded. "You really did read my essays."

He nodded. "Once I began to think seriously about building a schoolhouse I referred to some of your essays for direction. After all, you are clearly much more informed on this subject than I."

Charlotte felt dizzy. She recalled the salon Willa hosted last year at Hartwell House when she'd argued publicly funded education would strengthen society. The occasion also marked the first time she'd laid eyes on Willa's incomparable cousin. She'd been aware of him from the moment he'd bounded into the room, all sleek elegance and masculine assuredness. Back then, though, he'd seemed to react to her ideas with cynicism. Yet now, here he stood, putting into action what Charlotte had only dreamed of until now. She might be a forward thinker, but he was the true progressive.

"You were so passionate in your beliefs." He cradled her jaw in his hand. "How could I not respond to your passion?"

The burning intensity in his amber-green eyes caused her pulse to howl under her skin. She reached up to devour this enigma who could be both imperious and surprisingly kind, who was so much more than she could ever imagine.

Cam met her lips almost ferociously, driving his tongue inside her mouth with demanding strokes. His hands roamed over her body, touching and kneading, pulling her tight against his solid length, their bodies intertwined. They stumbled against the wall, sidestepping work tools, which littered the floor, doing a clumsy mating dance, feeding on each other while twisting and turning, with her back against the hard surface first and then his.

Her insides churning, she pressed herself harder against him, wanting to lose herself in him. He groaned, his iron-hot man's flesh throbbing against her. She moaned in response, pushing closer, melding her body to his.

"Oh, Lord, Charlotte," Cam rasped, trailing hot, wet kisses down the side of her neck. "You undo me. You make it difficult for me to hold on to reason."

"Then don't." Breathless, she pulled at his cravat, anxious to feel the bare skin beneath it.

His hands moved over her sides to her bottom, massaging the soft swells. When air whooshed over her legs, she realized Cam had hitched up her skirt. He reached into the soft dampness between her legs. Startled, Charlotte thought to stop him. But then Cam touched her in a way that made her arch and scream softly from the pure pleasure of it.

"You feel so good," he crooned into her ear, his breathing labored. "Charlotte, Charlotte. What you do to me." Stroking and teasing her with his fingers, he brought his lips back to her mouth.

"We can do it together, you and I," he said against her mouth, reaching in again to taste her. "Come and join me. We can make this mill town an example for others to follow."

A hurricane of need raged inside of her. Her body felt like it was hurtling toward an unknown destination as his words resonated in her mind. They *could* do it together. What a team they'd be.

She grabbed his shirt out of his breeches, flattening her breasts against him while running her hands under his shirt to feel the warmth of his skin. Cam dropped to his knees in a swift graceful movement. Hitching up her dress, he hooked one of her legs over his shoulder exposing her to his gaze. She froze when a rush of cool air blew over her most intimate area.

Something soft and wet touched her where his fingers had been. *His tongue.* A shock of pleasure reverberated through her. She fell back against the bookcase, moaning and squirming under Cam's expert touch. The image of him standing much like she did now, with another woman on her knees giving him satisfaction, passed through her mind. Only now that magnificent imperious creature knelt before her, fiercely offering indescribable pleasure. She began to tremble, unsure of how to handle the swirling sensations barreling through her.

He seemed to understand. "Yes, Charlotte," he crooned, still laving her. "Let it go for me. Give in to the pleasure." He intensified the movements of his tongue, adding gentle glides of his teeth. The mounting pressure made Charlotte let loose a strangled scream of wonder. Tremors overtook her until the tension in her muscles shattered. Sensual euphoria undulated through her in waves of warm, rippling pleasure. She floated blissfully on a suddenly calm, sun-kissed sea. When she came back to herself, her shaky legs sank to the sturdy floor. Cam shifted around, pulling her onto his lap as he came to a seat with his back against the wall.

"Sweet, Charlotte. So sweet," he murmured, wrapping his arms around her and burrowing his face into the side of her neck. "We'll make a good team, you and I."

Her senses still reeling, she leaned into his warm strength. He tightened his arms in a possessive embrace, offering safe harbor to her spent body.

Nestled against him, she reveled at the feel of his clamoring heart beneath her cheek. What a mistake it was to let things go so far with Cam, but she couldn't bring herself to regret it. What had just occurred between them was beyond anything she could have fathomed. Shutting her eyes, she sucked in his scent, memorizing the feel of his strong body pressed up against hers, clinging to a moment that could not last or be repeated.

After a few minutes, she took a deep breath and pulled away, ignoring the keen sense of loss she experienced after leaving the warmth of Cam's arms. She felt his eyes on her as she stood and tidied her clothing, fussing with the details because it gave her an excuse to avoid his gaze. Pushing to his feet, he moved to help her right her clothing, but she edged away.

"Charlotte, I intend to go and call on your brother." Cam cleared his throat, seeming to mistake her silence for embarrassment. "To ask him for your hand in marriage." He put his hand under her chin, gently forcing her to look up into his glistening eyes and sculpted masculine features. "If you'll have me."

Her heart stopped. "No." She backed away, searching for a safe distance from his piercing radiance.

"No?" he echoed, confusion in his eyes.

"No, I will not have you." Her chest throbbing, she struggled to make her voice firm. "I thought I had already made that abundantly clear."

"That was before you allowed me certain intimacies." Fierce emotion lit his eyes. "I took liberties with your person."

She staggered to the window, which put the table between them. "Come now, this was a pleasant interlude." She forced the words out despite the anguish wringing her body. "Very like what you enjoy with Mrs. Fitzharding."

He bolted to her side, grabbing her arm and pivoting her around so that she had no choice but to face him. "It was nothing like that and you know it."

"I know nothing of the sort." Scratching behind one ear, she spoke in a calm tone, which belied the calamity she felt inside. "Please don't make this into more than it is."

"More of it than it was?" The chords of his throat pulsed. "Am I to believe this meant nothing to you?"

Forcing herself to hold his gaze, she contorted her features into a mask of calm. "I am surprised a gentleman such as yourself would make so much of it."

Vulnerability flashed across his face before his expression steeled. "Tell me, will the stable boy have his face between your legs by this evening?" When Charlotte gasped in shock, he brought his lips to her ear. "Will you let him let him satisfy you as I have? Do you think he can?"

"Stop." She fought to stop the shaking in her voice, to keep from shattering into a million pieces. "The answer to your proposal is no. No. No. No."

Cam's demeanor changed. He approached her with predatory coldness, his face statue-like. "Very well then. How are we to proceed, Miss Livingston? Am I to be allowed to indulge in more *pleasant interludes*?" His voice dripped with false civility. "May I look forward to finding pleasure between your delectable thighs during the occasional stolen moment?" His long, elegant fingers reached out to tantalize her breast through her clothes and, despite everything, her body sang under the soft ruthlessness of his touch. Ribbons of pleasure streamed to the pit of her belly, prompting the sensitive place between her legs to ache for him again. He flicked a gentle finger over the eager point of her breast, his mouth curving with brutal satisfaction at the evidence of his effect on her. "Will your body continue to say yes, even when your mind says no?"

"Such base language and cruelty are beneath you." Instead of shoving his hand away, or giving him a well-deserved slap across the face, she dropped her hand to where his still rested on her breast. Cupping his hand with both of hers, she brought it to her lips and placed a tender kiss on the inside of his palm.

He flushed and jerked his hand away as though touched by fire. He turned his back, and the wide frame of his shoulders trembleds. "I apologize." He turned to face her, anguish lighting his eyes, his voice strained. "I am a scoundrel of the worst kind. As you have had the misfortune to witness on more than one occasion."

Charlotte smiled, knowing she would never believe the worst about him again. "You are far from a scoundrel, Arthur Stanhope." She gestured around the schoolroom. "You are the most decent and honorable of men. The room in which we stand is proof of that. Any lady would be proud to call you husband."

"Why then do you refuse me?" His searching gaze caught and held hers, making it impossible for her to look away. "Despite your efforts to pretend otherwise, I know you care for me."

"It is for the best. Please believe me." She forced herself to breathe through the ache in her lungs. "There are factors of which you are unaware. Circumstances I dare not share with you."

"What is it, Charlotte?" Capturing her hand, he held it to his chest with both hands. "Have you compromised yourself with Fuller? If that is what concerns you, worry about it no more. We can overcome it."

Her mouth went slack. "You could put something as serious as the loss of my virtue aside?"

For a moment he seemed unsure, but then a look of fierce determination crossed his face. "If that's what it takes to win you, then yes. Whatever is required. Come and share my life with me, Charlotte. Please."

"You will never know what your offer has meant to me." Her throat tight with love for him, she gently withdrew her hand from his clasp. "If I were at liberty to accept it, I would without hesitation."

His jaw clenched. "This isn't the end of it."

"Yes," she said sadly. "It is."

Chapter Nine

"It was beyond imagination." Charlotte reached for another breakfast roll. "Truly breathtaking."

Cam watched her animated eyes gleam with excitement. "Definitely breathtaking," he murmured from his seat next to hers. She flushed in response, casting a furtive glance around the table to make sure no one else had heard.

His chest expanded as he watched Charlotte. Another part of his body followed suit when he remembered the taste and feel of her, the indescribable joy of giving her pleasure. Here, finally, was a woman who both challenged his intellect and filled his senses. Although he'd left her alone on the ride back yesterday, he still fully intended to make her his marchioness. Even though seducing Charlotte was proving far more difficult than he'd anticipated, he fully expected to triumph in the end.

He could already envision them married, and reveled in the idea of her inhabiting his life, and bed, for the remainder of his days.

"I should like to write about it. All of it," Charlotte said. "The town, the school."

Gazing at her, he sat back in his chair. "Perhaps you should wait until the school is up and running."

"Perhaps." She considered his suggestion over the rim of her cup of chocolate. "That way I will truly be able to communicate how well the students are doing."

Willa smiled at her friend's zeal. "You are already assuming the children will thrive in school."

"How could they not?" She sipped her chocolate with great enthusiasm. "Children are made to learn. They absorb everything so much more quickly than adults."

Digby, the butler, entered the breakfast room. "Your Grace, you have a visitor."

Hartwell tossed aside his cloth napkin. "Who is it, Digby?"

"The constable from the village, Your Grace. He says it is an urgent matter."

"Constable Henley?" Willa looked at her husband. "What could he want?"

Hartwell shrugged his soldiers. "Show him in, Digby."

A man of average height entered the room. He carried a little extra weight around his middle and a serious look on his face. "Your Grace."

"Good morning, Henley," said Hart in a friendly manner. "What brings you around so early in the day?"

Henley flushed as he looked over at Willa and Charlotte. "Perhaps Your Grace would like to speak away from the ladies. My news is of a delicate nature."

"It is quite all right, Henley." Hartwell flashed an amused

look at the glint of irritation in his wife's eyes. "My wife will demand to hear the news as soon as you take your leave so she may as well hear it firsthand from you."

"Very well, Your Grace." Henley cleared his throat. "The Ludders are agitating."

"We are aware," answered Hartwell. "The marquess and I just returned from examining the damage done to our mill near Manchester."

"Yes, Your Grace." The constable shuffled his feet. "But I regret to inform you there have been a series of attacks over the last several days in Lancashire and Derbyshire."

Cam frowned. "How widespread has it become?"

"My lord, I fear the threat is so serious in Nottingham that 120 stocking frames were destroyed in a fortnight." Henley twisted his cap between his hands. "Three hundred special constables have been assigned to patrol the factories."

"I see. That is concerning." Hartwell rose. "Fortunately, Cam and I have already posted armed guards at our factory."

Willa breathed in. "Oh no, Hart. I hope it does not come to that."

Paling, Charlotte rose from the table and walked to the window. "No good can come of any of this," she said almost to herself. "It will end badly."

"Is that all, Henley?" asked Hart.

"No, Your Grace," he said casting another quick look at the ladies.

"Speak freely, Henley. Get on with it."

"Your Grace, it is my sad duty to inform you that we believe none other than Ned Ludd, the despicable leader of the Luddites, is in the vicinity." Henley spoke quickly, seeming anxious to finish the task of delivering his distasteful news.

"He was spotted as recently as a sennight ago in Northwich."

Cam inhaled. "That is but a day's ride from here."

An anguished sound escaped from Charlotte's throat, causing them all to look at her by the window.

"Miss Livingston, are you all right?" He went to her side, surprised that someone as sensible as Charlotte would be so distressed by Henley's news. "There is no cause for alarm. You are more than safe here."

She regarded him with apparent confusion then appeared to recover herself. "Of course, I am. It's just—" she stopped and looked into his eyes. "Oh, Cam, people will be killed," she whispered. "It seems as if the worst is truly happening now."

Cam's heart clenched at the anguish he saw in her soft blue eyes. He wanted nothing more than to take Charlotte into his arms and comfort her. Instead, he could only offer calming words.

"I received news of a government directive this morning. We are sending 12,000 troops to affected areas to quell the agitators." He rushed on when he saw the horror in her eyes. "No, it is a good thing. You must trust me on this. The risings must be put down quickly and decisively. Fewer people will be hurt if the government response is overwhelming and implacable."

She nodded, but the way she bit her plump lower lip suggested he hadn't quite convinced her. Retreating back to the window, she became very still.

• • •

Anxious to see Nathan, Charlotte stole away to the stables

as soon as she could. She found him in a stall brushing down a magnificent grey. Stroking the coarse fur on the beast's twitching neck, she admired its powerful muscled form and elegant carriage. "What a splendid creature."

"Hartwell purchased her at Tattersall's." Nathan brushed the animal's glistening flanks. "She was delivered this morning from London."

"His Grace, you mean. Nathan, you must take care to address the duke properly."

The brush stilled. "He is not here at this moment is he, Charlotte?" Scorn tinged the quiet words. "It's only you and me. Have you come up here to give me lessons in deportment or is there another reason for your visit?"

Stung, she crossed her arms. "Since when must I have a reason to spend time in your company?"

"It's apparent you have something on your mind, Lottie." Moving around the mount, he resumed brushing in long, firm strokes, from the animal's arched neck all the way to its hindquarters. "Why don't you just come out with it?"

She glanced around to make sure they weren't being overheard, and saw they were alone except for a few grooms at the far end of the cavernous stable. "The constable came up to visit."

"I heard." His masculine, work-roughened hands slid over the mare's pale gray coat.

"It might not be safe for you here any longer. The Luddites are on a rampage, and Cam says the crown is calling out 12,000 troops to protect the factories."

His arm paused. "Cam is it now?"

Ignoring the implication, Charlotte rushed on. "The constable says they have reason to believe Ned Ludd himself is in the vicinity."

"How did you find your visit to Camryn's factory? I hear it's quite impressive."

"There is going to be no stopping the machines, Nate. It was so clear to me. If you could have seen it—"

"I have seen it, Lottie, as you well know." His soft blue gaze probed her face. "I also understand that you and Camryn went off together alone."

Frowning, she leaned back against the stall rail, propping her elbows over it behind her. "Who informed you of that?" Nathan had not driven the coach yesterday in anticipation of the horse delivery. The second coachman had gone instead.

"All of the under coachmen are part of my staff, Charlotte. I hear what happens."

"They would have no way of knowing that." She curled her lip. "I would guess it was Molly who gave you that little bit of information. I should have her dismissed."

"Yes, you are, after all, a baron's daughter." He shook his head. "You should get that poor girl put out so she will have no place to go. But she is comely, so I suppose she can always toss up her skirts for a shilling."

"There is no need to be rude," she said sharply, her face heating. "Why do you ask about the marquess? It sounds to me as though you and Molly are very amiable toward one another. Perhaps too much so."

"Even if that were the case, it should not be of concern to you." He spoke in a low, biting tone. "She is a servant, after all, which means she is of my class."

Charlotte's temper flared. "Why are you being so churlish?"

Anger flashed in Nathan's blue eyes. He stopped

brushing and stepped toward her. "Are you tired of fighting for the poor and the beleaguered, Charlotte? Did their concerns escape your mind once your marquess had his hand down your blouse?"

She slapped him, hard and fast, reacting almost before she knew what she was doing. "How dare you!"

Snatching her wrist in an iron hold, he leaned in, his tone dark with warning. "Do not ever do that again. I am not your servant, Charlotte. You'd best not forget it."

"Take your hands off her."

The low, taut snarl made the hair rise on the back of her neck. She spun around. His boot-clad feed planted wide apart, raw violence etched in every line of Cam's granitic face.

"Lord Camryn." Nathan's mouth twisted into a daring sneer. He tightened his grasp on Charlotte's wrist even as she tried to wrestle it away. Alarm twisted her stomach.

"Cam, he isn't hurting me." She spoke in calm, soothing tones despite the nervous fear rioting in her stomach. "It is a simple misunderstanding."

"He dares to insult you with his insolence." His long fingers curled into fists by his sides, his savage gaze locked on Nathan. "And he still has his hands on you."

The strength went out of her legs. He'd heard Nathan's crass insult. Of course, both she and Cam knew it had gone much further between them yesterday in the schoolroom.

"Do not be a fool," she said to Nathan with quiet desperation, trying to wrest her arm away. "Think, Nathan, think."

A cold calm seemed to come over him. Abruptly releasing her, he leaned a shoulder insolently against the side of the stall. His eyes remained locked with Cam's, still lit by a blatant look of challenge. Terrified one of the men would erupt, she positioned herself between the two.

Turning to Cam, she put her hands flat against his hard, tense chest. "Escort me back to the manor, my lord. Please."

Cam maintained his visual standoff with Nathan. "Apologize to the lady."

Nathan's answering laugh curled her blood. Cam's furious heartbeat slammed beneath her hands. She whirled her panicked gaze over to Nathan, settling an imploring look on him.

His eyes darted away. "My apologies, Miss Livingston," he finally said tonelessly.

Furor still seemed to reverberate through Cam, as though a maddening din still clamored in his head. He looked down to where her hands were still splayed out across his chest.

She pulled her hands away. "There now, it is done." Charlotte forced lightness into her voice. "Come, Camryn. The misunderstanding is all cleared up." When he still did not move, she ran her hand over his tense arm. Heat burned through her at the feel of Cam's muscles twitching under her touch.

"Please, Cam, please," she said in soft, intimate tones. He spun around and stalked out of the stable. Charlotte cast Nathan one final look of warning before hurrying after him.

"Cam!" She ran to catch up with him, but had difficulty keeping pace with his strident steps. "Stop please or at least slow down before I trip over these blasted skirts."

He halted, hands on his hips. "What is it, Charlotte?"

"Please, I implore you not to speak of this to Hartwell. Nathan could lose his position."

"You would protect him, after he insults and misuses you?" He directed a bitter laugh toward the heavens. "I begin to see why you decline my suit. Obviously, I don't know the first thing about treating you with the contempt you so clearly think you deserve."

"You don't understand."

"Why do you let him treat you so? Do you feel guilty because you were to the manor born and he was not? Does it assuage your guilt to let the lower classes insult and degrade you?" He shook his head with obvious disgust. "You are not the woman I thought you were."

Charlotte's stomach cramped. "You do not know me at all. You cannot."

He uttered a derisive sound. "On that we agree. The person I perceived you to be is the smartest and most humane woman I have had the pleasure of becoming acquainted with, a woman who speaks her mind, who is full of visions for the future that fire my blood and take my breath away. A woman who satisfies every hunger in me, who answers questions in my very soul I did not even know I had." He spat the words out, as though he found them distasteful. "Not a weak or fearful woman who refuses to reach for what she wants. Not a liar. Not a woman who cowers in front of any man, much less a servant."

Charlotte's world spun. She had that effect on him? "You do not understand."

"No, I don't," he said bitterly. "And you won't explain it to me, will you." It was not a question. By now he knew what to expect from her. Cam brushed by her, stalking toward the manor.

Tears gathered in her eyes. Watching a blurry image of

the retreating golden warrior fade into the afternoon light, it was all she could do not to run after him and throw herself into his arms, begging him to hold on to her forever, even though it could never be.

. . .

That evening, Charlotte pleaded a headache and took supper in her room. Her head actually did pound and she didn't feel capable of facing Cam. Not when his words still reverberated in her mind and her body ached for his touch. Not when she longed to throw caution away, to launch herself into Cam's arms and trust him with the truth. She replayed his words over and over again in her mind. She fired his senses? She spoke to his soul? That she could affect him so was both exciting and overwhelming. And impossible. Unfathomable because it put someone she loved at risk and she could not chance it.

Splayed facedown across the bed, a tap at her chamber door punctured her misery. Expecting Molly, she was surprised to see Willa instead, a look of concern marring her perfect face.

"Are you unwell?" she asked, coming across the room.

"I've made a mess of things." She flopped ungracefully over onto her back, staring up at the velvet burgundy canopy above her bed. "Mostly because I am the most hopeless liar alive."

Willa climbed carefully up on the bed, still managing to look elegant despite her growing girth, and propped herself up against the carved wood bedpost. Charlotte switched positions to lie down next to Willa's seated form.

"I knew something was wrong." She reached over to stroke Charlotte's hair in smooth, comforting motions. "You have seemed out of sorts for days now. Will you tell me what is paining you?"

"No. It is to do with Cam." She swallowed back the tears knotting at the back of her throat. "He's your cousin, practically your brother, really. It would put you in an awkward position."

"Hush," she said firmly. "As your friend, you must let me help. Has he been hateful to you? If he has, I'll put a stop to it."

"I wish he'd been hateful. That would be so much easier." Feeling soothed by the comforting movements of Willa's hands over her hair, she sighed. "It's the opposite. He wants to marry me."

"That's wonderful!" Willa exclaimed with a delighted laugh. "I knew you two would suit. We will be cousins."

"I refused him."

"What?" Her smile melted. "Why? Anyone can see the two of you are besotted with each other. Even Hart sees it and he doesn't notice anything unless it's connected to industry."

"Or you."

"Charlotte, marriage to the right man can be wonderful. Sometimes I still cannot believe how fortunate I am to be Hart's wife. And now you have that chance with Cam."

It was easy to see how much her beautiful friend loved her husband, how well suited the duke and duchess were. A pang of longing knifed through her. "How did you know Hartwell was right for you? Of all of your suitors and the offers you received, how did you know to choose so wisely?"

"It wasn't so difficult." Willa let out a quiet laugh. "Aside from fortune hunters, Hart was the only man who ever asked for me."

Charlotte's mouth fell open. "How is that possible? You're easily the most beautiful woman in London. And you didn't marry until you were three-and-twenty. I always assumed you declined other suitors before Hartwell."

Willa smiled ruefully. "It's a long and sometimes unpleasant story. Someday perhaps, I shall tell you all about it. But not now. At this moment, I am most anxious to know why you would spurn Cam's offer."

"I have secrets, Willa." The words came tumbling out. "Blasted, ruinous secrets about my brother that could be devastating and hugely embarrassing for someone like Cam, were we to marry." Sitting up, she faced her friend's shocked expression. "You said yourself that your cousin is gaining prominence in the Lords. If he married me and all was revealed, he would be ruined. His political career would be in tatters. His reputation destroyed."

"I'm speechless." Willa put a hand to her throat, a look of astonished disbelief carved into her face. "What terrible secret could Shellborne possibly have?"

"I have already said too much." Emotion roiled in her chest. "But now you know why I can never marry Cam. He would hate me in the end and I couldn't bear that."

A frown line marred the space between Willa's perfectly arched brows. "Charlotte, there must be a way. Perhaps if you confide further in me we could find a suitable solution."

"No." She shook her head with adamancy. "There is no way. I have already said too much."

After Willa left her, Charlotte kept replaying their

conversation. It had been such a relief to be able confide in her friend. But now that sense of release gave way to a feeling of despair. Voicing her concerns aloud made them seem even more insurmountable.

Restless, with little desire to be left alone with her thoughts and craving her friend's comforting presence, she went in search of Willa. Disappointed to find the upstairs sitting room empty and dark, she went below stairs where a servant directed her to the back terrace. She quickened her step in that direction, anxious to escape her blackening mood.

Her heart lifted when she spotted Willa standing on the terrace, but she halted abruptly when the duke also came into view. Hartwell stood tall and dark with sharp-cut features that made him look intimidating, but the way his whole being softened when he gazed at Willa robbed Charlotte of breath.

One hand resting on his wife's burgeoning belly, the duke stroked his wife's cheek with the other. Charlotte couldn't hear what he said, but Willa gave a throaty laugh and looked up at him with luminous eyes, placing her own hand over her husband's, where it rested on her cheek. He murmured something and she laughed again as Hartwell dipped to kiss his wife's neck. The moonlight cast a bluish glow over the lovers, the night shadows dancing across them when they moved.

Hartwell took his time, moving his lips down his wife's neck to the upper swells of her breasts. When he finally moved languidly back up his wife's neck, Willa put her arms around him and eagerly met his lips. Their kiss was full and gently passionate, an unguarded moment between husband

and wife, an exclusive communion no one else could share.

Watching them, Charlotte grasped the difference between this and what she had witnessed between Cam and Maria Fitzharding in the garden last spring. That act had been purely physical and completely devoid of intimacy. It seemed hollow and meaningless compared to the robust grace of Willa and Hartwell's mutual demonstration of love. The unexpected exquisiteness of the moment stabbed at her heart. What must it be like to be loved so completely by a man?

"She is the world to him."

The smooth timbre of Cam's voice reverberated through her, the heat of his body behind hers radiated over her neck and back. "Yes." She locked her gaze on Hartwell and Willa, now in a loose embrace, murmuring to each other.

"He fought for her. Did you know that?" The words, low and deep, were like velvet across her senses. "They almost lost each other because another man had been obsessed with her for years."

She hadn't known that. Willa had been married for a few months when Charlotte first met her. Perhaps her friend had made the vaguest reference to it during their talk earlier this evening. It occurred to Charlotte that she'd like to hear the story someday.

She remained rooted in her spot. Although Cam wasn't touching her, he stood close enough for his musky masculinity to wrap itself around her.

"Hartwell destroyed the man. Ruined him completely."

The couple's embrace ended and the duke took his wife's hand to lead her inside. They disappeared into the manor, still unaware they were being watched, their soft laughter and murmurs growing fainter. The warmth of Cam's breath brushed her cheek, his voice so faint it was almost a whisper. "Would you fight for love, Charlotte? No matter what the cost?"

Her chest felt painfully hollow. "I don't know." But of course she already had. Just not in the way he meant.

"Don't you?" His face lowered to the side of her bare neck. The warmth of his lips, the roughness of the skin on his cheek, slid across her sensitive skin. He inhaled, as if savoring her essence. "I would, you know. I would not just fight. I would claw and scrape for it. I would, apparently, suffer untold humiliation for it. For you."

A tear slipped down her cheek. Closing her eyes to shut out the pain, she whispered, "Don't. Stop, please."

"I find," he said in a strained voice, his lips still against her neck, "that I cannot stop." He kissed her neck and lingered there, as though it was the only spot on earth worth paying attention to.

Her body rushed with physical pleasure. She shook her head, a sob escaping her throat. "This is impossible."

Placing his large hands on her shoulders, he turned her to face him, his intense face just inches from hers. "Tell me why," he said fiercely. "Tell me."

She heard the urgency in his voice and wanted to answer it, but could not. "There is another."

"Liar."

The tears continued to flow. She gave up trying to stop them. "There is another."

Cam's eyes clouded. "Liar," he said softly. He made no effort to stop her when she pulled away from him and ran back to her room.

• • •

She stood in the schoolroom watching the laughing children tumble outside to play. Charlotte tried to follow but could not find the door. Feeling helpless, she banged on the walls and wondered why no one seemed to hear her.

She peered out the window, catching sight of Cam coming to greet the children. His golden-green eyes glittered when he smiled, leading them in a game. The children crowded around Cam, the sounds of their happy shouts and excited chatter drifted toward her. She tried to call out to them, but could not find her voice. Determined to find a way out, Charlotte fought back tears of angry frustration.

The banging grew louder, confusing her, since she'd stopped slamming her fists against the walls. Cam seemed to hear the noise. Still surrounded by the children, he stopped and looked toward Charlotte, his eyes glistening with recognition. Smiling, he extended his hand and called her name. Charlotte. *Charlotte.*

She opened her eyes, struggling to answer as the fog between deep sleep and misty wakefulness began to ebb. It took her a moment to realize she was abed in her chamber with the form of a large man standing at the foot of her bed. She blinked, trying to clear her vision, bringing Cam into full view.

Concern lit his eyes. "Charlotte, what the devil! You gave me such a fright." He exhaled, shoving both hands through his unruly hair. "Why did you not answer when I knocked on your door?"

"I was sleeping." Still groggy, she pulled herself into a

sitting position with a yawn. "I hadn't planned on entertaining visitors."

Cam's glance dropped to the jiggle of her unfettered breasts loose beneath her thin cotton gown. Flushing, he immediately lowered his gaze and turned away, but not before the hot flash of desire in his eyes curled Charlotte's toes.

Now fully awake, she reached for the dressing gown from near the foot of her bed. "What are you doing here?"

Molly appeared in the doorway wearing her nightclothes. "Miss, are you all right?" Out of breath, she darted a look at Cam. "Oh, my lord, you have found her."

"Found me? What is going on, Camryn?" Pulling on her dressing gown, she glanced out of the dark window. "What time is it? Why are you in my bedchamber?"

Cam nodded to Molly, his back still to Charlotte. "Please inform His Grace that Miss Livingston is unharmed and undisturbed." Molly nodded and hurried away in the direction of the stairs.

"What is going on?" Alarm rolled in her stomach. "You're frightening me."

When he turned to face her, she registered his state of undress for the first time. His white linen shirt hung loosely over breeches as though he'd pulled it on in a hurry. Tawny-colored hairs dusted the strong expanse of chest left bare by his open collar. He wore the snug white breeches that seemed to outline every lean, hard curve. And his feet and lower legs were bare.

Her mouth watered. Aside from her father and brother, she'd never seen a man's bare calves. His were rounded with muscle and sprinkled with the same coarse hairs that licked his throat. His high-arched feet were smooth, with long, elegant toes topped by trim, clean nails.

"There was an intruder," he said. "He made it above stairs before one of the night footmen saw him."

She clutched her dressing gown around her. "Someone got in?" She shivered at the thought of a strange man lurking outside her unlocked bedchamber door.

"He made his escape, unfortunately." Clearly agitated, Cam stalked around her room, stepping into her separate dressing room to give it a sweeping glance. "Hartwell has the staff conducting a search of the house and the grounds. We must make certain it was just one intruder and that he is indeed gone."

"Was anyone hurt? Willa?"

"No, no. She is fine. So far it appears the staff is also unhurt and accounted for." He strode across the room, checking the windows, eyeing the door to the small balcony she'd left slightly ajar. "Charlotte, it is not safe to leave this door open and unlocked."

"I like a bit of fresh air," she answered, her thoughts elsewhere. "Who could it be do you think, Cam? What do they want?"

He paced across the room. Coming to a stop with his hands on his hips, he faced her with a somber gaze. "It could be the Luddites. We cannot exclude the possibility."

Putting her hand over her mouth, she sank down to sit on her bed. "Oh, no. I hope it has not come to that." She looked up at him, considering the ominous implications. "To trespass upon a duke's domain, to threaten his family."

A low clatter sounded on her balcony. She jumped up as Nathan let himself into her room through the balcony door.

His blue gaze swept from her to Cam, narrowing at the sight of another man in her room.

"What the?" Rage colored Cam's face. With a furious roar, he leapt at Nathan, landing noisily atop the man, pummeling him in a violent fury.

Nathan went after Cam, too, unleashing the pent-up anger Charlotte knew had built for years. The two men hacked at each other with brutal ferocity, throwing blind, untutored punches fueled as much by anger as surprise.

"Stop it!" Panicked, Charlotte dodged the haphazard blows while trying to pull them apart. "Stop it before you kill each other!" The men fell to the floor, rolling across it together in a violent embrace, thumping into furniture, toppling a small table that clattered to the floor. "Stop it, Cam! Nathan! Stop right now." She blanched when she saw blood, uncertain of whom it belonged to.

"Good Lord, Cam! Don't be an idiot. Stop all of this before you kill each other. Nathan Fuller is not my lover. He is my brother."

Chapter Ten

It took a moment for the words to penetrate Cam's fog of fury. He'd waited a long time to pummel the man who'd kept Charlotte from him.

Not her lover. *Her brother.*

Elation ballooned in his chest. Giving Fuller one final shove, he rolled into a sitting position, his bent legs splayed out in front of him, his feet planted on the floor. "What the devil do you mean?"

"My brother." She sank down on the bed, her tone one of weary resignation.

He stared at her. "How is that possible?"

"Are you daft?" Gripping a nearby chair, Fuller hauled himself to his feet, his hand coming up to gingerly assess his bloodied nose. "There is only one way it usually occurs. I am her father's by-blow." He inhaled a harsh breath. "Is that clear enough for even you to understand?"

Cam studied Fuller, for the first time really taking in

the light blue eyes and long, trim frame, which now struck him as familiar. So like the man's sister. He felt like a fool. Had he ever bothered to look, really look, he would have hit upon the truth, which had been right there in front of him all along. Physically, Fuller resembled his sister far more than the shorter, rounder Shellborne did. Now Fuller's cultivated manner began to make perfect sense. He'd been born a baron's son.

"That explains why you don't have a servant's bearing." He gingerly touched his tender lip. "If you were acknowledged and your father saw fit to educate you, why the devil are you in service?"

"My sire did not acknowledge me." His lip curled. "He allowed my education with a governess but no further. Everyone at Shellborne Manor accepted that I was his issue. Regardless, he died without making any kind of provision for his bastard son." Fuller narrowed his eyes. "Now that we have settled that, perhaps you would care to explain what you are doing in a state of undress in my sister's bedchamber?"

Cam heaved himself off the floor, not missing the ominous look on Fuller's face. "There was an intruder in the manor. I came to assure Char...uh...your sister's safety and wellbeing."

Fuller's brows knit. "An intruder?"

"You also have some explaining to do," Charlotte said to her brother. "Why are you stealing into my room in the dead of night?"

Cam swung around to look at her, surprised by the sound of her voice. He had almost forgotten her presence. The excitement of the evening shone in her radiant eyes, contrasting with the heightened color of her cheeks. Her flimsy wrapper clung to the soft contours of her sweet breasts and the subtle flare of her hips, leaving little to the imagination.

Praise heaven she didn't wear a nightcap. Her silky, straight tresses tumbled loosely about the shoulders, streaming down the small of her back like a satin curtain. The cinnamon-colored locks were much longer than he'd anticipated. The glistening strands draped over her exquisitely rounded bottom. Heat pooled between his legs.

Thankfully, Fuller and his sister were focused on each other. A sheepish expression replaced Fuller's usual dark countenance. "I came to apologize for my base behavior earlier today in the stable."

She crossed her arms, a movement that hoisted and jiggled her breasts and made Cam's mouth go dry. "It was unworthy of you."

A slight smile tugged at Fuller's surly lips. "Yes. And knowing how obstinate you are, I surmised if I did not come to you, you wouldn't come to the stable, perhaps for weeks, to punish me for my boorish behavior." He quieted, looking toward the open door at the sound of strong, purposeful footsteps approaching in the hallway. Fuller spun around and leapt through the balcony doors just as Hart appeared in the doorway. Cam stepped toward the duke, attempting to shield Fuller's exit from the duke's view.

Hartwell's forehead rose at the sight of Cam's disheveled appearance and bloodied lip. "Are you well, Miss Livingston?"

"Yes, Your Grace." Bright red spots painting each of her cheeks, Charlotte tightened her wrapper around those lovely curves. "Quite well. Thank you."

The duke's dark gaze surveyed the chamber, his inspection pausing at the overturned table, before landing squarely on Cam. "What happened to you?" He spoke over the bridge of his nose, his haughty, authoritarian manner reminding all present of his ducal status. "If I may ask." Only, of course, it was more of a command than a question.

"I'm afraid I tripped when I came to check on Miss Livingston. In the dark and all, you understand." Cam shrugged one shoulder. "Frightfully clumsy of me."

Biting her lip, Charlotte looked to the floor, clearly embarrassed by the flimsy excuse. Granted, it wasn't the most graceful lie, but he'd had to come up with it on rather short notice.

Hart's eyes narrowed, his glance skipped between the two of them. "I see," he finally said in a tone that suggested he didn't believe one word of the ham-fisted tale. "Are you certain you are unharmed, Miss Livingston?"

"Yes, of course, quite," she said, tugging on her left earlobe.

She really was the worst of liars. Cam knew how the scene looked. His unkempt appearance and swelling lip suggested she'd had to fight off his unwelcome advances. The thought caused a wide grin to spread across his face.

The duke's brows seemed permanently arched. "I fail to see what you find so amusing, Camryn."

Cam merely shrugged and brushed off his clothes.

Charlotte winced. "I assure you, Your Grace, all is well."

Hart's midnight-blue eyes looked thoughtfully at her for a long, silent moment. "I am pleased to hear it." His gaze drilled into Cam, who responded with a careless smile. "I would be most displeased if Miss Livingston experienced any distress while under my roof."

Returning his full attention to Charlotte, the duke said, "Footmen will be stationed along the corridor for the remainder of the evening. Rest assured no one will be able to enter your bedchamber unchallenged."

"Thank you," she squeaked.

"I bid you good night, Miss Livingston." Hartwell turned to go. "Camryn, do join me for a brandy in my study." It was a ducal command rather than a friendly invitation, but Cam had no fear of his old friend, even at his most imperious.

With an exaggerated stretch and a forced yawn, he said, "Actually, I think I shall turn in. This evening has been most exhausting." He bowed toward Charlotte, making no effort to temper the wide grin on his face. "Good night, Miss Livingston. I hope you sleep well. I know I shall."

• • •

Rain greeted the morning, casting Fairview Manor in a soft mist, which Cam hardly noticed when he sauntered into the breakfast room. Hartwell sat alone at the head of the long mahogany table brooding over a cup of coffee.

"Good morning." Surveying the offerings laid out on the sideboard, he piled baked eggs, ham cakes, kidney pie, sweet buns, and warm rolls onto his plate before settling down at the table. Peering into his old friend's dark face, he asked, "Why so glum, Hart?"

"Perhaps because an unknown intruder broke into my home last night." The duke leaned into the table, propping his chin in his hand while focusing his blue-black eyes on Cam. "You are extremely cheery today."

"And why not?" He took a large bite of baked eggs and reached for his coffee. "It's a beautiful day."

"If one prefers damp and rainy weather."

He glanced toward the window, his brows shooting up when he spied rivulets of water clinging to the glass. "Funny, I hadn't noticed."

Hart eyed the generous helping of food on Cam's plate. "May I ask what inspires your lust for food this morning?"

"I feel awfully close to being leg shackled, my friend." Grinning, he leaned forward, pointing with his fork. "Look at it as a condemned man's last meal." He guffawed at his own joke.

With a motion of his hand, Hartwell dismissed the two footmen in the room. The door closed behind them, leaving Cam alone with the duke. "You and Miss Livingston, I presume?"

"You presume correctly."

"Am I to understand the two of you came to an understanding last evening?"

"Not precisely." Cam took another bite. "However, I will bring her around."

One side of Hart's mouth twitched upward. "How exactly do you propose to do that?" He eyed Cam's swollen lip. "If last night is any indication, you might not survive another effort to persuade her."

"She'll come around. I will see to it without delay."

Hartwell's face darkened. "Heed me. I will not allow Miss Livingston to be subjected to unwelcome advances. She is a guest in my home. If you dare to compromise her—"

"Then I will be forced to marry her. Exactly!" Cam sat back in his chair, relishing a surge of triumph. "And, of course, we will have to be quick about it."

Crossing his arms, Hartwell leaned back against the carved wooden back of his chair. "Your idea of a courtship is to compromise Miss Livingston into marrying you?"

"Brilliant, isn't it? Although, I much prefer the term seduction. After you caught me in her chambers, it occurred to me that I've been missing the most obvious way to make Charlotte my wife." Publicly compromising her would achieve his goals as handily as a private seduction, perhaps even more so. "By the way, nothing improper happened last night. But if I have my way, it will soon."

"You plan to purposely compromise Miss Livingston in order to get her into your marriage bed." Hart shook his head. "You are aware that you are a marquess, are you not? You hardly have to stoop to trickery to catch a woman."

"Why not?" Cam scraped the last bit of eggs onto his fork. "It worked for you and you're a duke."

Hartwell scowled. "That is different."

"How so?" Cam swallowed his food. "You compromised my cousin. I caught you. You were forced to marry her. I am simply suggesting a similar scenario to hasten my courtship as well."

The duke stiffened. "Unlike what you are suggesting, the circumstances surrounding my unexpected betrothal were indeed accidental. And I was not forced to marry Willa. I did the honorable thing and offered her marriage."

"Yes. As I recall, it was either that or face me on the dueling field, and we both know I am a better shot. So really what choice did you have?"

"Yes, thank goodness," Hartwell said, smiling softly. "There was no choice."

"Anyhow, it might not come to that." Cam stretched, straining his arms high into the air. "I believe last evening has altered the situation between myself and Miss Livingston."

"How so?"

"It is complicated. Let us just say the circumstances between Miss Livingston and myself have changed. I have reason to be hopeful." He looked toward the door impatiently. "The ladies are certainly getting a late start this morning."

Hartwell rose, tossing his napkin aside. "My wife remains abed. She is fatigued after the events of last evening. I have a meeting with my steward to discuss security matters after last night's breach." He headed through the breakfast room doors. "Miss Livingston has already taken her morning meal."

"What?" Cam shot to his feet. "Why did you not say so?"

"I just did."

He followed Hartwell out into the hallway. "I wonder where she is."

"I believe she mentioned taking a turn in the galleries above stairs," Hartwell answered as he disappeared in the direction of his study. Anxious to see Charlotte, Cam bounded up the steps, taking them two at a time.

Fairview was opulent by any standards and the manor's generous wood-paneled gallery, with its stucco ceilings, false domes, and high-arched windows, was no exception. The longest room in the manor, it ran the entire width of the house. Its walls were lined with Belgian tapestries intermixed with ancestral portraits of the past Dukes of Hartwell. Willa often strolled in the gallery when inclement weather kept her from her daily walk through the gardens. Charlotte, it seemed, had adopted the same habit.

A burst of warmth shot through Cam's body when he found her striding through the galleries at a determined gait. Her simple moss morning gown brought out the blue of her incandescent eyes, the soft folds clinging to the enticing turn of her breasts before falling straight down, skimming the rest of her quiet curves. The hair he now knew to be long and silky, truly her crowning glory, was pulled up, leaving just a few soft tendrils to fall about her slim elegant neck and delicate shoulders.

His pulse drummed at the sight of her. He was continually surprised by his reaction to her. There were far more beautiful women, but none who fired his blood the way Charlotte did.

He fell in step beside her. "Miss Livingston, may I join you?"

She favored him with a cautious smile. "Of course."

"And how are you this morning?"

She slowed her steps. "I owe you an apology."

"Whatever for?"

"For not being truthful about the nature of my relationship with Nathan." She stopped to face him. "I have been dissembling with you. Of course, you were already aware since I am a terrible liar."

"That you are," he agreed, letting his eyes run appreciatively over her. "Are you aware that you scratch your ears when you are lying?"

Her eyes widened. "I do no such thing."

"Indeed you do. A scratch behind the ear, a tug on the earlobe. It's a dead giveaway whenever you prevaricate."

She looked heavenward. "There really is no hope for

me."

He put a gentle hand on her arm. "Will you share with me what happened with your brother? How could your father, or Shellborne for that matter, allow him to come to this?"

Pain crossed her face. "You know the circumstances surrounding his birth."

"Of course, but it is hardly unusual." He grimaced. By-blows were not a subject one generally discussed with ladies of quality. "There are many gentlemen who raise their... uh...base-born children alongside their legitimate offspring. If not that, then they are duty-bound to provide for them."

"Father didn't do all he should have for Nathan." The lines around her mouth tightened. "He should have been educated to a more respectable life, as a barrister or perhaps a solicitor."

Cam frowned. "Fuller said last night that your father accepted him."

Charlotte told him the full story as they walked. Her father had fallen in love with the butler's daughter, but hadn't learned she carried his child until after marrying Charlotte's mother. So he'd arranged a marriage to the local blacksmith, Tom Fuller, a decent working man who'd long carried a torch for Elizabeth and who agreed to raise her child as his own.

When Nathan turned six, the baron brought him to live at Shellborne Manor where he shared their lessons with the governess. But Charlotte's mother had resented the preferential treatment, so when Hugh had left for Eton, she'd refused to allow Nathan to go as well. As a result, he'd stayed behind to train as the estate steward.

"I think Father saw Nathan's potential and hoped he would eventually become Hugh's steward." The gentle patter of soft rain sounded as they passed an expanse of tall, arched windows. "But Hugh and Nathan never got on. Nathan excelled at everything. Hugh did not. It rankled Mother that the son of her rival could best her own son."

"Her rival? I thought you said the affair with Fuller's mother ended."

"It did, but I suspect Mrs. Fuller remained the great love of Father's life and Mother always knew it." She flushed, casting a quick glance at Cam. "There, I have said entirely too much. Now you see how lacking in discretion I truly am and why Mother fears my loose tongue."

"You are forthright and honest." The words were tender. "Those are qualities to be admired."

Her color rose even higher. "You cannot blame Hugh, I suppose. Mother's attitude was bound to rub off on him."

"But not on you."

"No." Her eyes glistened. "Nathan is my older brother and I adored him from the first."

"Knowing how it was between the brothers, why did your father make no provision for Nathan when he died?"

"He left him nothing. Perhaps he meant to and never got to it. I've always thought he was frightened to do so because of Mother." She blew out a breath. "As soon as father died, Nathan left Shellborne Manor. He worked in a mill for a time, but he missed estate life. So he came to work for Hartwell."

"With your help."

"Yes." She stopped walking and faced him. "But the duke and Willa know nothing of our connection, and Nathan desires that it remain so."

"Why? He would receive better treatment if people knew the truth of his birth."

"I suppose it is easier for him that people simply think of him as the duke's coachman rather than the unacknowledged base-born son of a baron. He has a keen mind." Pride filled her voice. "I can foresee him eventually becoming Hartwell's steward."

He halted and reached for her hand. "What of us, Charlotte? Dare I hope this new honesty between us can lead to a future?"

She shook her head, watching his hand flirt with her fingers. "No, Cam. I wish it were that simple, but it is not."

"Tell me why," he said. "I know now there is no other. We have something special here, Charlotte. It is not always this way between a man and a woman. You must not cast it aside lightly."

She took his hand into both of hers, running her slim, tapered fingers over the rough curves and edges where soft skin melted into hardened calluses from years of riding. Her feathery touch sent a jolt of electricity through him. He would never let her go.

"I will not lie to you. You deserve so much better than that." She raised her eyes, locking her azure gaze with his. "The circumstances that prevent us from marrying have not changed. No one is sorrier of that than I."

Cam brought her hand to his mouth to press a quiet kiss into her open palm. "Tell me what those circumstances are. We shall work them out together." The words were urgent. "I am a marquess, Charlotte, who wields a great deal of power and has widespread influence. Whatever it is, we can manage it together."

"That is just it." The words were heavy with regret. "There are secrets in my family that I cannot share."

"Whatever it is, it cannot be so awful."

"You are someone of importance in the government," she said. "You could be minister one day. And then you will be able to achieve true greatness. You can help the workers. Everyone will look to your mill town and emulate you. Nothing can taint that. Nothing is more important."

"You think to protect my political career? Is that what this is about?"

"It is about the good you will do for so many people when you are a minister. Perhaps even one day you will be prime minister." She turned away from him. "My family's secrets would ruin you."

He put a hand on her shoulder to turn her back to face him. A wave of determination moved through him. He could not lose her. He would not. "How bad can it be? Surely you exaggerate. I can withstand a little embarrassment, Charlotte. You must let me decide."

"No, once I tell you, you are tainted with the truth. You will be forced to choose between me and your honor." She shook her head adamantly. "I will never force you to make that choice. Loving me cannot be the cause of your ruination."

Her crystal-blue eyes glistened with such honest determination his chest ached. "Do you love me, Charlotte? You said you would not lie to me. Do you?"

She exhaled. "Yes."

"Then fight for us."

"I am fighting for you, Cam," she said. "For your future.

To keep my family safe."

"You do not trust that I will keep your family safe?" The steel of her voice ignited a quiet panic deep within him. "Your family becomes mine when we marry. They will have my protection."

Her face softened. "Of that I have no doubt. That is why I cannot allow it. You must have no connection to the Livingstons, ever."

A maid appeared at the end of the hall. "Miss Livingston? Her Grace requests your presence in her chambers."

She nodded to the girl. "I am coming." She looked back to Cam. "I am not a silly, hysterical woman. You know this. You must trust me."

He felt her slipping away. "Are you certain you can do this, Charlotte? Are you prepared to see me court other women and perhaps marry one of them?" He leaned down, coming face-to-face with her, trying to ignore the light floral smell raking his senses. "Have you asked yourself how you will feel when another woman carries my child in her belly? When all along you will know it should have been you in her place?"

She stiffened. "I must go. Willa is not well this morning."

"This is not over."

"I will always want the best for you." She regarded him with quiet calm. "I wish you every happiness."

Reluctantly releasing her, he leaned against the gallery wall and crossed his arms, his iron look following Charlotte's retreating figure. Oh, he planned to be happy all right. He didn't care what her secret was. He wouldn't be diverted from his plan to make her his. The only difference now was that the matter of seducing Charlotte had just taken on an entirely new level of urgency.

Chapter Eleven

"Who is that?" Charlotte asked.

A well-appointed, blacked-lacquer coach came into focus as she and Willa came around a bend during their daily walk.

Willa craned her neck for a better look. "Why, I think it's Selwyn's coach. Hart said he might come for a few days." She let out a sigh of relief, pushing an errant curl off her flawless face. "Thank goodness. We need a diversion. You are so good to spend my confinement with me, but I fear I have been selfish, cooping you up here entirely too long without amusement."

"Nonsense." Charlotte thought of the pleasure of seeing Cam every day. "I have been able to catch up on my writing. I've even begun my article about Cam's mill town."

As they entered the great hallway, the duke stepped out of the drawing room to greet them. "Here they are now." Hartwell offered Willa his arm, leading them both inside the drawing room. "Willa and Miss Livingston are returned from their walk. Darling, Selwyn is here and he has brought his lovely sister."

Standing to greet them, David Selwyn sketched a bow before turning and beckoning his sister to come forward. "Your Grace, Miss Livingston, allow me to make known my sister, Miss Margaret Selwyn."

Miss Selwyn was striking, with lustrous golden hair and large grey eyes. The fashionably low décolletage of her peach gown displayed the generous curves of her dainty form to great advantage.

"Your Grace." She dipped a deep curtsy. "It is an honor and a pleasure to meet you."

Willa returned a generous smile. "Welcome, Miss Selwyn. His Grace and I are very fond of your brother. It is a true pleasure to at last make the acquaintance of his sister." The duchess tossed Selwyn a look of friendly recrimination. "Mister Selwyn, where have you been hiding this lovely creature?"

"My sister has been traveling on the Continent," he said with a warm smile. "She is just returned."

Miss Selwyn turned to Charlotte. "Miss Livingston, when David told me you were here," she said in a breathless voice, "I was thrilled beyond all measure. I have read some of your writings. It is a rare treat indeed to have the opportunity to meet you in person."

Pleased and surprised by the compliment, Charlotte smiled. "Why, thank you, Miss Selwyn. How good of you to join us." A footman appeared with tea and Willa directed them to their seats.

She turned to Selwyn. "I hope you are going to honor us

with your presence for more than a short visit."

Selwyn sat in a chair opposite Willa and crossed his legs, one knee over the other. "His Grace has invited us to stay for a few days, with your leave of course."

"You have it, with pleasure." Willa opened the caddy and sorted out the tea leaves before nodding to the waiting footman to pour the urn of boiling water into the china teapot. "Charlotte and I were just talking about a need for diversion. And you have brought your lovely sister, too. It is a wonderful surprise."

Footsteps sounded in the cavernous hall just before Cam strode into the room full of vigorous energy. His riding clothes hugged the strong curve of his backside, highlighting the enticing indentation to the side of each firm swell. Cam's amber hair was windblown, his angled cheeks flushed from his exertions.

Charlotte's heart faltered every time the man swept into the room. In the week since the revelation about Nathan, he'd been polite, engaging, and charming. Once or twice she caught him giving her a discreet considering glance, but he hadn't attempted to be alone with her. Cam's apparent acceptance of her rejection should relieve her, but it left her insides feeling barren and desolate.

"Ah, here's Cam now," said Willa. The marquess stopped short when he realized new guests had arrived.

Selwyn stood, a broad smile on his face. "I see your valet has yet to learn how to cut a gentleman's hair."

Cam flashed a wide, genuine grin. "It is the secret to my strength." He assumed a fighting stance with fists raised at the ready. "Care to test my theory?"

Willa rolled her eyes and interrupted their friendly

blustering by gesturing toward Margaret. "Cam, Mister Selwyn has brought his sister along. Have you met Miss Margaret Selwyn?" The smile on Cam's face stiffened almost imperceptibly as his gaze slid to the lovely Margaret.

She smiled prettily and dipped her chin in a show of practiced modesty. "My lord."

He bowed. "Miss Selwyn, we meet again."

Willa's eyes widened. "The two of you know each other?"

Miss Selwyn's luminous face brightened. "Yes, the marquess came home with David quite often during breaks from university. I was just a girl the first time he visited." She fingered a tendril of hair. "It has been what...almost three years since your last visit? That was shortly before he came into the title."

"Indeed." The cool, courteous words lacked Cam's usual geniality. "I was just the Honorable Mister Stanhope back then."

"And where is your family home, Miss Selwyn?" Charlotte asked, forcing a friendly tone despite the jealousy raking her insides. What kind of connection did Cam have to this gorgeous creature?

Selwyn's sister kept her large grey eyes fixed on Cam, appearing not to have heard Charlotte's question. Her brother answered for her. "Just outside of London, in Richmond, Miss Livingston."

Miss Selwyn blinked those endless lashes of hers. "It was a wonderful house party." She looked to Cam. "We had a most lovely time. Do you recall, my lord?"

"I do, Miss Selwyn." Cam's face remained stone-like. "It was memorable."

"I was such a child then, just barely seventeen." Her luminous eyes still fixed on him, she let out a soft lilting laugh.

It was obvious Selwyn's comely sister wanted Cam. Charlotte fought a mad urge to pull the chit's golden hair right out of her head. Instead, she pressed her lips into a smile and sipped her tea.

Cam took a position by the hearth with one elbow propped on the mantle. Despite the casual stance, Charlotte detected tautness behind his courteous expression. Selwyn's sister clearly affected him somehow.

She suppressed a sigh. Well, why not? Even she could see Miss Selwyn, with her petite frame, fair hair, and delicate features, embodied the ideal Ton beauty. Men no doubt appreciated her lush, curvaceous body. Charlotte shoved a loose tendril of hair away from her face. The lady's visit had just begun yet her jaw already hurt from clenching her teeth.

• • •

Miss Selwyn's charms were on full display that evening at supper. Her sea-green silk gown enhanced a full bosom and smooth expanse of creamy skin. The wide round neck of her gown was trimmed in silver, which highlighted Miss Selwyn's slate-grey eyes, while soft tendrils from her upswept golden hair framed her face.

The lady spent the entire meal tittering at any remark Cam happened to utter, hanging on to his every word, especially when conversation turned to the Luddite risings.

Miss Selwyn's eyes widened when she learned of the attack on Cam and Hartwell's mill. "Oh, my," she exclaimed breathlessly. "Those Luddites are frightful."

"What of the thousands of government troops brought in to quell the machine breaking?" Selwyn asked over a glass of wine. "Has it helped?"

"Somewhat," Hartwell said. "But one wonders what will happen once the troops are withdrawn."

Miss Selwyn gave a dainty shudder. "They should hang every one of them."

Her brother said, "One wonders if they will ever capture Ned Ludd."

Hartwell gave a footman a mere fraction of a nod. The man moved forward to refill the duke's glass. "They have not even been able to ascertain whether the man is real."

"It is easy for an imaginary man to elude capture," Cam said.

"An imaginary man?" The worshipful look Miss Selwyn gave Cam made Charlotte want to roll her eyes. Instead, she chomped down, a bit too forcefully, on the veal in her mouth.

"Some say the Luddite risings can be traced back to one man and a single incident," Cam said. "This Ludd fellow worked in a mill somewhere, perhaps in Leicester. They say he broke two stocking frames in a fit of rage."

Miss Selwyn's eyes widened. "Was it done purposefully?"

Selwyn nodded. "Some say it is so."

"But others say Ludd was a simple man, actually the village idiot, so that it was not purposeful," said Cam, taking a bite of boiled beef.

Willa shifted in her seat, trying to find a comfortable position. "How ironic it would be if a village idiot's careless actions launched this rebellion."

Charlotte, who had listened to the exchange without

comment, finally spoke. "However it began, the movement it launched is very real. Its grievances are not without merit."

Miss Selwyn's eyes widened so much that those never-ending lashes almost touched her delicate brows. "Surely you do not approve of machine wrecking, Miss Livingston."

"No, but their concerns will have to be addressed," she said, wondering if Miss Selwyn practiced that expression in her mirror. "We cannot have a countryside full of people reduced to beggary because there is no work. They must have a way to feed their families and light their hearths."

"Exactly right, but violence is not the answer and it must be dealt with harshly," said Cam. A pang of disappointment cut into Charlotte's belly when his glance slid away from her to settle on Miss Selwyn. "If this Ned Ludd does indeed exist, he needs to be stamped out. The sooner, the better."

Charlotte couldn't have been more thankful when the interminable evening finally came to an end. Unfortunately, she faced more of the same the following morning when the group set out for an early morning ride.

"Thank you," Miss Selwyn said to Nathan as he helped her mount her steed. She and David joined Cam, Charlotte, and Hartwell. Willa's condition prevented her from participating.

Charlotte rarely noticed clothes, but even she could see Miss Selwyn wore the most exquisite riding habit with its delicate clinging fabric the color of a soft blue sky, embroidered cuffs and a rich lace accentuating the neck line. The matching hat was made of silk and adorned with feathers. Charlotte ruefully glanced down at her own simple riding apparel—plain white shirt and skirt, suspenders, and her red spencer.

It didn't surprise her that, before long, Margaret and Cam were riding side by side. Tossing her blond locks, Selwyn's sister laughed in dulcet tones at something Cam said. It didn't help matters that the stylish beauty also gave every appearance of being a skilled rider. Fortunately, the gentlemen seemed to pay her little attention. They challenged each other to race, joking and taunting each other as they must have when they were at university together. Charlotte smiled at their camaraderie. How fortunate men were to be able to go away to be educated.

They engaged in a series of jumps, and, like Charlotte, Miss Selwyn held her own in the sidesaddle. She laughed easily when the men exchanged good-natured insults, joining in with their banter, her calculating eyes twinkling in Cam's direction in a way that prompted Charlotte's belly to simmer with envy.

Selwyn pulled his mount up alongside hers. "You seem lost in thought."

"I was just ruminating over my latest essay," she lied. "If I do not focus on it, I fear it will be late getting to the publisher." At least that last part was true enough.

"As a great admirer of your work, I look forward to reading it."

"Why, thank you," she said, genuinely pleased by the compliment. "Some would say I am far too radical."

"Miss Livingston, I am sure those who say such things are from the peerage." He placed his hand on his chest. "I am not a gentleman. My family has done very well for itself, but I continue to be aware of the difficulties faced by the operative class."

Charlotte smiled, thinking of how much she liked

Selwyn's warmth and friendly manner. "You are more of a gentleman than many who are born to it."

Her horse pranced. Selwyn's hand shot out to steady Flame, and then he snatched his hand back, apparently fearing he'd overstepped. "I do beg your pardon."

She reached over and patted his arm. "Please, it is nothing. No harm done."

His jaw relaxed. "I am used to riding with my sister. She has only recently learned to ride. She was determined to do it well. I have often reached over to steady her mount." He gave her a rueful look. "I suppose it is the older brother in me."

"She is most fortunate to have you as her protector." Charlotte's horse pranced again, snorting from its nostrils. "My mare is eager for a run. Would you care for a quick turn? Say to that old tree stump and back?"

He smiled at the challenge. "Indeed. Lead on, Miss Livingston."

• • •

Sounds of their laughter filled the air as Charlotte and Selwyn spurred their mounts forward. His nostrils flaring, Cam stared hard at the two retreating riders. The way Charlotte had touched Selwyn's arm had not escaped his notice.

A gentle feminine cough demanded his attention. He dragged his eyes from Charlotte and Selwyn to find Margaret at his side. Once he took notice of her presence, she smiled radiantly. "I see you are an even finer rider than when you graced us at Richmond, my lord."

"I'm astonished by your considerable riding skills, Miss Selwyn." He forced himself not to steal a look in Charlotte's direction. "As I recall, you had a fear of riding and rarely indulged."

"You've discovered my secret. I was so moved by your devotion to the sport." She reached over to stroke her steed's neck, moving her delicate gloved hand in slow up-and-down motions. "I have practiced daily for the last three years as I knew you would appreciate a woman of great skill when it comes to being mounted."

Cam's brows raised a fraction, confusion clouded his brain. Had she intended the rather scandalous double entendre or was it the innocent remark of an inexperienced young lady? Even the manner in which she stroked her horse seemed suggestive. He pushed the unfathomable notion out of his head. The young woman he remembered was an innocent. She had, however, also been calculating and ambitious, even at such a tender age. He'd learned that the hard way.

"Bravo, Miss Selwyn." Anxious to be away from her, he searched for Charlotte and found her serious gaze fixed on them. She met his eyes and cocked an eyebrow before turning away and spurring her horse into a gallop.

Cam grinned, his loins stirring. Now seemed like an excellent time to employ a bit of seduction. "If you'll excuse me." He urged his mount to follow after her. The stallion's hooves pounded the ground, easily catching up with her mare. He cantered alongside Charlotte for several strides until he realized she had no intention of slowing down. Pulled out in front, he turned his stallion into the path of her horse, forcing Charlotte to slow down and ultimately come to a stop.

"What is the matter with you?" Charlotte said sharply as she brought the mare under control. "Are you trying to get me thrown again?"

He gave her a sly, playful smile. "What was that look for?"

"What look?"

"The one you threw my way when I was talking to Miss Selwyn." He reached over and brushed a finger over her brow. "The arched brow and all."

"Oh, that," she said in a dismissive tone, sliding off her horse. "I could not help but notice she seems enthralled with you."

Cam dismounted in one smooth motion, his mouth widening into a delighted grin. "Do I detect jealousy, Charlotte?"

She looked at him with unsmiling eyes. "Perhaps."

Emotion tugged in his chest. This was the Charlotte he found hard to resist, the one who told the truth. His grin vanished. "You have no reason to be."

Her eyes glistened as she forced an uneven smile. "I have no right to be. I am well aware of that. Still, I should not like to witness your courting another woman." She stroked her horse's neck. "If it were not for Willa's babe, I would remove to Shellborne Manor and leave you to court Miss Selwyn."

Cam's heart winced at the deep pain in her sky colored eyes. He resolved to hurry the seduction to spare his beloved any more distress. Her brother, Shellborne, needed to be on hand when Cam made his move. He made a mental note to ask Willa to invite the baron down for a few days. To Charlotte, he said, "I have no intention of courting Miss

Selwyn."

She turned to walk, holding her mount's reins as the animal followed behind her. "Why ever not? She would make a perfect marchioness, an ideal political wife."

Cam followed. "And what of her brother?" he asked, unable to tap down his jealousy. "Would he make an ideal husband?"

She frowned. "Do not be absurd."

"You seem to enjoy his company."

"As do we all. He is all that is amiable." Her tone grew grave. "As is his sister."

He watched her walk on ahead, taking in the simple brown riding skirt and white shirt with suspenders she usually favored. Her snug red riding jacket hugged her breasts, its scooped neckline and buttons emphasizing her gentle curves. He caught up with her after a few quick strides. "Margaret Selwyn is not you."

"On that we agree. She is lovely."

He came to an abrupt stop and faced her. The last thing he cared to discuss was either of the Selwyns. Instead, wanting her to remember the indefatigable heat between them, he asked her the question which had nagged him for weeks.

"Charlotte, tell me about that night you came upon me with Maria Fitzharding. How did you feel when you saw us together?"

Her brows lowered. "Why in the world would you bring this up now?"

"I have often wondered."

Charlotte took a deep breath. "I was jealous of her."

"Jealous?"

She looked straight at him with clear blue eyes. "I envied her ability to give you pleasure. And I thought you were beautiful. I still think you are the most beautiful man I have ever seen."

Cam forgot to breathe. He gaped at Charlotte, taking in the endless pools of her eyes and her flushed cheeks. His body pounded with hunger, his man parts burning for her. He reached out but she stepped away, using a large rock to mount her horse in one easy motion. In a swift moment, she was galloping back to join the others, leaving a stunned Cam behind, struggling to control his inflamed body.

He forced several deep breaths to calm the painfully urgent throbbing between his legs. Good Lord. He'd end up a bedlamite for certain if he didn't manage to seduce her soon.

· · ·

"It is breathtaking." Charlotte looked in wonder at the ruins of the old abbey where the group would picnic today. They wandered near the ruins for a closer inspection while the servants set up the meal. The agreeable summer day seemed perfect for an outdoor luncheon.

She looked at what remained of the ancient structure. Much of the old gray masonry had been stolen away over the years, but a lone tower remained intact for the most part, surging majestically against the lush serene landscape.

Hartwell followed her gaze. "The monks are said to have chosen this spot for its calm and solitude."

"I can see not much has changed," said Hugh Livingston, swatting a fly away. Her brother's florid cheeks were even redder than usual and his face glistened with moisture. Poor Hugh. He did seem to perspire an awful lot. She wondered why Willa had unexpectedly invited him to Fairview for a fortnight. He'd arrived yesterday, thrilled to be included in the intimate ducal gathering.

Her thoughts were distracted when Cam's arm shot out to steady Miss Selwyn, who still managed to look graceful while staggering on the old abbey's uneven surfaces.

Clutching his arm, she favored Cam with a grateful smile. "Oh, thank you, my lord," she said, her voice more breathless than usual. Cam returned the smile not seeming to mind that Miss Selwyn kept grasping this arm while the group continued its exploration. Her loss of footing seemed more strategic than accidental. In the week since her arrival, the lady seemed to make a habit of being stuck to Cam's side.

Charlotte turned her attention back to the abbey, running her hand over what remained of the depleted stone wall. "Just look at the stone work. It is so ornate." She bent her head to examine the intricate details. "What is this?" She pointed to some indecipherable marks etched into the floor.

"I see you have found our local mystery." Hartwell came over, with the rest of the group following. "This is the church floor. No one has been able to determine what these markings were meant to signify."

"How long has this been here?" asked Selwyn.

The duke ran his hands over the stone. "The abbey has stood for more than 430 years. The monks lived here undisturbed for about two hundred years."

Cam sauntered over, mischief lighting his eyes in a way that made Charlotte's stomach flip. "Until your ancestors tossed them out?"

"This land passed into the Preston family when the Hartwell dukedom was created just under 215 years ago."

"What became of the monks?" asked Miss Selwyn, who of course, had followed Cam over. She tossed a quick glance Cam's way, her dainty forehead wrinkled with interest.

Charlotte could not help but admire the performance. Miss Selwyn was smart enough not to act the fool with Cam, having apparently deduced the marquess preferred a female of some substance. As far as Charlotte could tell, Cam's behavior towards Miss Selwyn seemed unchanged. He maintained a polite distance but he was a man after all. And a virile one at that. Her stomach knotted. Cam might not be interested in courting the lady as of yet, but surely it was only a matter of time before he succumbed to her abundant charms.

"Are you an admirer of history, Miss Livingston?" Selwyn knelt beside Charlotte to examine the etchings on the floor.

"Yes, I find it fascinating," she said, grateful for the distraction. "To think of the people who walked here before us. I wonder what they thought and how they truly lived." She looked up at him and smiled. "No doubt you think me a boring bluestocking."

Rising, he offered his hand to help her stand. "I could never think you boring, Miss Livingston." He gave her a kindly look. "Indeed, your mind always seems to be at work. Whether you are thinking about your writings or contemplating the meaning of history."

"You are not scandalized that I am not interested in the latest color of ribbon in the village store or latest fashion plates?"

He answered with an appreciative laugh as they continued to explore the ruins together. After a while, they were joined by some of the others. Anxious to examine the tower up close, Charlotte wandered away from the group. She walked through the arched entryway and into the tower. The interior was small and hollow, opening up to the other side.

She walked through and almost bumped into Cam, who leaned up against the outside wall with his hips thrust forward and his legs apart. He wore his well-worn brown Hessians and the weathered leather breeches that outlined the firm lines of his thighs. Flashing Charlotte a cocky smile, he pulled her beside him and out of the view of the rest of their party.

"Whatever are you doing?" she asked trying to ignore the way his familiar masculine smell quickened her pulse.

The sun shone through his unruly golden mane. He winked at her. "I am hiding from the lovely Miss Selwyn."

Charlotte's heart soared, but she forced herself to look at him with false indifference. "I do not understand your continued reluctance. Miss Selwyn is lovely and she does seem quite taken with you."

"Do you think so?"

"Yes, and she's dainty and pleasingly formed," she said, making a barely veiled reference to Margaret's generous curves.

"Hmm. I find I prefer a woman of stature." Cam's flashing amber eyes slid down Charlotte's body, warming her all the way down to her toes. "As to curves, I prefer the mystery of discovering them for myself, rather than having them on display for every man to see." They stood side by side against the wall, but Cam spun around to face her, his body coming to a stop inches from hers. She pressed back against the wall, her heart fluttering as his long fingers came up to toy with the top of her bodice.

She caught her breath. "What are you doing?"

"You began this conversation." His gaze remained on the movement of his fingers. "I am merely replying to your inquiry." His fingers feathered over the sensitive, exposed skin on the upper swells of her breasts, making her nerves frolic under his touch. "A gentlewoman blessed with quiet curves has secrets of the flesh known only to her husband. How fortunate for him that he alone of the male species will ever see her thus." He bent to put his lips at the sensitive spot where her neck met the smooth curve of her shoulder and sucked lightly.

She gasped at the delicious sensation. Her reckless hand crept up to caress the thick strands of Cam's hair as his lips blazed a hot path up her neck to her earlobe.

"Only he will have the privilege of uncovering every soft curve, each sensitive spot." Cam's warm breath tickled her ear. She trembled at the subtle flick of his tongue. "And he should honor that privilege and treat it with the extreme care and delicacy it deserves."

Heat rose in her body. She closed her eyes, savoring his touch and smell, waiting to feel his lips on hers. She should run of course, but she had no defenses against Cam's enticements. And he knew it. "Surely, you can't still think to seduce me."

"If you can't tell for certain"—he nibbled the sensitive skin at her neck—"then clearly my technique needs improvement."

She shivered with pleasure. If his technique got any better, she was liable to burst into a ball of flames.

It felt like forever before the smooth brush of his mouth settled on hers. He kissed her gently at first, soft, languorous lips moving over hers. She sighed when he intensified the kiss, his tongue coming in to mate with hers, stroking deeply. She felt the love in his kiss and could not help but return it. Urgency burning in her, she opened her mouth more fully, welcoming his attentions. A satisfied groan sounded in Cam's throat.

A voice rang out. Charlotte realized someone was calling out their names. "It is time to eat," she heard herself say, pulling away. Her heart leapt at the look of raw desire she saw in his eyes, but he made no move to stop her. Her pulse still pounding, she willed her shaky legs to stay firm enough to carry her back to the group.

Rejoining the others, Charlotte sank down in a spot next to Selwyn, hoping no one would notice how her body still strummed from his touch. Cam ambled up a few minutes later, barely suppressing a frown when he saw her sitting next to Selwyn. With a jaunty smile, he settled himself on her other side.

Miss Selwyn, who watched his approach, smiled warmly at Cam. Then her cool grey gaze slithered over to Charlotte and rested there for a moment.

• • •

"Wellington has crossed the Pyrenees. It won't be long now before the allies reach Paris." The duke lounged in his chair, his long legs propped up on another chair. Selwyn and Cam joined him on the terrace for after-dinner port and cheroots. A lazy summer breeze wafted over them, carrying the sweet-and-spicy floral scents from the gardens.

Cam sprawled in his chair. "I shall be happy when this bloody war on the Peninsula is over."

"Where is your brother these days, Cam? Do you hear from him?" asked Selwyn. He sat in a less relaxed fashion than the other two men, leaning forward at the table propping his elbows on it.

"Not overmuch." Staring into the darkness, he bottomed out his glass of port. "According to the last word we had from him, he's with Wellington."

Hart took a long drag on his cheroot and tilted his face upward, his eyes following the curling grey path of the exhale smoke. "Has he recovered from his battle injuries?"

"Edward's latest letters to our mother suggest he has, but I won't be satisfied until we see him in the flesh."

"Charlotte tells me she would like to write an essay on the men who come back from war," Selwyn said. "The ones without means or title who suffer war injuries and are left to fend for themselves."

"Charlotte, is it?" Cam turned to look at Selwyn, his jaw tightening. The man seemed permanently attached to Charlotte's side these days.

"Miss Livingston, of course." Selwyn's face flushed. "I beg your pardon."

Refilling his glass, Cam focused on the swishing, dark amber liquid. Selwyn had been panting around Charlotte for days. The man was a complication he didn't intend to tolerate. "Tell me, Selwyn, do you fancy Miss Livingston's advocacy of the common man will extend to her bedchamber?"

The sharp intake of Selwyn's breath pierced the night. "I beg your pardon?"

Straightening, Hart swung his booted feet off the chair and leaned towards Cam. "What the devil are you about?"

"I'm wondering if Selwyn has it in his mind to court the daughter and sister of a baron."

Selwyn stiffened. Although they were longtime friends, the men at the table were not social equals.

Cam tossed the amber liquid down his throat, relishing the burn and fiery sensation streaming into his chest and gut. "Tell us, do you hope to marry one of your betters?"

"Camryn, that's enough," Hartwell said.

Selwyn met Cam's gaze straight on. "Am I poaching, Camryn? If so, then I apologize." He stood in a stiff movement. "I was led to understand there was nothing between you and Miss Livingston." He turned with a slight bow to Hartwell and walked back into the house, his bearing upright and unbowed.

Groaning, Cam dragged both hands down his face, well aware he'd just insulted his longtime friend. "Devil take it."

"That was well done, you ass." Hartwell settled back in his chair, puffing on his cheroot. "How do you plan to set it to rights?"

Cam bottomed out his drink, placing the empty glass on the table with a hard *clank*. "Leave off."

"It appears you must resolve the situation with Miss Livingston immediately." Hartwell exhaled curling, silvery smoke in small, neat circles. "Unless you'd prefer to end up on a dueling field."

"I don't know what possesses me when it comes to

Charlotte." He collapsed back in his chair. "The idea of her anywhere near another man drives me to bedlam."

Hartwell's dark eyes gleamed with amusement. "Ah, Cam, it seems you are finally completely and totally afflicted."

He peered at his friend through bleary eyes. "Surely, this is not how it was for you and Willa?"

"You'd better marry the lady." Hartwell chuckled. "It's the only cure."

The beginnings of a severe headache stabbed at the base of his skull. He huffed an exasperated breath. "I'm trying."

Chapter Twelve

Three days later, after everyone retired for a nap before supper, Charlotte slipped out of her bedchamber. Passing the billiards room, she stopped and doubled back, looking in at the intimidating wooden table with its bright green cloth.

Billiards was on the agenda this evening after supper, and she winced at the idea because she played so dismally. The thought of making a fool of herself in front of flawless Margaret Selwyn sounded more distasteful by the minute. She looked around, and seeing no one in view, stepped inside and picked up a mace.

After arranging the wooden balls, she stabbed at them with the thin wooden stick, cursing when she missed the balls altogether. Repeating her efforts several times, she barely managed to hit the balls with a weak, essentially useless bump of her mace.

"Blast it!" Biting her lip, Charlotte concentrated on hitting the ball with something remotely resembling accuracy.

"It is all about mental focus and concentration."

Startled, she spun around to find Cam lounging against the doorjamb, his forehead wrinkled with amusement. She grimaced. It was just her luck to be caught at her most ungraceful. "Obviously, I lack those talents."

"Not at all." He advanced into the room. "Surely, they are required when writing your essays."

"I've been giving it my best so as not to make a complete fool of myself this evening, but as you can see," she gestured to the balls on the table, "it is not going well."

He grinned and walked over to grab a mace. Setting the balls, he leaned over with the casual agility of a seasoned billiards player and lined up his stick. "You must focus on your grip and aim." He struck his stick forward, launching a ball, which slammed into the other balls, sending three of them in different directions. Two hit a bank, crossed back over the table, and dropped into separate pockets.

She looked heavenward. "I can see this evening will be a spectacular embarrassment for me."

He set the balls up again. "Nonsense. Of all people, you can do anything you put your mind to." Propping his chin over his hand on the end of his stick, he said, "Try again."

She bent over the table with her mace, feeling awkward and self-conscious with Cam watching her from the opposite end of the billiards table. She made another stab at it and this time her cue completely missed its target.

"Blast it, blast it, blast it!" She threw her stick down on the table.

Cam's chest rumbled with laughter and the gold in his eyes sparkled. He came around to her end of the table.

Picking up her abandoned mace, he handed it back to her. "You must begin by learning the proper stance. May I?"

He came up behind her, pushing lightly on her shoulder to lean her forward over the table with her stick. "The proper stance is critical to a good billiards stroke."

He bent over with her, his body lined up directly behind her, close enough that they were almost touching, his body heat intermingling with hers. "Billiards is a complex game. However, once you learn the basic rules and positions, you must approach your shot with confidence." His long, strong fingers adjusted hers on the stick. "Keep your focus and follow through with your shots. Always appear relaxed and confident as it will help your stroke."

The smooth timbre of his voice resonated in her ear. "You should feel at ease, yet totally sturdy and well balanced." Then she was off to a poor start because she felt decidedly off balance and much too warm.

"Allow me." Cam's firm hands settled on her hips, adjusting her stance. "Yes, just like that. Very good. Now plant your feet." He knelt down to position her slippers, his warm fingers brushing her stocking-clad ankles. "You need to visualize what you want to happen next. Your grip must be comfortable and relaxed. That's it." He stood and murmured in her ear, running his hand over her arm to relax it, leaving goose bumps in its wake. "Don't tense up halfway through because your perfect shot will fall apart."

"Now, show me your grip." His musky, clean scent encased her in a cloud of masculinity. "Wrap your fingers around the stick and hold it gently."

Now thoroughly hot and agitated, she gave up trying to breathe normally. Wrapping her fingers around the stick in a slow, deliberate manner, she could not help smiling with satisfaction when she heard the sharp intake of Cam's breath.

His lips touched her ear. "You must hold the shaft with gentle yet firm fingers. If you grip too tightly, these muscles will tense up." He feathered his fingers over her forearm. "Then you lose all control."

She'd already lost control. Pivoting to face him, she leaned back against the pool table, their bodies inches apart, her entire being flushed and aching for him.

Cam's eyes glittered. He cupped her cheeks and bent down to rub his firm, soft mouth against hers. When she parted her lips, he drove his tongue inside her mouth, thrusting in and out in sensual, suggestive movements. His hands smoothed down her sides and around to cup her buttocks in strong, sure movements. Lifting her to sit on the edge of the billiards table, he plundered her mouth with ruthless, breath-stealing intent.

Need flared in Charlotte. She kissed him back feverishly. Their tongues danced with each other, sucking and nibbling. She drove her hands through Cam's hair, gripping its thick, coarse texture with abandon. She felt a tug at the shoulder of her day gown followed by the cool rush of air over her exposed breasts. Warm hands closed over them as his mouth continued its onslaught on hers. Charlotte arched back with a moan as his hands massaged her tender flesh, his fingers teasing the hardening points.

Somewhere beyond their revelry, Charlotte heard a muffled cry of surprise. She froze in horror, realizing someone stood behind her in the doorway. Cam pulled away, looking up with unfocused, passion-hazed eyes. Recognition and then regret flashed across his face. Automatically, he helped Charlotte pull up the bodice of her dress. She leapt off the billiards table, spinning around to see who had come upon them.

Miss Selwyn stood in the doorway with her perfect little mouth frozen in the shape of an O. Her cheeks were flushed, but the calculated calm in those cool gray eyes sent a frisson of fear rippling through Charlotte. Miss Selwyn took a step back, whirled around, and slammed the door behind her as she rushed from the room.

"Oh, Lord. Now we've done it," Charlotte cried. "She is going to ruin me. She's probably telling Hugh what happened at this very minute."

"No, she will not." He spoke with cool certainty. "Miss Selwyn won't breathe a word of it to anyone."

"How can you say that?" Panic ballooned inside of her. "We don't know what she'll do."

Shoving both hands through his rumpled hair, he stared hard at the door. "Miss Selwyn wants to be a marchioness. If she shares what she witnessed, I'd be honor-bound to offer for you. Her chances of marrying a marquess would be quite ruined then, wouldn't they?"

A sick ache knotted in Charlotte's stomach. "So you are considering marrying Miss Selwyn?"

"I did want to marry her once. Very badly." Leaning over to corral the balls on the billiards table, he spoke in an almost offhand manner. "I quite fancied myself in love, but she rejected my suit."

Charlotte's throat squeezed. Here she stood, her body vibrating from his touch, the taste of him still on her lips, while he discussed the woman he'd likely take to wife. And he had once loved the woman. Perhaps even still did. She pictured Miss Selwyn, resplendent in a wedding gown, and then later, with that lovely, lush figure swollen with child. Cam's child.

"So tell me, Charlotte. What should I do? Shall I marry you to save your reputation?" He paused and locked eyes with her, an inscrutable look on his face. "Or do I offer Miss Selwyn marriage to keep her from ruining you?"

Chapter Thirteen

Tearing off his white linen shirt, Cam cursed aloud and splashed his face with water, his head still swimming with the sweet floral scent and soft heat of Charlotte's skin.

Standing before the small basin in his chamber, he welcomed the shock of cold water against his heated skin. Anything to settle his blood. The way she'd moaned and writhed under his touch made his body tense anew. He splashed his face again, running his wet hands over the back of his neck, trying to tap down his bodily reactions.

He'd been right about her response to passion. She'd reacted to his touch with such eager fervor his prick had swollen to the point of pain. He'd been close to shoving up her skirts and taking her innocence right there on the billiards table. All in all, the seduction had been going quite well. Until Margaret interrupted them. Cam groaned. He'd finally put a stop to Selwyn's attentions toward Charlotte only to have the man's intolerable sister thwart his well-laid plans.

The day after their unpleasant encounter, Cam had sought Selwyn out, issuing a very proper and heartfelt apology. He'd blamed the liquor for his rude comments, and, as expected, Selwyn had accepted the apology with his usual good-natured grace. But it wasn't going to be as easy with the man's sister. Margaret was a calculating social climber who now possessed ammunition to use against him. No doubt she'd make her move soon.

As if his thoughts had summoned her, Margaret slipped into his chamber without knocking. Closing the door, she rested her back against it. The generous cut of her square neckline elucidated the smooth cream of her shoulders and fullness of her ample bosom, as did the emerald pendant necklace snuggled deep in the valley between her breasts. The cool metal of her eyes ran over his bare torso with obvious appreciation.

Grabbing a hand cloth, he vigorously mopped his face and neck. "You shouldn't be in here."

She moved toward him with a certain swagger, like a stealthy big cat closing in on her prey, who believes the outcome of the hunt has just changed in her favor. Reaching out to run a cool hand over his bare back, she said, "I should like to be married at St. George's Hanover Square."

Stepping out of her reach, he tugged his shirt over his head. "I wish you good fortune with that."

"During the season, I think, with the finest families in attendance." She wandered past him, the soft muslin of her cream-colored gown floating over her womanly curves, and eased down onto his bed.

Worry pulled in his chest and across the back of his

shoulders. Should someone discover Margaret alone with him in his bedchamber, she'd be thoroughly compromised and her brother would have every right to expect him to offer marriage.

"It should be a large, elaborate wedding. I plan to be the envy of the Ton when I become your marchioness."

"As I recall, I offered you the position four years ago and you declined." He reached for his boots.

"Yes, and you are even more appealing now then you were then."

He sat in a red velvet chair by the unlit hearth to pull on his boots. "I'm sure my newfound attractiveness is directly related to the title I've gained since I proposed marriage."

"Why did you not tell me you stood to inherit the title?" Margaret's pale, delicate hand wandered across her décolletage. "My answer would have been different."

He gave a harsh laugh. "No doubt." Pulling on his boots, he stood.

"You thought to marry for love?" she asked wide-eyed. "Did you expect me to accept you as you were, with no title? People of our sort do not marry for love."

Shaking his head, he headed for the door. "Good-bye, Margaret."

"I will tell everybody what I saw in the billiards room." The words were sharp, the sweet, seductive tone abandoned. "You will be forced to marry her."

Cam pulled the door open and paused to look back at Margaret. He saw a well-formed woman, with pleasing curves and a lovely face. Once he'd lusted after her, had been anxious to bed her, but looking at her now he experienced a profound sense of relief she'd rejected his suit all those years ago. "You think I would prefer marriage to you rather than be forced to offer for Miss Livingston?"

"She is a shapeless thing and rather ungainly for a woman. I seem to remember you have a fondness for curves." Margaret toyed with the pendant of her necklace which fell deep into the valley between her breasts. "As your wife, I would be most accommodating. I would allow you any liberty."

Distaste crawled over his skin. "Unfortunately, Miss Selwyn, I'm now a marquess, and, as such, must give great consideration to my bride's ancestral line." He sharpened his tone. "Miss Livingston is the daughter of a baron, while you, I fear, are common in every way."

Margaret paled. "How dare you —"

"Oh, I dare," he said, stepping out of his chamber and slamming the door behind him.

• • •

After dinner the following evening, the gentlemen retired to the games room. Charlotte knew little about the impromptu gathering, only that the old university friends were looking forward to it and that Hugh had been included. To beef up their numbers, a few men from the local gentry were joining them as well.

It was a welcome development when Miss Selwyn retired for the evening, pleading a headache, probably because Cam wouldn't be around for her to bat her cow eyelashes at. To Charlotte's relief, the woman had apparently chosen to ignore what she'd witnessed in the billiards room, carrying on at meals as though nothing had happened. This evening, happy to have private time alone with Willa in the duchess's sitting room, Charlotte welcomed the break from Miss Selwyn's grating presence.

"Do my feet not look like they belong on a sow?" Willa complained looking at her swollen limbs.

Charlotte helped her put them up. "You need to elevate them. That's all," she said, trying to sooth her. Although she had to admit to herself that she'd never seen such bloated feet. Pregnancy was taking its toll even on the beautiful duchess. "I am certain the duke finds you as lovely as ever. He still looks at you as though he cannot quite believe his good fortune."

Willa laughed, her chocolate eyes shimmering at the mention of her husband. "No doubt I shall be safe from his attentions this evening. I expect him to be deep in his cups when the gentlemen's party comes to an end."

"I've never known Hartwell to overindulge." Charlotte sat in a comfortable large chair opposite Willa.

"He does not, but this evening they play an old imbibing game from their university days." Willa shook her head indulgently. "It is silly, really. None of them will be able to manage their drink as they did ten years past."

Charlotte smiled at the thought of Cam in a drunken state. "It is true, I suppose, that most men never lose the boy in them."

"They take it quite seriously. Hart says Cam could always outdrink everyone else." Willa shifted her swollen body, trying to get comfortable. "Apparently, my cousin is determined to prove he can still best them all. Hart says he's never seen Cam the least bit foxed. "

"I suppose Cam can do anything he sets his mind to."

"If you can imagine, it was that nice David Selwyn who suggested the game." She looked heavenward. "And he is supposed to be the calm, rational one in their little group."

Sitting back, Charlotte laced her fingers over her chest. "I'm just grateful for the respite from his lovely sister."

"She makes no secret of her interest in my cousin."

"And she's so comely I want to scratch her eyes out."

Willa laughed. "Charlotte!"

"Or maybe I should pull her eyelashes one at a time." Jealousy burned in her chest. "But of course I won't. Instead, I shall sit by and watch her ensnare Cam."

Rubbing her distended belly, Willa said, "Are you certain there's no way the two of you can be together?"

Charlotte scowled. "Do you think I'd allow that baggage to trap Cam if there was a way out of my predicament?"

"I suppose not." Willa yawned. "Still, I find the idea of Cam marrying anyone other than you quite distasteful.

"You are fatigued," Charlotte said, pushing to her feet. "I should leave you to your slumber."

"No," Willa protested, even as her eyelids fluttered shut. "Stay."

Charlotte kissed her cheek. "You need your rest. After all, your body is in the midst of a very important undertaking."

"Mm," Willa said drowsily. "I'm cooking up the heir to the dukedom. I hope he looks like Hart."

"And if it is a girl?"

"He'll spoil her terribly." Her eyes fluttered shut.

Charlotte summoned Clara to help her mistress ready for bed. Leaving Willa in the care of her maid, she retired to her chamber to work on the essay about Cam's mill town.

She planned to make another trip there in three weeks' time, when a picnic would be held to celebrate the mill's success. She looked forward to the opportunity to speak with the workers, students, and townspeople.

Sitting at the escritoire, she quickly became immersed in work. Much later, after many words and reworked sentences, she put down her quill to stretch her cramping fingers and decided to ring for tea. Pulling the rope absentmindedly, she quickly became engrossed in her writing again. After a while, realizing Molly hadn't responded to her summons, she welcomed the opportunity to stretch her legs. Rolling her neck out, Charlotte headed to the kitchen to ask for the tea herself.

On her way, she passed the cards room where the raucous laughter and high voices suggested the men's drinking game was well under way. Approaching the kitchen, Charlotte heard light laughter and conversation. Cook, along with Molly and some other members of the household staff, sat around the table enjoying a cup of tea and some biscuits. Nathan sat with them.

Standing in the shadows, Charlotte watched her brother flirt lightly with a plump, red-haired girl she recognized as Miss Selwyn's maid, whose freckled cheeks glowed with pleasure under Nathan's attentions. Some of the bolder maids sent appreciative glances her brother's way and glowering ones at the fleshy ginger top who'd drawn his interest. Nathan always drew more than his fair share of feminine attention.

Pausing to take a drink of tea and toss a full biscuit into his mouth, Nathan seemed at ease with the servants, still managing to exude a sense of confidence and authority while interacting with them. Sadness tugged heavy in her chest that fate had put one of her brothers at the servants' table, while the other kept company with a duke and marquess just a few chambers away.

"Oh, miss." Molly leapt to her feet when she spotted Charlotte. "Are you needing something?" The other people at the table moved to rise as well.

"Please be at your ease." Charlotte gestured for them to remain seated. "I've come to collect a cup of tea. As soon as I fetch it, I shall be out of your way."

Cook bustled over to prepare the kettle. "I'll have Molly deliver it to your chambers just as soon as it is ready, miss."

"No need." Charlotte advanced into the room. "I will just wait for it, if you don't mind."

The staff exchanged awkward glances, not sure what to make of a baron's daughter in the kitchen with them. She smiled, trying to set them at ease. "I suppose the state the gentlemen are in, they are not terribly in need of your services this evening." Most of the assembled staff smiled, still casting unsure glances around the table to each other.

"Aye, they are all in their cups already," affirmed Nathan.

"Who, may I ask, is winning?"

Nathan gestured toward one of the footmen. "You will have to ask old Lionel here. He's the one in service in the card room this eve."

Lionel's chest puffed with pride. "Aye, miss. The duke is holding his own. But the marquess has had a few rounds of bad luck. He's ape drunk, if you don't mind my saying so. We just carried him to his chambers. Quite out of it, he is."

Miss Selwyn's maid popped up at the mention of Cam's name, her freckles brown against ashen cheeks. "Oh, I forgot.

I must go."

"But your mistress retired with a headache several hours ago, did she not?" Charlotte asked.

"Ah, y...yes, miss." The maid's chin wobbled. "It is... just that I really must go!" She scurried from the room, her rotund form moving with surprising swiftness. She seemed oddly nervous, but then, working for Margaret Selwyn would put anyone on edge.

A few minutes later, Charlotte headed back to her room with a steaming cup of tea. Approaching the card room, she saw Selwyn standing in the hallway alongside Miss Selwyn's maid, a look of consternation on his face.

"You must come, sir," the girl said with a great deal of urgency. "I have looked for Miss Selwyn for the past half hour and she is nowhere to be found."

Charlotte halted, ducking back behind the corner. The sudden movement caused her tea to lap over the rim of the cup, spilling a few drops of the scorching liquid onto her hand. She bit her lip to keep from crying out. Charlotte righted the teacup, blowing on her hand to cool the slight burn.

Why would the maid lie to Selwyn? She most definitely had not spent the past half hour looking for his sister. She'd left the kitchen not more than ten minutes ago. A vague sense of alarm stirred in her.

"Perhaps she is in the library," Selwyn said to the maid. "It is possible she is looking for a book to read."

"Ah...n-no, sir. I checked there," the maid answered with obvious uncertainty. "Yes, I did, sir, checked the library, I did."

Charlotte grimaced. The maid was a blatant liar and a

poor one at that. It wasn't possible she'd found time to check the library since leaving the kitchen.

"The only place I have not searched, sir, is the bedchambers." The words were stilted, almost as if they'd been rehearsed.

"But I thought you said you checked my sister's room—" Selwyn stopped abruptly, blanching. He looked back at the door where the raucous drunken men still carried on.

All except for Cam.

"I am sure nothing untoward is going on." But Selwyn did not sound convinced. His eyes drilled into the maid. "Tell me again where you have looked."

Realization slammed into Charlotte. Miss Selwyn was up to something and the thickheaded maid was in on it. What could that greedy wench be plotting? She ran the events of the evening over in her mind. There was only one thing Margaret Selwyn wanted: Cam.

The footman's words came rushing back. "*The marquess is ape drunk, quite out of it he is.*" Yet, just this evening, Willa had said how well Cam could hold his liquor and that Hart had never seen Cam foxed. And David Selwyn had arranged the game. Selwyn? Could he be in on whatever scheme his sister had in mind? She immediately dismissed the notion. He had seemed genuinely puzzled and concerned about his sister's whereabouts.

Struggling to organize her thoughts, she forced herself to think. Where was Cam? Up in his bed and Selwyn seemed poised to head to the bedchambers in search of his sister. A chill sliced through her. Her legs tingling, she turned and almost ran back to the kitchen, trying to balance the teacup to avoid spilling it again. She came to an abrupt halt as she entered the kitchen. The staff looked up in surprise to see her back among them.

"Is your tea all right then, miss?" Cook asked.

"What? Oh, yes quite, thank you," she said, putting the tea down while searching out Nathan. She found his eyes fixed on her, one brow cocked.

"I am afraid my escritoire has shifted most uncomfortably and I require immediate assistance to right it." She focused on Nathan, pretending not to notice when one of the footmen stood up. "Mr. Coachman, if you please. I am in most urgent need of your services."

Nathan's frown lasted just a second. By the time he stood up, a blank mask had replaced it. "Of course, Miss Livingston," he said, his voice tinged with a sarcasm that only she could detect.

"What is this all about?" Nathan demanded once they were well out of earshot of the others and hurrying up the stairs.

"I am not certain." She felt breathless, almost light-headed. "But I think Miss Selwyn is up to something and I need you to accompany me to Cam's chamber."

Nathan frowned. "Camryn's chamber? Whatever for?"

"Just help me, please." Her hands trembled as they slid along the carved, wooden banister. "I will explain everything later."

When they reached Cam's bedchamber, Charlotte pushed the door open without knocking, praying they weren't too late. The scene that greeted them shocked her, even as it confirmed her worst suspicions.

Clad only in a diaphanous shift which showcased her full, barely clad breasts, Miss Selwyn was comfortably ensconced in Cam's bed, her long, golden curls fanning out across the pillow like angel's wings. Cam's limp arm was draped over her waist, but Charlotte immediately saw he wasn't awake.

"Well, I'll be—" Nathan began.

Catching sight of them, Miss Selwyn jerked upright. "What in the world?" Her grey eyes narrowed at first, but then she lifted her chin, exposing a creamy expanse of neck as satisfaction settled over the lovely contours of her face. "Well, Miss Livingston, as you can see, the marquess and I cannot stay away from each other." She stretched and snuggled closer to Cam's inert body. "And now that I have been so scandalously compromised, it won't be long before the banns are being read."

Outrage clouded Charlotte's vision. "Compromised?" Her nostrils flared. "I don't know what you mean, Miss Selwyn. I have seen nothing. What about you, Mr. Coachman?"

"I?" Nathan's eyebrows rose. "Not a thing, Miss Livingston."

Footsteps sounded in the hallway. Charlotte ducked her head out the door to see Selwyn, Hartwell, and Hugh heading their way. Slamming the door, she whirled around to Nathan. "Hurry, help me get her into Cam's dressing room before they discover her here."

When he didn't immediately move, she pushed him toward the bed. "Hurry, Nathan, don't just stand there. Help me move her." She grabbed the counterpane and flung it off the woman. The movement brought a grunt from Cam, who shifted in his drunken sleep.

"Get away from me, you skinny bluestocking!" Miss Selwyn hissed, trying to grab the cover to shield herself.

Nathan advanced, looming over her, amusement lighting his features. "Come now, Miss Selwyn, do not be difficult." He reached to pull her up out of the bed.

"Don't touch me." She drew back, panic shining in her eyes. "You're just a servant. Don't you dare put your hands on my person."

Nathan laughed, but the sound held no amusement. "It wouldn't be the first time now would it, Maggie?" Miss Selwyn gasped when he hauled her up as if she weighed nothing, a dangerous glint glittering in his eyes. "And as I recall, you weren't protesting the last time I laid my hands on you, moaning maybe, but definitely not complaining."

Charlotte didn't have time to be scandalized by her brother's words. "Hurry, Nathan." She pushed them both toward Cam's dressing room. She managed to get them all inside, slamming the dressing room door shut just as the door to Cam's chamber swung open, followed by the sounds of muffled voices.

"He is alone." It sounded like Selwyn, the relief evident in his voice.

"Sir, we must look around," said a squeaky, uncertain voice. Miss Selwyn's maid. Charlotte looked back at Margaret who glared back with a look of pure hatred in her eyes. Nathan held Miss Selwyn firmly around the waist with one hand while the other remained clamped over her mouth to keep her quiet. At that moment, Miss Selwyn struggled and made a muffled sound from behind his hand, her eyes blaring.

"What was that?" said Selwyn's voice.

The grim voice of the Duke of Hartwell. "It appears someone is closeted in the dressing chamber."

Charlotte panicked as footsteps clicked their way. How would she explain why the three of them were in the small, dark room? She glanced back at Miss Selwyn's state of undress. Her interference with the woman's scheme would be pointless if the men found Margaret half-naked in Cam's dressing room. Heat rose in Charlotte's chest. She couldn't — *wouldn't* — allow Margaret to win Cam this way.

Footsteps paused outside the dressing room door. Charlotte looked around wildly, desperate for a way out of this mess. Seeing none, she took a deep breath, opened the dressing room door, and stepped out into the Marquess of Camryn's bedchamber.

Chapter Fourteen

Four bleary pairs of eyes gaped at Charlotte.

The men were flushed, their clothes slightly askew from the evening's excesses. Selwyn's rounded eyes were edged with relief, likely because the lady stepping out of the closet and into disaster wasn't his sister. The duke's eyebrows lifted, his glance darting between Charlotte and Cam. Miss Selwyn's maid was slack-faced. But it was the expression on Hugh's face that truly alarmed her, especially as the booze-filled flush in his ruddy face deepened into a distressing shade of purple.

Cam chose that moment to begin to stir. "What the devil?" He groaned and blinked repeatedly, his face scrunching up in confusion when he saw five pairs of eyes staring at him. It was at that moment that Charlotte realized Cam wasn't wearing any clothes. When she'd pulled back the counterpane to drag Miss Selwyn out of the bed, she'd unwittingly uncovered most of Cam's impressive physique as well.

Her eyes were riveted when he stirred like a lazy cat, his bare, sculpted body glistening as the firelight flirted with it. The counterpane cover dipped dangerously low, revealing the enticing shadow of hair surrounding his manly anatomy.

Cam realized it just in time. "Bloody hell." He sat up, grabbing the counterpane to shield himself. The sudden movement appeared to cause him great pain. Wincing, he grabbed his head with a groan.

Hugh stepped forward, his face almost the color of an eggplant. "Yes, what the devil indeed!" he choked out, appearing close to a complete eruption. "Perhaps you would care to explain why my sister is here in your room with you, with you—" He gestured agitatedly towards Cam's obvious state of undress.

Cam's eyes narrowed. "Your sister?" His gaze floated over to her, surprise registering in his face.

Hugh's venomous glare suggested he'd like to both shoot Cam *and* run him through with the sharpest, longest blade available. "Perhaps you would care to explain Charlotte's presence in your bedchamber."

"I was getting him a dressing gown," she uttered, knowing just how weak her excuse sounded. Hartwell, Selwyn, and Hugh all looked at her empty hands. Miss Selwyn's maid peered around the room, probably in search of her mistress.

"I couldn't find it," Charlotte said weakly, answering their unasked question. A long, uncomfortable silence settled over the room. Charlotte grappled for a way to rescue the situation, but despite all the alternating scenarios and haphazard excuses crashing through her head, nothing formed into a cohesive thought.

She took a deep breath and stepped forward, praying no more sounds would be forthcoming from the closet. "I came to check on my betrothed."

All eyes in the room swung over to her.

"Your betrothed?" Hugh sputtered.

"Yes." Charlotte's heart clamored as she tried to inject her words with calm indignation. "We meant to ask for your approval this evening, Hugh. But seeing as though you are all in your cups, it seems rather pointless. Really, you all ought to be ashamed of your behavior." She blinked repeatedly, trying to summon tears, which, considering her very real distress, wasn't entirely difficult. "I hope you are pleased with yourselves. You have totally ruined our surprise."

Hugh's overgrown eyebrows squished together. "Your surprise?"

"Yes," she lied, clenching her hands together to stop from scratching behind her itching ears. "Why do you think Willa invited you here so suddenly? It was for our big announcement."

Hugh's mouth hung open. "You and the marquess have reached an understanding?"

"Ask Her Grace if you doubt my word." She squared her shoulders, making a mental note to get to Willa before Hugh did.

"Is that so, Camryn?" her brother asked sharply, the color in his face easing into a less disquieting shade of red. "Have you made my sister an offer of marriage?"

An almost unbearable stillness hung over the room as they all looked expectantly at Cam. Charlotte rubbed her arms, praying he was sober enough to comprehend the dire nature of their predicament.

The cloud of confusion in Cam's amber-green eyes gave way to a wicked gleam. "Ah, yes." Grinning like a Cheshire cat, he held a hand out to Charlotte. "Congratulate me, gentlemen. Miss Livingston has agreed to make me the happiest man in England."

Relief weakened her legs. Determined to continue playing her part, she waved away the hand Cam offered. "Remember yourself, my lord. You are in your cups and not decent to be seen by anyone at this moment." Charlotte's voice trembled, but the men seemed to take her admonishment to heart. All except for Cam, who made a very poor attempt to look sheepish.

Hartwell cleared his throat. "Well, I say, this calls for a drink." He bowed toward Charlotte. "In honor of your betrothal of course, Miss Livingston."

"Of course," she said drily.

It all seemed to be sinking in for Hugh who realized the match he'd ardently hoped for was coming to pass after all. "Well, yes indeed." A broad smile broke out across his face, the red in it returning to an almost natural color. "This most definitely calls for a celebratory drink. Charlotte, I trust you are coming?"

"I've had enough excitement for one evening. I shall retire to my bedchamber," she said. "But why don't you gentlemen have a drink in our honor. Though it hardly seems as if you need an excuse to indulge."

Her glance kept flitting over to the dressing room door. She needed to get Miss Selwyn out of Cam's bedchamber before the woman stirred up any more trouble.

Selwyn turned to follow the other two men out. "My sincerest felicitations, Camryn. You are a fortunate man, indeed." He cast a warm smile in Charlotte's direction as he exited the room, leaving the door slightly ajar to protect what was left of her tattered reputation.

Cam's warm, golden gaze flashed, his insouciant grin widening. "My dear, I wanted to marry you anyway. I am flattered you would go to all of this trouble to compromise me."

"Oh, Cam. I did not know what else to do." Deep distress cramped her stomach. "Now you are going to be bound inextricably to me."

He sat up, the sleek muscles in his arms flexing from the effort. "Charlotte, there is nothing I would like more than to be inextricably bound to you." He held out his hand to her, his dancing eyes full of flirtatious intention. "And I confess, I would not mind getting totally bound to you starting right now."

Nathan charged out of the dressing room with a lethal look on his face. "Keep your drawers on Camryn," he growled. "Unless you want her other brother to finish the job of killing you."

Cam's forehead shot up. "What are you doing in my dressing room?" His mouth fell open when a disheveled-looking, barely clad Miss Selwyn tumbled out after Nathan.

Charlotte spotted the woman's gown folded neatly on a stool by the bed. She breathed a sigh of relief that nobody else had noticed it before now. She snatched up the dress and pitched it at Miss Selwyn, before pushing the woman back into the dressing room.

"What in blazes do you think you are doing?" Miss Selwyn snapped, her usually perfect golden curls all askew. She tried to slap Charlotte's hands away. "You are not going to lock me back in there."

"Do not tempt me." Charlotte gave Margaret one final shove into the dressing room. "Cover yourself. I won't have you parading in front of my betrothed looking like a common trollop."

"I won't let you get away with this," Miss Selwyn said, her voice trembling with fury.

"Don't push me. You've no idea what I'm capable of." Charlotte slammed the dressing room door on the woman's flushed, outraged face.

Cam slumped back against the plump pillows. "I must be dreaming. Either that or I'm still foxed out of my mind." He shot Charlotte a naughty glance. "As long as none of it is actually happening, I might as well enjoy this hallucination." He held open the counterpane, beckoning her, revealing an enticing flash of hard, masculine thigh dusted with amber hairs. "It's never too early to anticipate the marriage bed, and I can't tell you how much I've anticipated seeing you divested of all of those troublesome garments."

Nathan's face flushed. "It is no dream, you bloody arse." He started toward Cam. "And I am going to give you a thrashing that will most definitely wake you up."

Choking back a laugh, Charlotte clutched Nathan's arm. "He's foxed, Nathan. Let him be."

Her brother hesitated, looking the other man over in an assessing way. Cam jauntily cocked a questioning brow in response.

The loopy behavior brought a reluctant smile to Nathan's face. "I believe he's more than foxed, Lottie."

"What do you mean?"

"It appears our cunning Miss Selwyn has given him

something a bit stronger."

Violence roiled in her chest. "Why...that...I will throttle her!" She bolted for the dressing room door.

Grabbing her around the waist, he hauled her back to where she started. "Calm yourself, little sister. Enough is enough. You've won this round. Let the lovely Miss Selwyn be." The dressing room door opened. Fully dressed, Miss Selwyn stepped out, patting her hair into place.

"What did you give him, you witch?" Charlotte lunged for her, but Nathan tightened his hold on her waist.

Recoiling, Miss Selwyn scurried for the door. "Stay away from me, you plain sack of bones."

Charlotte broke free and hurtled after her, slamming the door shut just as Miss Selwyn pulled it open. "You will go nowhere until you tell us exactly what did to Cam."

"Nothing." Holding her hands up in a defensive posture, she backed away. "I swear it."

"Just tell her what she wants to know, Miss Selwyn," Nathan said. "Your scheme is quite ruined anyway."

A fleeting look of uncertainty crossed her face. "Fine," she huffed. "It was just a silly sleeping draught. He'll be fine in the morning." She gave Charlotte a disdainful look. "Until, of course, he realizes he is betrothed to you."

Charlotte thought she heard Nathan chuckle. When she glared at him, he held up his hands in innocence.

Miss Selwyn drew herself up. "He loved me, you know. He worshipped my body." She cast a disparaging look along Charlotte's tall, slender form.

Charlotte wanted to pummel her. "He worshipped you to such an extent that you needed to trap him into matrimony?"

"He may have been reluctant at first." Miss Selwyn's cold grey gaze drilled into her. "But I can assure you, once he was in my bed, I would have won him over. I am precisely the type of wife a marquess should have. I would make a perfect marchioness." Her laugh chilled the air. "Do you really think you have saved him by keeping him from me?"

Charlotte winced. In Miss Selwyn, Cam would have had the perfect political wife— beautiful, smart, engaging. Cam might have eventually been won over. In trying to save him, Charlotte might have propelled Cam onto a course he would soon hate her for.

"Do you think a wife with radical thoughts like yours will help further his political career?" Miss Selwyn said. "And furthermore, he is now stuck with a shapeless bluestocking for a wife."

Cam stirred into a languorous stretch. "Margaret, pardon me for saying so, but when you stand next to Charlotte like that, you do look a little, dare I say, fat?"

Nathan guffawed. Miss Selwyn's face flushed a crimson red. She opened her mouth to speak, but no words came out. Finally, she clamped her lips together and stomped out of the chamber, slamming the door behind her.

Cam watched her go with a confused look on his face. "I say this is a most interesting dream. Charlotte and Margaret in my bedchamber." He yawned extravagantly. "I just want Charlotte alone, only my beautiful love," he said softly, drifting off to sleep. Charlotte's heart skipped a beat, a warm, all-encompassing love for him welled up in her chest again. Tears stung her eyes.

Nathan misunderstood. "Don't cry, love. Whatever draught she gave him, your marquess will be just fine in the morning. He'll have a headache perhaps, but I suspect he will be no worse for it."

A horrible new fear swept over her. Eyeing Cam's sleeping form, she asked, "Do you think he'll recall we are supposed to be betrothed when he awakens?"

Nathan's eyes darkened. "Do not worry, Lottie. We will all see that he does. You can be certain of that."

She suddenly felt exhausted, weary right to the bone. Light-headed, she swayed on her feet.

Nathan caught her. "Come on, little girl," he said, using a childhood endearment. "It is not every day that a lady becomes betrothed. Obviously, the excitement has had an effect on you."

Leaning on her big brother as they walked toward the door, she still had one nagging question. "Nathan, how did you manage to keep that awful woman quiet in the closet?"

"It wasn't difficult," he said with a laugh. "Let's just say Miss Selwyn decided to make the best of the situation."

For the first time, Charlotte took note of her brother's swollen mouth and mussed hair, but she was too spent to summon any reaction beyond mild shock. Sighing, she let Nathan guide her back to her room.

• • •

Late the following morning, Cam found Charlotte taking one of her brisk walks along Fairview Manor grounds. Beyond the estate's magnificent gardens were endless uncultivated fields punctuated by tree-lined areas and clusters of dense woods.

"There you are," he said, pulling her up against him.

"You aren't running away from me again, are you?"

"Cam." She pushed away. "We mustn't."

"Oh now, I will have none of that." His eyes twinkling, he snuggled her against his lean, molded form. "Do say you won't deny me the sweet honey found only upon the lips of my betrothed."

Relenting, she allowed her body to fall against him. A part of her was relieved he remembered their betrothal, the other profoundly fearful because she had no choice but to tell him the truth now. Before their betrothal went any further.

His lips sought hers, opening them and reaching in to taste her. He kissed her so thoroughly, so deliciously, that her legs turned immediately to butter.

"Charlotte," he murmured, his lips moving to her throat, playfully nipping and licking her.

She wanted nothing more than to lose herself in him, yet somehow she found the strength to pull away.

His eyes clouded. "What is it, now?" The beautiful planes of his face hardened. "Surely you don't mean to break our betrothal?"

"No, I fear I will never be able to bring myself to leave you again." Her heart ached with the depth of her love for him. "I cannot wait to be your wife."

He grinned, flashing a wide row of pearly teeth. "I am relieved to hear it." He reached for her again and wrapped his arms around her waist so that their lower bodies were all but melded together. She could easily feel the evidence of his devotion to her. Heat suffused her body.

"So tell me, darling, why are you frowning? You're not worried I feel tricked into this engagement. You know I have desired it for quite a while."

She licked her lips. "No, it is not that. I should tell you what happened last night."

He swooped down to kiss her, his hands still holding their bodies together. "No need. Your brother, Fuller, was kind enough to fill in the particulars before pointing me in your direction just now. He was concerned I wouldn't remember our betrothal."

She examined his face, trying not to be distracted by the feel of his hardening flesh against her belly. "And did you?"

He smiled softly. "How could I not? Admittedly, there are serious gaps in my recall of last evening, but our betrothal is not something I could ever forget, under any circumstances." Still clasping her against him with one hand, Cam's other hand wandered to Charlotte's bodice and his fingers feathered along the upper swells of her breasts. "As your husband, I cannot wait to discover the delicious mysteries you are hiding."

"And what of Miss Selwyn?"

"Fortunately, she and her brother departed early this morning. It seems Selwyn recalled an urgent appointment." He bent to kiss her décolletage. "She is a reaching, deceitful, calculating witch," he murmured against her chest, immersed in his task. "I cannot wait to show you how grateful I am to you for saving me from her machinations."

Charlotte melted into his touch, warmth spreading through her. "I could not have done it without Nathan."

He reached in to cup her bare breast beneath her blouse, his finger running over the tip, which immediately tightened. "I will thank him as well, but will definitely have to find some other way to show my gratitude."

"Stop, please." She forced herself to pull away from him. Adjusting her blouse, she said, "I must tell you my family secret so you will enter this union with your eyes completely open."

Frowning, he reached for her, but she sidestepped and angled her body to elude his grasp.

"If you must tell me, please do so quickly so we can return to what we were doing." The hungry heat in his eyes made her heart go heavy in her chest. Would he still want her after he learned the truth?

"I must have your word as a gentleman that what I'm about to confess goes no further. You must keep my secret safe no matter how much it pains you."

Appearing somewhat startled by the intensity of her demeanor, he inclined his chin. "Of course."

"It has to do with Nathan."

"Go on."

"There is no easy way to do this, so I will just say it." Her insides trembling, she took a deep breath for courage. "Nathan is a Luddite. And more than that, he was one of their leaders, an organizer of their efforts."

"How can that be?" Frowning, he rubbed his chin. "Fuller isn't a mill worker."

"He was briefly, when he first left Shellborne Manor."

He blanched, his arms dropping to his sides. "It cannot be."

"You must comprehend his position." Chills shivered through her body, her fingers cold. "Conditions were abominable and the weavers were losing everything."

"A Luddite?" He pressed a fist against his mouth. "Fuller is a leader of those machine-breaking killers?"

"Not a killer. Never that." The words were urgent, desperate. "Nathan possesses a strong sense of fairness and justice. He is propelled by right and wrong."

"Right and wrong?" Cam stared at her. "Are you suggesting it is right to vandalize and destroy industry? That it is *just* to kill those who champion or embrace progress?"

"No, of course not. It was an error in judgment perhaps—"

"An error in judgment?" His voice rose in strident disbelief. "They ambushed and murdered that mill owner in Marsden, Charlotte. That is murder. Not a damned error in judgment."

He didn't understand. Maybe he never would. But she had to try. "He is not a killer. Nathan has not had a hand in any deaths. I swear it."

"Is that what he tells you?" He regarded her with a new watchfulness, a profound wariness that stung her. "Has it ever occurred to you that he is lying?"

"He is my brother. I know him. Nathan was there at the inception of the rebellion. Yes, he is one of the leading, founding members." She swallowed hard against the rising panic in her throat. "But, no, he does not believe in violence against people. And he has come to believe machine wrecking is useless in the face of progress."

"Are you saying he is reformed? Did he find the righteous path before or after he attacked our looms?"

"He had nothing to do with the machine breaking at your mill because he has pulled away from the Luddites." She wiped cold, damp palms against her skirt. "He believes they have gotten out of hand. That their efforts are futile in any case."

"Does that mean he has broken with them?" A muscle jerked in his neck. "Will he work with the magistrate to identify the guilty?"

"He does not believe violence is the answer." She shook her head slowly, the words quiet with resignation. "But no. He will never turn traitor to the workers. He stays among them to try to coax them to take a different approach. He will lose all influence if he leaves the movement outright."

"Is that what he tells you so that both of you can sleep at night?"

Angry defiance flared in her. "Do not take that tone with me. You pushed for this entanglement, not I. I told you to leave it be." She struggled to level her tone. "Look at how hard Nathan works, how much he has advanced at Fairview Manor in just a short period of time. Surely you do not believe he sneaks off in the night to break machines?"

Cam studied her, a frozen expression on his face. Finally Charlotte couldn't bear the heavy silence. "Say something."

He exhaled, his face haggard. "What do you want me to say? That I am staggered by the depth of this betrayal?"

"That is not fair." Unshed tears ached in her throat. "I have never been disloyal to you."

"How you must have mocked me." He pressed his palms against his eyes, his voice both weary and tinged with hurt. "Did you laugh, Charlotte, while I raged against the machine breakers? Did it amuse you to hear us speak of the troubles at the supper table when you knew the culprit was right there under our noses?"

Desperate to make him understand, she reached out to touch him. "No, it wasn't that way."

He recoiled. "By God, how you and your law-breaking

brother must have laughed. To think Hartwell unknowingly financed the attacks against his very own interests."

"I have never found any of this remotely amusing." A jagged piece of iron seemed to be twisting hard in her chest. "How can you even think such a thing, much less suggest it?"

He searched her face with a pained expression. "Has it all been a lie? Were you willing to warm my bed in order to protect your brother?"

She ached to throw her arms around him, to reassure him of her love. "You must know I would never whore myself for anyone, not even Nathan."

"I championed the effort to make machine wrecking punishable by death, Charlotte. How my political enemies will gloat should they learn of this mockery." He shook his head and paced away from her, dragging both hands through his hair in a familiar gesture that made her heart twinge. "Perhaps they will even accuse me of treachery. And now that I know the truth, if I marry the Luddite's sister and keep quiet, I will, in fact, be a traitor."

His words were a vise clamping down on her heart. "Why do you think I have avoided a connection with you? I knew the untenable position this would put you in."

"Untenable?" He gave a cracked laugh. "Yes, I suppose you could say it is untenable to harbor a murderer."

"No, never a murderer!" she cried. "You must believe me. Nathan aspires to be Hartwell's steward. The duke's current steward is nearing retirement. Nathan has already begun doing some of the books. Why would he work so hard to better himself if he intended to stay actively involved in the rebellion?"

"I hope for your sake Fuller speaks the truth. Machine wrecking is now punishable by death. If Fuller is caught in the act, I give you my word as a gentleman that I will see him hanged."

Chapter Fifteen

Unusually high, sweltering temperatures settled over Fairview, with not even the slightest breeze to stir the stiff summer air.

The doctor who came to see Willa took one look at her swelling limbs and promptly ordered her to remain abed for the remainder of her pregnancy.

A sense of tense quiet hovered over the manor after the latest distressing news from the mill. Machine breakers had attacked again. The armed guards Cam and Hart hired after the last incident managed to repel the crowds, but not without bloodshed. Three protesters had been killed in the melee and the angry crowd managed to get to one of the mill security guards. He'd been beaten and seriously injured before one of his fellow guards managed to frighten the rioters away by firing his weapon.

The news, which she'd learned of from Willa well after Hart and Cam rushed off to inspect the mill, sickened her.

It was the kind of escalation they had all feared. And for Charlotte, it heightened the growing fear she had no future with Cam. His reaction to the revelations about Nathan had been as virulent as she'd expected. And she hadn't even told him all of it. She'd revealed just enough of the truth so he would know marrying her could deeply impact his future.

Despite the unusually warm temperatures and lack of a companion, she still undertook her daily walks. She had not seen Cam for three days and the exercise was a way to work off the brittle tension building within her. Exhaling, she increased her pace, striding over Fairview's fields, going further than she normally did. Small beads of sweat gathered on her upper lip as she pushed onward, uncertain of how long she had walked. So lost was she in her thoughts, that she didn't hear the approaching horse until it was almost upon her.

She spun around to see Cam sitting atop his stallion, silhouetted by the sun. He slid off his horse, his Hessians thudding when he hit the ground. The two of them looked at each other for a moment. He wore an inscrutable look on the strong curves of his face, his shining gaze holding hers. Then, in two quick strides, he was in front of her, pulling her into his arms.

The wave of relief that washed over Charlotte almost knocked her off her feet. He murmured her name and crushed her lips under his, his tongue invasive and demanding. Desire surged and overflowed in her. She vaguely worried that she must look and smell less than pleasing in the summer heat, but if Cam noticed, he gave no indication. His mouth moved to her throat, devouring it, softly calling her name.

Embracing his head and face, she pulled him closer.

"Cam? What is this?"

She felt him smile against her neck. "Can a man not seek comfort in the arms of his betrothed when he is returned from an arduous journey?"

Her heart soared and clenched at the same instance. He was troubled and had sought her out for what? Comfort? Warmth? She cupped his face and looked into his eyes. "Was it so very awful? Were more hurt than you feared?"

He feathered his fingers along her temple, his eyes clouding. "The anger is palpable now. The tension is everywhere." He sighed. The stress of the past few days had deepened the lines around his eyes and mouth. "We've hired more armed guards to patrol the town as well. The Ludders are turning their anger on the people who work in our mill."

She searched his face. "Cam, if you like, I will cry off on our betrothal. I know the news about Nathan is too much."

He tightened his hold on her. "All I could think of while I was gone was how much I wanted to return to you and put things to rights." His wry smile melted her insides. "Somehow you have become home to me, Charlotte. If I let you go, where will I go? What would I do?"

"Truly?" The heavy weight in her chest took flight, leaving her heart feeling buoyant. "But what about Nathan?"

His jaw tightened. "I do not like it, Charlotte. I cannot lie." He pulled away from her, shaking out his shoulders, stretching his arms and neck, which she imagined were tight from both travel and tension. "I have spoken to Fuller. He informs me he'll have no hand in any future violence. He said, as you did, that he has not sanctioned the machine breaking for quite a while."

He fixed a hard stare on her. "I gave you my word that

I would not turn him in based on his past associations. But I warned him if he breaks the law going forward, I won't lift a hand to stop him from being hanged." He grasped her shoulders and held her gaze. "Do you understand me? If we marry, those are the terms I can live with. The question now is, can you? If your brother breaks the law again, you must agree to let the law deal with him without any interference from either of us."

She nodded tremulously, her heart clamoring. It was a tremendous compromise on Cam's part and she knew it. "Are you quite sure?" she whispered, still in disbelief. "You must be certain."

"I am certain that I love you, Charlotte Livingston." His full, open smile dazzled her. "I love your passion, your honesty, and, yes, even your unswerving loyalty to your brother. I shall be a fortunate man, indeed, if I am the recipient of that level of love and devotion."

Her heart swelled. She had never truly felt joy until now. "You already have my love and devotion. You have all of me. It has been so from the very first."

He held out his hand to her. "Come, let us return."

She put her hand in his, glad for the radiating warmth of his golden presence. He mounted and pulled her up, settling her sidesaddle, the edge of her body up against his. He put the strength of his arms around her, holding her close, urging Hercules on. Twisting to embrace him, she relished the feel of his toned body pushed intimately up against hers.

Cam grasped Charlotte with one arm while his other hand held the ribbons to guide the stallion. He impelled the animal into a run, everything around them passing in a heady blur as they picked up speed. They raced into the still air, summoning a refreshing wind, which blew against them, engulfing both in a sense of runaway rapture. Longing to touch him, she nuzzled his neck. Before long, light kisses gave way to soft nips and licks.

She felt his body react to her caresses. His hand slipped down from its grip on her waist, going to her bottom and lifting her with a forceful gentleness against the strength of his hunger for her. He kissed her, his tongue plundering her as though he could not get enough. She pushed herself against him, famished for more, for the promise of where their passion would propel them.

Pulling his lips from hers, he slowed his mount to an easy walk. "If we persist," he said against her mouth, his voice hoarse, "we shall have a devil of a time explaining why two experienced riders could not keep their seat."

She sighed and put her hand up to her hair, tossing her bonnet away so it would not impede their kisses. Her hair pulled loose and fell about her shoulders and waist.

He swallowed hard. "You are a shameless temptress." Pulling Hercules to a halt, he dropped the ribbons, his hands going to her lustrous hair. He ran them through all the way to her waist before taking her completely into his arms again for a brazen kiss.

He dismounted, pulling her down with him, kissing her as he held her body up against his. He walked her backwards toward an old oak tree with their bodies meshed together, arms intertwined as their mouths devoured each other. His musky, masculine smell engulfed her. He tasted like sunshine and freedom and unlimited possibilities.

Cam dropped down with his back against the tree and pulled her down astride him on his lap. She felt a strong hand on her bottom, and then her skirts were being eased up. His fingers went to her soft folds, and she cried out when he reached the intended spot.

She moaned at his touch, pushing herself towards his hand, needing him beyond all else. He murmured her name when she cried out with pleasure. His fingers drove her to madness, her body on fire and trembling.

His tongue sought hers with intense reaching motions. Charlotte was hungry for all of him. Her hands went to his breeches and pulled at them. Groaning, Cam helped her, pulling at the fastenings, freeing his anxious man's flesh. She wrapped her fingers around his hardened length, amazed at its soft-iron feel and rubbed herself over the satiny tip.

Cam almost bucked when she did. He stilled for a moment, looking at her. Wild desire clouded his eyes. "Charlotte," he said in short, hard gasps. "This is not the place for a lady's first time. I can't take you here like a common wench."

The thought that he might stop was unbearable. "Please, Cam." She squirmed on top of him, making him groan again.

Steady hands went to her hips stilling her movement. "If you keep doing that, I will be unable to stop."

She looked at him, the wild tawny hair, the way his carved lower lip grimaced with the effort of stopping. So she moved again, covering his face with nips and kisses. "I'm relieved to hear it. Don't stop."

His eyes glittered. "I am nothing if not obedient." He lifted her while adjusting his own position. Balancing Charlotte atop his hard flesh, he guided her down onto him. She felt him at her entrance and then the full, gloved feel of him coming into her. A sharp pain shot through her.

Charlotte squeezed her eyes shut, taking a deep inhale. She hadn't expected such intense discomfort. How in the world was that supposed to fit inside her? Cam stopped moving. Despite the strain of their coupling, Charlotte's insides screamed in protest. Her eyes flew open to find that burning amber gaze fixed on her face.

A muscle twitched in his jaw. "You are in pain. We'll stop." He began to move out of her.

The idea of Cam leaving her made her crazed. "No. Stay with me. Don't leave me now."

He brushed tender kisses over her cheekbones and brows. "I will never leave you, Charlotte."

He froze when she clutched his shoulders and pushed down, blotting out the discomfort until he was completely inside of her. Wanting to see him, she kept her eyes open. Cam watched her face, wincing when she cried out at the burning pain, which signaled the loss of her innocence. Despite the discomfort, the robust feel of him inside of her made Charlotte want to weep with relief.

He seemed to be fighting the urge to move inside her. "Give it a moment," he soothed. He feathered more kisses along her throat. "Go easy."

Lost in the sensation of having him inside her, Charlotte didn't really hear the words. Locking eyes with him, she began to move on instinct. He automatically jerked into her in response. He groaned and seemed to catch himself because he stopped moving again. She did not. She kept moving but had an awkward rhythm and realized she didn't know what to do. Frustration and some sort of unmet need welled up inside of her.

He seemed to understand. "I've got you, my love. I've

got it." He gave her a long, intense kiss and then grasped her hips, helping her adjust the rhythm. His capable, long fingers caressed her bottom, guiding her up and down the length of him. She could sense it when he finally let himself really go, thrusting upward through her body.

They moved in a rhythm of the ages, punctuated by soft moans and the primal slapping sounds of hot, wet strokes. Charlotte moved atop him, relishing the feel of him moving inside her, gasping when pleasure seemed to overwhelm her senses. She lost all control when her muscles released, the involuntary contractions shooting through her shuddering womb. Cam kissed her hard when she cried out and the warm ripples of her climax quivered over her body. He pumped furiously into Charlotte, letting out a quiet roar when he released himself inside of her.

Sensation still roiling deliciously through her body, Charlotte closed her eyes, savoring this small, perfect moment when everything in the world was just as it should be. Except for one thing. "Show me how to pleasure you."

His chest rumbled with amusement. "Oh, you give me great pleasure, Charlotte, unbelievably so." His mouth closed over hers in a hot, lingering kiss.

"That is not the pleasure I mean."

"Hmm?" He pulled her bodice down, revealing her modest breasts. His eyes glistened with appreciation. "Such beauties. It wouldn't do for me not to pay them proper attention." Lowering his head, he licked across a tender point. "What kind of pleasure do you mean?"

"I happen to know firsthand there is another type of... amorous activity you enjoy." She squirmed atop him trying not to be distracted by the feel of her nipple between his teeth. Arching into his mouth, she added, "I would like to give you that now."

He jerked his head up. "Charlotte, it is not necessary," he said incredulously when he took her meaning. "I cannot fathom a lady such as yourself doing such a thing. Why, you've just been introduced to the pleasures of the flesh. I would never ask it of you."

"You did not ask. I want to." Triumph surged through her at the feel of his male anatomy firming beneath her bottom. "I don't want there to be anything you've done with another woman that we haven't experienced together. I do not want any female to have that claim on you."

"I assure you, no one has ever had a claim on me as you do." His face softened, taking on a radiant glow. "I love and desire you as I have no other woman."

Heat shimmered through her chest. "Truly?"

"Truly."

Wriggling out of his lap, she jumped to her feet and offered him her hand. Taking it, he stood up. "Shall we return?"

"Not just yet." Pushing him up against the tree, she began to slide down his body. "Show me," she demanded.

And so he did.

• • •

"Do tell, Camryn. When do you plan to wed my sister?" asked Hugh Livingston, a shrill undertone to his voice. "I must inform our mother, and there are, of course, the marriage settlement details to be worked out."

Cam sat with splayed legs in a large leather chair in the

billiards room where Shellborne had sought him out. "I've arranged for the banns to be read at our parish church at Camryn Hall for the next three Sundays." Cam swallowed some brandy. "I trust you will do the same at your parish church?"

"Of course." Shellborne coughed. "There is, of course, the matter of Charlotte's dowry."

"Yes." Cam eyed the swishing dregs inside his brandy glass. "I am not in need of Charlotte's money. Whatever figure you've set aside for her dowry is more than adequate."

Relief relaxed the baron's features. "And there is, of course, the issue of pin money."

The man might be a pest, but Cam appreciated his determination to ensure his sister's future. "I will arrange for my solicitor to provide a personal annual allowance for Charlotte once she becomes my wife." He couldn't wait for that to happen. His mind wandered back to yesterday, when she'd demonstrated what an apt and enthusiastic lover she could be. Then there'd been revelation of Charlotte's nude form at the pond, where they'd gone for a swim afterward. His mind feasted on the memory of her lean yet surprisingly supple body, smooth expanses of creamy skin punctuated by the soft curves of her hips and round perfection of her pert breasts. "I am sure you will find the allowance to be more than generous," he heard himself saying.

"Yes, undoubtedly," said Shellborne. There was an awkward pause. "Furthermore, in the event of your death—"

Cam wondered how soon he could get Charlotte alone again. His guess about her unbridled reaction to passion had been correct. He couldn't wait to have her again, to hear that little, muffled scream she uttered when she reached her release.

He realized Shellborne was looking at him expectantly. "What? Oh, yes, of course Charlotte and any children we might have will be protected in the event of my death." Perhaps he could steal into her chamber this evening. He frowned. Hopefully, her other brother didn't make a habit of climbing into her room at night. Cam certainly didn't want a repeat of their previous encounter. Last time nothing improper had happened. Tonight, Nathan would have excellent reason to kill him if he came upon them in Charlotte's chamber.

The changing expressions on Cam's face seemed to make Shellborne nervous. "She will, naturally, be entitled to the right of dower."

Cam squinted at Shellborne, trying to focus on what the little, round man had just said. The scrutiny caused Charlotte's brother to shift uncomfortably in his chair. Cam forced himself to process Shellborne's words. "Yes, yes. My marchioness will be entitled to one-third of the income from Camryn Hall in the event of my death." He pushed to his feet, stretching his cramped legs. "However, I will also set aside a generous jointure to assure Charlotte's complete comfort and financial independence after I am gone. In addition, I will arrange a town home in Mayfair and a country estate for her in the event of my demise. Portions will also be set aside for the children." He paused, trying to mask his impatience. "Anything else?"

Shellborne took a quick sip of his brandy, which had remained untouched until now. "No. I shall look forward to reviewing the contract once your solicitor draws it up."

Cam poured himself another brandy. Turning, he held

the decanter in Shellborne's direction. The baron shook his head, declining the silent offer of a refill. "There is another related issue," Cam said. "Perhaps now is an opportune time to discuss it."

"What might that be?" Shellborne crossed his arms, before uncrossing them again.

Cam tossed back some brandy, enjoying the warm, smooth feel of the fiery liquid sliding down his throat. "It is in regards to Nathan Fuller."

"Nathan Fuller?" His tone was as bland as the expression on his face. "The duke's coachman?"

"And your brother." Cam strode across the room, dropping into a chair opposite Shellborne. "Let us not waste time by dissembling. I am aware Fuller is your father's by-blow."

"I see." Flushing, Shellborne scratched the thinning, random strands atop of his shiny pate. "I fail to see how that is relevant to anything."

Cam leaned back, draping his arms over the back of his chair. "Fuller is dear to your sister. Consequently, he is of concern to me."

"I see."

"I was wondering, Shellborne, if you approve of Fuller's political activities?"

"Political activities?" The baron's eyes widened. "I beg your pardon?"

Cam wasn't surprised the baron appeared unaware of his brother's clandestine activities. "What do you know of your brother's movements since leaving Shellborne Manor?"

Charlotte's brother shrugged. "All I know is that Fuller worked at a mill in Leicestershire. But he ran into trouble there." He released a long exhale. "Not that that was any surprise. He has never known his place."

Cam bit back a retort. "In some families, the two of you would have been raised as the brothers you are."

"My father, the late baron, did not acknowledge him," Shellborne said, his voice chillier than Cam had ever heard it. "That was his choice."

"Indeed it was." Cam shifted back to his real focus. "What became of Fuller after he left Leicestershire?"

"I had no idea where he was until I discovered him here, in service to His Grace." Shellborne stood, bringing the discussion to a close. "As you've no doubt surmised, we are not close."

After Shellborne excused himself, Cam closed his eyes and ran the baron's words over again in his mind. Something about the exchange unsettled him, as though he was missing the key piece to a puzzle. But he couldn't, for the life of him, put his finger on precisely what it was.

. . .

This time, when Cam came to Charlotte's chamber in the middle of the night, she expected him. He let himself in as if it were already his right, disrobing in quick, efficient movements. She watched with hot curiosity, her body craving him now that she fully comprehended what she'd missed all of these barren years. He pulled his white linen shirt over his head, the movement causing the muscled contours of his chest and stomach to stretch and ripple.

When he bent to shed his breeches, the fires light glowed over the sleek lines of his narrow waist and across the indentations at his hips. Naked, he turned toward her and the impossible fullness of his engorged flesh sprang proudly from a nest of tawny curls. He eased his weight onto the bed next to her and even the mattress seemed to groan with admiration.

Pulling her into his arms, he kissed her soundly. His tongue moved into her mouth, branding her with every stroke. He stopped and pulled back, his amber eyes shining in the firelight. "Will you take off your sleeping gown?"

Heat suffused her, but she was eager for him. Sitting up in the bed, she pulled off the thin white gown. Propped up on his elbow, he watched with obvious appreciation. It still surprised her that Cam wanted her above all others. That he, who could have any woman, had chosen her.

He ran a warm hand over her bare back, leaving tingling sensations in his wake. Sitting up, he moved behind her, pulling Charlotte's sitting body back up against his. His hands stole over her breasts from behind, coaxing them into fine points as he kissed and nipped her neck. "I trust Fuller does not make a habit of sneaking into your chamber at night."

With a contented sigh, she leaned back into the smooth hard warmth of his body. A throbbing sensation began to build. "If he does, I'll be terribly compromised."

"It's fortunate we've already decided upon marriage," Cam said raggedly, his breathing becoming shallower.

Marriage. Guilt niggled in her chest. Had she been right not to tell him the entire truth? She hadn't revealed everything, convincing herself she protected both Cam and Nathan by not doing so. Perhaps now was the time to tell him. But then he lifted her, sheathing himself inside of her from behind in one smooth, quick stroke, and all rational thought tumbled out of her mind.

"Oh," she said responding to the combination of surprise and sensation. There were no words to express how wonderful it felt. "I did not know it could be done like this."

Cam gave a rough laugh as she began to move experimentally atop him. "Yes, just like that," he ground out. "There is so much we have yet to explore together, my love." He scraped his teeth lightly along her back in a sensual movement that made her tingle and shiver. Cam helped her move, thrusting upward into her, hard and fast.

A conflagration of fire and passion flooded through her. She began to move faster, the tension inside her growing. Cam moved with her, helping her keep the rhythm of her quickening movements. He ran his hands over her back and shoulders, around to cup her breasts, and then to the place between her legs, rubbing and coaxing. When she cried out, Cam came with her, both hurtling over a precipice that rendered all thought impossible.

Later, they made love again, enjoying the newness of each other's touch, the preciousness of what they'd found together, their bodies and limbs still intertwined when they finally dozed off. It seemed as if they'd barely closed their eyes when Charlotte awakened to the flickering, reddish haze of a new day.

She stretched with a satisfied sigh before rolling over to Cam. "Wake up," she crooned, running her hand over the curly amber hairs on his chest. "I shall be utterly and completely compromised if Molly finds you here."

Cam stirred, groaning as he pulled Charlotte closer. "It cannot possibly be morning yet." He ran his hand over

Charlotte's belly. "And I am not done ruining you." His voice went deep with intent as his hand crept lower.

Her skin jumped with excitement at his touch, but she forced herself to grab his hand, impeding its progress. "Look, the day is upon us." She gestured toward the window. "You cannot be found here. Poor Hugh will have an apoplexy for certain this time."

Cam uttered a grumpy sound and reluctantly swung his legs over the side of the bed. Sitting up, he glanced out over the red dawn visible through the window. "Morning came entirely too quickly. I'm as tired as the devil." He twisted around to grab Charlotte, pulling her across to sit on his lap. "I suspect my weariness is entirely your fault, my future marchioness."

"I am practicing at being a competent wife." She wrapped her arms around his neck. "I do like to excel in all things."

"I'm a most fortunate man." Their mouths met. They took it slow, sliding their tongues against each other in deep, leisurely movements, drawing out their pleasure in each other.

She finally pulled away and stood up to draw on her dressing gown. She reached for Cam's clothes. "Come now," she said pulling at his hand.

He rose and began to dress. As he fastened his breeches, something about the flickering, orange hue of the new day distracted him. His eyes widened in realization.

"By God, that is not the sun." Pulling on his shirt, he raced toward the door. "Those are flames. The stables are on fire!" Before Charlotte could react, Cam flew out into the hall and barreled down the stairs yelling, "Fire, fire!"

Someone else had apparently seen it, too. A bell began to

peal and urgent shouts erupted beneath Charlotte's window.

Fear blasted through her. "Nathan," she whispered struggling to pull on the gown she'd worn just a few hours ago. She prayed he'd escaped his sleeping quarters above the stables. Finally dressed, Charlotte burst into the hallway, rushing down the stairs and out the door. Sprinting toward the blazing structure, she was swept up in the stream of servants running in the same direction as shouts and curses filled the air.

A massive ball of flames engulfed the north side of the stable. The shooting blaze roiled into the sky. Billowing smoke formed an ominous halo around the vicious orange, yellow, and white flames. Coughing grooms led the horses to safety. Their faces were covered with soot and the whites of their eyes floated in the amber-tinged darkness.

Terror seized Charlotte, paralyzing her lungs. She looked around wildly almost sobbing her brother's name. She grabbed at one of the groom's arms. "My bro...Nathan Fuller, the coachman. Have you seen him?"

"No, ma'am," he said before turning his attention back to the two horses he rushed to safety.

She became aware of Hartwell calling out orders. She had never seen the duke looking less than flawless in his appearance. But this evening, his long, dark hair, usually pulled back in a queue, hung loose, somehow softening his sharp features. His white shirt was over his breeches. Something about seeing the usually immaculate duke in a state of dishabille, silhouetted against the surreal, reddish haze of the mammoth flames, heightened Charlotte's mounting distress.

The acrid air snaked into her lungs making it hard to

breath. Intense heat slapped across her skin, moistening it with sweat and fear.

She saw Cam then, his height allowing him to stand out above the people around him, his wild leonine mane tousled and free. He commanded the staff to form water lines and they were soon passing buckets to help douse the fire.

Cam joined one of lines, helping pass the buckets. His fine white lawn shirt bared some of his chest, which, like the smooth planes of his face, glistened in the scorching heat.

Charlotte ran to him. "I cannot find Nathan."

Cam shouted some commands down the water line and then turned his attention back to her as he passed the buckets onward. "He's a strong and able man, Charlotte. Surely, he managed to escape." He shouted to be heard above the roaring flames. More urgent calls came from down the water line and he sprinted in that direction to see what was amiss. Calling back over his shoulder, he called, "Wait here. I'll find him, Charlotte. You have my word."

More people continued to arrive. Word of the crisis must have reached the tenants. Someone grabbed her arm. She turned to see Hugh.

"Have you seen him, Charlotte?" Hugh cried out, his voice thick with emotion.

"No!" Charlotte's lungs burned. "Have you?"

Hugh's eyes were rounded with fear. The orange light of the flames cast a sickly hue over his face. He shook his head slowly, sadly.

Charlotte couldn't breathe. Her stomach twisted into painful knots. She choked back a sob and looked toward the fire. Where could Nathan be? No one who remained inside the stable could survive the inferno devouring it.

"Miss Livingston?" She turned to see Digby, the butler. "Is it Mister Fuller, the coachman, that you seek?"

She nodded, coughing from the smoke burning into her lungs. "Have you seen him, Digby?"

If it perplexed the butler to find Charlotte overwrought over the well-being of a servant, he showed no sign of it. "Yes, Miss Livingston. I am certain I saw Fuller running toward the manor just a few minutes ago." A grateful sob escaped her throat. He was safe.

It was Hartwell who first saw the smoke coming from the manor house itself. Charlotte only realized something was amiss when she heard a thundering, animalistic cry and turned to see the dark duke hurtling toward the manor to where his wife lay, mostly alone and vulnerable, her body impossibly swollen with his child.

Cam sprinted behind Hartwell, his unruly hair more wild than usual, his face glistening with perspiration and his damp white shirt darkened with soot and sweat. Charlotte scrambled after them, but both disappeared in the throng of people.

She could smell the new flames before she saw them, the air laden with the sharp smell of smoke interlaced with a pungent citrus aroma. She reached the orangery in time to see Cam and Hart running in with massive drapes torn down from a nearby formal room. They batted at the blaze, trying to smother the fast-moving flames that licked, threatened, and sometimes succeeded in jumping to a neighboring orange or lemon tree.

Cam threw a chair through one of the palladium windows, shattering the glass. The two men tossed the burning tree plants out of the broken windows. Others, servants and tenants, streamed toward the orangery. Some on the outside had already formed a bucket line, and the containers of water passed through the windows into the orangery to quell the flames. It seemed the duke had spotted the fire in time. He and Cam had managed to confine it mostly to the orangery, preventing the destruction of the massive historic manor.

A bloodcurdling scream rang through the air, and Charlotte immediately recognized it as Willa.

Hartwell knew it too for he raced out of the orangery, rocketing up the massive stairs, his glistening, soot-blackened face a mask of fury and dread. Cam and Charlotte were right on his heels. They tore through the endless corridors towards the family wing where Willa remained on bed rest.

As they rounded the corner near the family apartments, the rancid smell of smoke assaulted Charlotte's nostrils. The smell of fire clearly emanated from the vicinity of Willa's chambers. She choked back a sob. What if they were already too late? Then a shadow came around the corner, followed by the sight of Nathan, disheveled and damp with perspiration, carrying a moaning Willa in his arms.

The duke cursed and reached for his wife. Nathan lowered his eyes as he handed Willa into her husband's anxious arms.

Charlotte rushed to her side. "Are you all right?"

Willa coughed. "Yes, yes, it was the smoke. I was overcome." She looked up into her husband's worried face. "I screamed when I saw the flames. Truly, I am fine." A group of house servants who had rushed up after them now stood in the hallway, a respectful distance away.

Cam turned to them. "There is a fire in the family wing. Quickly, another water line."

"No," said Nathan.

Cam's face hardened. "No?"

"What I mean to say is there is no need." Nathan rubbed the back of his hand against his forehead. "I managed to put out the fire. It was just the curtains in Her Grace's chamber."

Suspicion gleamed in Cam's amber eyes. "And what, pray tell, were you doing here? What business do you have in the family wing, much less Her Grace's *bedchamber*?"

Anger and resentment flashed across Nathan's face. His retort was drowned out by a cry from Willa. She writhed in Hartwell's arms, clutching her stomach, her face contorted in pain.

The duke blanched. He strode across the hallway and kicked open the door to the nearest guest chamber. "Mrs. Chalmers," he bellowed to the housekeeper as he entered the room with Willa in his arms. "Have this chamber prepared for Her Grace." The housekeeper scurried in after the duke while Nathan hurried down the hallway and around the corner.

Charlotte rushed after her brother, alarm filling her chest as she swept down the stairs after him. "Nathan. Nathan!"

He halted abruptly. "What is it?"

"What is going on?" she asked trying to catch her breath. "Why were you in the duchess's bedchamber?"

"I went to save her." He looked around to see if they were alone and then led Charlotte a few steps back into the empty, darkened library. Closing the door for privacy, he said, "This was no accident, Charlotte. It was a Luddite attack."

"No." Shaking her head with disbelief, she put a hand to her chest. "How can you know? You cannot mean you are a part of this."

His face darkened. "Of course not. I saw faces I recognized in the crowd."

"Machine breakers," she breathed.

"Yes, and one was headed for the main house. I knew he meant to cause harm."

Relief flowed through her. "Thank God you got to Willa in time."

"Do you have so little trust in me, Lottie?" His voice was gentle in its reproach. "Did you really think Ned Ludd had taken up the cause again?"

Guilt scoured her chest. "No, of course not, forgive me. It's been such a trying evening."

"You weren't alone in thinking it." He rubbed the side of his head wearily. "Some of the Ludders who saw me this evening didn't realize I'm now the head coachman here. Like you, they surmised I'd come back to lead the charge."

"They still see you as their leader. You are Ned Ludd. There can be no other."

A dark emotion passed over Nathan's face. "It is well past time for Ned Ludd to vanish forever and truly become a myth." He looked at her with troubled eyes. "I never wanted any of this, Charlotte. I just wanted justice."

"I know."

"This," he gestured into the air with his hand, "is not what I had expected. The violence, the killing—" His voice trailed off before turning brisk and businesslike. "I must go. The fire is under control, but I must sort out whether we lost any animals and where to house the ones that survived." With a quick peck on Charlotte's cheek, Nathan slipped out of the library.

She sensed another presence before she actually saw him. Unease shivered through her, the hair on the back of her neck tingled. Forcing herself to turn around with as much calm as she could muster, she peered into the dim recesses of the long, rectangular room. Like almost everything at Fairview Manor, the two-story library was oversize and impressive, with stocked bookshelves soaring up the two floors.

Her searching gaze finally found him as he slipped from behind the stairs which lead to the library's second floor.

Shadows fell across the worn and disheveled figure. His amber hair was even more rumpled than usual, and his soiled, white lawn shirt hung loose over his trousers. He watched her through lowered lids, with the deceptively lazy gaze of a predator in repose.

"Cam." Her scalp tingled. "I did not see you there."

"Obviously." He took a slow, menacing gait toward her.

She took a reflexive step back. "What are you doing here?"

"I was following your brother. When I heard you coming behind me, I slipped inside here to stay out of the way."

"Oh."

"Yes, oh. It appears I was correct to be suspicious of the man."

Terror rained down inside of her. He'd overhead everything.

He watched her face intently. "Why did you not tell me, my dear, that I've already had the pleasure of meeting the illustrious and most elusive Ned Ludd?"

Chapter Sixteen

The underlying ice in his voice chilled Charlotte's soul. Gone was the twinkling amusement she adored in his sunlit green eyes, replaced by a hard stare that pierced her heart.

"I was trying to find a way to tell you," she said, surprised at how calm her voice sounded.

"Obviously you didn't try hard enough."

"What good would it have done?"

"What good?" His carved features contorted in anger. Lunging at her with the swift agility of a mountain cat, he grabbed her arm, hauling her to him. She went willingly, knowing he would never harm her. Not physically at least. She could smell liquor on him, intermingled with the musky, masculine aura that never failed to captivate her. Even now.

"It is a pity, is it not, my dear, that I did not learn of this before your brother and his ilk burned the stables down." His mouth was just by her ear, his hot breath a rough caress. "The rafters there would have been ideal for slipping a noose around your brother's neck and watching him swing."

Despair gutted through Charlotte, an anguished sound escaped her. A shadow crossed Cam's face. Abruptly releasing her arm, he strode over to pour himself a drink. Charlotte watched his back, the way the sleek turn of muscle rippled under the fine lawn of his shirt.

He turned back toward her, bitter disillusionment etched in his face. "I should have put it all together myself. Ned Ludd is known to be from Leicester. Fuller is from Leicester. The mythical idiot, Ned Ludd, worked at a mill there, as did your brother." Cam raised his glass in a mock salute, emotion glazing his eyes. "But he is no idiot, is he, Charlotte? That is where we got the story wrong." He gave a ragged laugh and threw back more drink, grimacing as he swallowed. "Congratulations, my dear, on a game well played."

Her hands curled into fists, the nails digging into her skin. "Cam, what will you do to him now?"

Uttering a low curse, he pivoted to hurl his glass against the wall. The shattering sound exploded into the air, the scattering shards tinkling away. She backed away when he stalked toward her with glittering eyes.

Alarm flooded her and she could think of nothing but warning her brother. Spinning around, she dashed for the door, her heart blasting in her chest. Cam's boots pounded behind her, closing in. She reached the door, blinded by tears, and tried to pull it open with jerky, panicked movements. Cam slammed up behind her. Thrusting both of his palms against the door, he boxed her in, effectively preventing her from leaving.

"Do you think to go and warn him?" His despairing

whisper sliced through her. "Is it always him you think of first, Charlotte? Even now?"

"Let me go," she gasped, her back to him, her forehead resting against the dark, cool wood of the door. "You have made it quite clear that I am now beneath your touch."

Pushing his body up against hers, he forced Charlotte flat against the door. "Oh, hardly that. Hardly that." Pained bitterness tinged his voice. His hips were against the small of her back and she shivered at the feel of his obvious arousal. Her body reacted almost violently, with a ravening need to be joined with him.

For one last time.

To push away whatever shattering inevitability awaited them on the other side of the massive wooden door. She knew better than anyone what Cam would be compelled to do once he left this room. And they both understood she could never forgive him for it.

Turning to face him, Charlotte let out a cry of need, her hands going to the sides of his hips to bring him closer to her. She melded herself against him, trying to assuage her hunger. Cam's questioning eyes burned into hers.

"Yes," she whispered, her pulse slamming against her skin. "Now."

Surprise flickered in his face. "Do not allow this. Tell me to stop."

She shook her head. "I want no more pretenses between us."

Abandoning any show of gentlemanly restraint, he made quick work of her bodice, shoving down the delicate fabric of her shift and the lace of her stays, leaving her bare to his gaze. Cool air bathed the engorged pink tips of her pale mounds.

He lifted her up against the wall and anchored her there. His head came down to ravish her softness. He took one bud into his mouth and toyed with it, suckling her, his teeth skimming the sensitive point.

Wrapping her legs around Cam's hips, she welcomed the feel of his hard flesh against her bare thigh. She clawed at his shirt, pulling it out of his breeches. Anxious to feel his skin, her hands slid up the smooth warmth of his back.

He pulled his lips away, watching his long fingers caress her breasts, their tips slick and glistening from his mouth. Handling them almost reverently, his deft fingers continued their sensuous assault.

Then he was unfastening his breeches. She half sobbed with relief when his manhood sprang out, stiff and massive, impossibly ready. Grabbing the skirt of her mangled dress, he bunched it around Charlotte's waist. Then he cupped her buttocks, clasping her bare skin in his firm, strong grip.

The moment Cam's hard arousal breeched her, Charlotte's greedy body clutched him, drawing him further in. With a quiet roar, he slipped into her in one quick stroke. She cried out, the fullness of being joined with him banishing the desolation inside of her. Cam thrust into her with a ferocity they both craved. Her body softened, taking as much of him inside her as she could. Both moved in a frenzy, their bodies quickly finding a matching rhythm.

His tongue plundered Charlotte's mouth. His unshaven face abraded hers, stinging her sensitive skin. She kissed him back hard, intertwining her tongue with his, tasting the lingering brandy and the depth of their shared desperation.

Pounding against each other, they exploded together, a wild and noisy climax, crying out with relief as sensation crashed over them in powerful waves. They stilled for a moment, panting and intertwined, slick with perspiration. Charlotte's body pulsated, her legs quivered.

Still intimately connected, Cam buried his face in her neck. "Did I hurt you?" he murmured, his voice thick with remorse.

She shook her head, unable to speak, her eyelids burning with unshed tears. Charlotte clasped him to her, both loving and hating him all at once because of what he would do next.

He released her with a tenderness that made her want to weep. Cradling her jaw with warm fingers, Cam brushed a kiss over her lips, this one gentle and sweet. He lingered as if savoring her taste, then stepped back to fasten his breeches.

He tucked his shirt into his breeches, watching her as she pulled her chemise up to cover herself. She knew she looked awful with her hair askew and tousled about her shoulders. Her lips felt swollen and her cheeks on fire from where his unshaven face had scraped her tender skin.

A knock sounded on the door behind her. "Miss Livingston?" came the tentative voice of Clara, Willa's maid.

"Yes." Clearing her emotion-swollen throat, she struggled to put her bodice to rights. "Just a moment."

"It is Her Grace, ma'am," Clara said talking through the door. "It is her time. The babe is coming, and she's asking for you."

"Yes, of course," she called back. "Please tell the duchess I'll attend her soon."

Cam's inscrutable gaze flickered over her, then shifted, and he seemed very far away. "I must go as well."

His tone was polite, distant, as though he had already left her. Cam's warm hand moved over her shoulder to ease her away from the exit.

She swallowed hard, a useless attempt to ease the strangled feeling in her throat. "What will you do now?"

"You know what I must do." Regret glinted his eyes. "It would be wrong of me to allow more people to die when it is within my power to put a halt to the violence."

He reached for the door and hesitated, turning to lock gazes with her. The fine creases around his sunlit green eyes seemed to have deepened overnight. "But also know this. There will never be another woman for me. I have already taken you to wife in every way that matters. When you leave me, there will be no other. You are the wife of my heart."

She choked back a sob, her heart swelling until it felt too big for her chest. She could almost appreciate the irony of it—the reformed rake faithful to a phantom bride.

Cam pulled the door open and slipped out without giving her another look. The sound of his boots clicked a persistent beat on the marble floors as he strode away.

Listening to the sound of his footsteps grow ever lighter, Cam's words from that afternoon not so long ago ricocheted in her head. There was one way, he'd said, to quash the burgeoning Luddite movement. "*You must cut off the head of the snake. Ned Ludd must hang.*"

Sorrow exploded inside of her chest. Sliding to the floor with her back against the door, a sob erupted from her chest, and she let grief overwhelm her.

• • •

Several endless hours later, after Willa delivered a healthy son, Charlotte went in search of her brother. She'd looked desperately for Nathan before attending to the birth, but he'd been nowhere to be found. She could only hope now that he'd escaped before Cam had run him to ground.

When she didn't find him at the destroyed stable or the barn where the horses were being housed temporarily, anxiety stretched hard in her chest. She returned to the house to find Digby overseeing the cleanup of the solarium.

"Have you, by any chance, seen the coachman?" she asked the butler, her heart pounding.

"No, ma'am, not since he rode out early this morning with the marquess."

Her heart faltered. "Mister Fuller left with Lord Camryn?"

"Yes, miss. Just after my lord summoned the constable."

The band of anxiety around her chest tightened, squeezing the air out of her. "Where did they go?"

"He's gone." Cam's sure, steady voice sounded from behind her. "And he's not coming back."

She turned to face him. He looked like he'd ridden hard, his face bronzed from too much sun, weariness deepening the lines in his face. His riding clothes were wrinkled, his boots dusty from the road.

"You sent him away."

He nodded gravely. "I took care of everything."

Anguish filled her chest. She'd known to expect it. But, until this moment, Charlotte realized she hadn't truly believed Cam would go through with it. At her core, she hadn't thought him capable of wounding her so deeply and irreparably. What a fool she was.

Stumbling past him, desperate to get away, she ran blindly through the hallway. Nathan was gone. Perhaps had already been hanged. Had his life been taken at the very moment she'd helped bring new life into the world?

"Charlotte." Cam's urgent voice broke through the grief pounding in her ears. "Charlotte, wait!"

Stopping, she turned abruptly and flew at him, anguished fury ripping her insides. "Wait for what? What is there left to say?" She pounded his chest with both fists. "I know you summoned the constable."

"Calm yourself." He caught her wrists in a gentle grip. "I must tell you what has become of Nathan."

"Do you think I care to hear the details? Haven't you done enough?" Pressure pushed down on her chest. She couldn't breathe. Breaking loose from his grip, she turned and staggered to the terrace doors, eager to get outside. Maybe she could draw a breath in the fresh air.

She ran into the garden and bent over, with her hands on her knees, gasping the warm, still air into her flattened lungs.

Cam ran up behind her. "Charlotte, love—"

"Stop." Bending over, she struggled for breath. Her skin felt like it was being stretched inside out. "I beg of you. Please just let me alone."

"I thought you might like to know where your brother is."

"Must you paint a vivid picture of Nathan swinging from a tree?"

"More like sailing on a ship."

"I hate you—" Her words stumbled. "Sailing on a... what?"

Cam's voice gentled. "Fuller has decided to seek his fortune in the West Indies."

"What do you mean?" She straightened and peered into

Cam's face. "How is that possible?"

"As we speak, he is on one of my trading vessels, which should be pulling out to sea at any moment."

She drew a big gulp of air that soothed her desperate lungs. "But Digby said the constable came."

"And informed me that there would be no trial once Ludd was apprehended. He'd have been strung up to the nearest tree as an example to all of the other agitators."

"You didn't turn him in when you had the chance?"

"And allow them to make a gruesome spectacle of him? He'd have faced a hangman's noose without benefit of a trial. What manner of justice would that have been?"

The truth hit her with a head-dizzying rush. "Nathan is free?" she whispered, hardly able to believe it.

He nodded. "I accompanied him part of the way to the port. Once Mister Fuller arrives on the islands, he'll find a clerical job awaiting him at our West Indies shipping offices. As it happens, I've just become a partner with the duke in that operation."

She shook her head, trying in vain to sharpen her dazed mind. "I don't know what to say."

"It won't be long before Mister Fuller is comfortably settled into his new life."

A mammoth wave of relief almost swept her off her feet. Cam's arm shot out to lend her strength.

"So as you can see," he said, "all is well."

"Yes," she echoed, still unable to trust the feeling of joy beginning to swell in her chest. "All is well."

Chapter Seventeen

Over the next week, summer began its fade into fall, the verdant trees gradually transforming into a brilliant riot of reds, oranges, and golds. The softened sun slanted over Cam's mill town, casting the sand-colored stone cottages in picturesque hues of golden light.

Inhaling the crisp country air, Charlotte surveyed the area, which looked much as it had when she'd last visited several weeks ago. No obvious scars from the rioting and turmoil were visible. Tables had been set out near the white stone church, where women bustled about preparing for the picnic, which all of the workers would be attending later in the day. The town itself appeared busier now. A tidy new store had opened, and the children had begun attending school.

"Does this place have a name?" she asked Cam as they strolled through the center of town.

"We haven't really settled on one, but I have a few

thoughts."

"Such as?"

"Charlottesfield has a certain cache. Or Charlottesford."

She smiled, shaking her head. "How you do go on."

"I've also considered Charlotteham."

"Definitely *not* Charlotteham. That sounds like a dish served at a country dinner table."

"Charlottesly."

"Stop," she said laughing as they reached the schoolhouse. "Let's go see the children at their studies."

"Sorry to disappoint you, love, but the pupils have the day off for the picnic."

"Oh." She made a moue of disappointment. "Well, I should still like to see it."

Although absent of children, the schoolroom felt very alive. Their artwork adorned one wall. She studied them, smiling at the most rudimentary ones, the bright colors and simple strokes obviously done by the youngest children. She walked along the sun-kissed room, taking in the smell of paint, fresh wood, and lingering scent of active children. The map on the wall caught her attention and her gaze darted to the West Indies.

"We shall hear from him soon enough," Cam's gentle voice said from behind her. "It has only been a fortnight."

"Yes, of course." Heaviness settled into her chest. "I shall never be able to repay you for what you've done."

"What is it, darling?" He drew her around to face him. "Why this sadness? I've seen it more than once since Nathan left us."

She lowered her gaze. "It is nothing."

"It is *not* nothing." He put a finger under her chin, tilting her face upward until she looked into his determined amber-green gaze. "We agreed there would be no more secrets between us."

"It is that I worry."

"About?"

"That my selfishness will end up ruining you." Her lungs felt sore. "Passion fades. And once it does you'll be left with a wife who is Ned Ludd's sister. If that were ever to become known, you would be destroyed."

"We've been over this." He drew a breath, slowly releasing it through his nostrils before continuing. "None of us can know what the future will bring, except that you and I will marry. You could already be carrying my child in your womb."

"You loved me enough to let Nathan go. Perhaps I should love you enough to let you go."

He laughed. *Laughed*. While she contemplated making the greatest sacrifice imaginable. "I fail to see what is so amusing," she sniffed, drawing away.

"You fool." He closed his long fingers closed around her upper arms, holding her in place. "I let him go for you, yes. But I didn't compromise my principles. In all likelihood, they were going to torture him and hang him without a trial. Allowing that to take place would have compromised my sense of right and wrong." He pulled her closer. "Do not act so beetle-headed. If anything, you helped me examine my principles and stay true to them."

She drew back to study his face. "But you said, when you left the library, after we'd—" She flushed at the memory. "That I knew what you must do."

"I'm no saint." One corner of his mouth lifted. "I wanted

to quell the violence. Sending your brother to the West Indies was no accident. He can hardly cause trouble from there."

"Still, you took a great risk."

"I couldn't let them string your brother up. He didn't stand a chance. Perhaps if there had been a possibility of him having a fair trial." Cupping her face, he planted a firm kiss on her lips. "I love you, Charlotte. You bring out the best in me, make me demand the best of myself. You cannot even consider leaving me."

"I love you, too," she whispered, the ache in her chest easing. "How could I not? Look at you. You are perfect."

He took her into his arms, holding her tightly to him. "We are getting married next week. Say yes and promise me you'll never even consider leaving me again."

"I do want to marry you as soon as possible." She snuggled into his warm embrace, inhaling his familiar, musky, masculine scent mixed with horses and leather. "I promise to never leave you. I doubt I could survive it."

"Then we are agreed. Finally," he said, pressing his lips softly to hers.

Remembering where they were, she pulled away. "Oh, Cam, now I can help you with your school project."

He grabbed her before she could move completely away from him. "Oh, no. You are not going anywhere." He pulled her close and kissed her deeply.

Exhilaration shot through her, happiness made her heart buoyant. "Cam, we mustn't. Not here. This is a schoolhouse."

"Balderdash. This is where people come to be educated." He drew her down to the gleaming wood floor, his skillful hands moving over her, doing their magic until her legs wavered. "And, as I recall from the last time we were here, we have a most important lesson to complete."

"As if I could forget." She sighed contentedly, sinking to the floor with him. "I wouldn't dream of arguing with such an accomplished instructor. After all, I am most determined to be an excellent student."

Epilogue

Leaning against the study door frame, Charlotte smiled at the sight of Cam on all fours with the twins scrambling across his back, squealing with delighted laughter.

"Neigh, neigh!" he growled in a falsely menacing voice, swaying from side to side in an attempt to throw them. His cravat was a mess from the game, and his hair was askew as usual. "I am too wild a horsey for you."

The scene was at odds with the serious backdrop of the marquess's study, with its Oriental rugs, dark wood paneling, and rich leather seating.

"Hold on, Caro!" Sophia garbled, her wild, amber curls bouncing, delight glowing in her soft blue eyes.

Caroline, more serious than her sister, held on with an intent expression in her golden-green eyes, her soft brown curls catching the air. Their father succeeded in gently throwing both of them to the carpet, ending the game with the girls giggling and squirming, trying to escape his tickling fingers.

"Well," said Charlotte with a wry smile. "It is good of you not to overexcite them just before bedtime."

He grinned at her from where he sat on the carpet, hands planted behind him as Sophia and Caroline climbed all over him as though he were a tree. "Girls, we should tell Mama to come and play horsey with us." A naughty glint flashed in his eyes. "Do you want to play horsey with us, Mama?"

"Yes, yes!" the girls squealed in unison. They jumped up and ran to her, each tugging on one of her hands.

Laughing, she knelt to draw them both into a big hug, peppering noisy kisses along their necks. "Perhaps another time," she said firmly, standing up. "Now you must run along to Nurse, who is waiting to give you your bath." The girls moaned, throwing a petulant look their father's way, looking for support.

Cam held up his hands, palms facing upward in a gesture of surrender. "We cannot go against both Mama and Nurse. They are far too fearsome." He growled, making a sudden move toward the twins. Sophia and Caroline squealed in anxious laughter and raced out the door to where their nurse awaited them.

Watching them go, Charlotte shook her head. "You shouldn't excite them so just before bedtime. It is not fair to Nurse."

"Are you going to spank me for being naughty?" Cam jumped to his feet and sashayed over to pull her into his arms for a long, unhurried kiss. Her heart did a little flip, as it always did when he touched her, even after two children and three years of marriage. She finally pulled away, remembering why she'd sought him out in the first place. "The post has come."

He eyed the letter in her hand. "Who has written to you?"

"It is from Nathan." Her heart floated in her chest. "Why did you not tell me he is now overseeing your West Indies trading operation?"

"Fuller has expanded the business twofold since he's been there. Hart and I have discussed eventually offering him part of the business."

"You continue to surprise me every day," she said softly, handing him a second letter. "This came for you."

"For me?" Taking it from her, he tore it open. "It's from Sebastian. His wife has finally returned home."

"*His wife*?" Charlotte exclaimed, forgetting all about her brother. "Sebastian has married?"

"Yes," he said absentmindedly, still reading the letter. "Of course."

"Of course?" She shook her head. "When? Why did he not invite us?"

"That would hardly have been possible. It was years ago. Well before we met."

"Sebastian took a wife *years ago*?" She put her hand over the letter to draw his full attention. "Why have I never heard of this before now?"

He looked up with a shrug. "You never asked."

"That's because I assumed—" She halted, embarrassed to voice the thought aloud.

His gaze sharpened with interest. "You assumed what?"

"That perhaps he had no interest in…um…females."

His brows furrowed with confusion, and then shot up when he took her meaning. "You thought Sebastian was a molly?" Cam threw back his rumpled mane and shouted a laugh. "Far from it, I assure you."

"Well, what did you expect me to think?" She put her fists on her hips. "No one ever mentions marriage around him and your family's silence on this particular issue seems quite deliberate."

His smile melted. "It is a sensitive matter. The marriage was not of his choosing."

"What happened?"

"The girl was but a child and Sebastian wasn't much older when it was arranged." Putting the letter aside, he slipped into a chair and drew her down to sit on his lap. "He only laid eyes on her that once, on the day they married."

She draped an arm around his neck. "Why did he consent to it?"

"He didn't have much choice." His deep sigh weighted the air. "The union was arranged to settle a gaming debt between my father and the Duke of Traherne.

"The Duke of Traherne?" She drew back. "Sebastian is married to the daughter of a *duke* and you never thought to mention it?"

"Who will one day be duchess in her own right through an act of parliament. There is no male heir."

"Astounding. Where has he hidden her all of these years?"

"Mirabella was in finishing school and then abroad." He nuzzled her neck. "Enough about that. Where were we?"

"It is nowhere near enough of that. I want the full story at supper." She pushed up from his lap. "Come along, Cook won't appreciate it if her creations are served cold."

He grabbed her hand, pulling her back down onto his lap. "Not so fast." He shifted to kiss her deeply. "We have not had a chance to play horsey, yet."

"You are incorrigible." Charlotte laughed, running her hand through his tousled hair in a hapless attempt to tidy it. "Besides, you have already taken me on the ride of my life."

Drawing her hand from his hair, he placed a warm, lingering kiss on the inside of her palm. "Ah, but this is still just the beginning." He gazed into her eyes.

"Let's go for a ride, my love. A long and glorious ride."

Acknowledgements

Writing begins as a solitary endeavor but many skilled hands are required to bring a book to publication and I must thank them:

First to my editor, Alethea Spiridon Hopson, for making this a much better book than it was when it came to her, and to my wonderful agent, Kevan Lyon, for bringing us together.

To Megann Yaqub for her incredible generosity and unwavering support, for reading every last word, many times over, from first draft to last, and for never failing to offer smart, insightful feedback.

To my husband, who told me I should be penning my own stories long before I thought I could, and for calling my work "art" from the very beginning. To my exceptional boys, Zach and Laith, who are the best thing that ever happened to me. Thank you for being patient while your mom pursued her writing dream. I love you more than I can say.

To my mother, for being unfailingly supportive of my writing, even though my books contain scenes that make her blush.

And, finally, to my father, a man of boundless intellect, who taught me everything I know about unconditional love, the pursuit of excellence, and living an authentic life. My only regret is that he passed before my writing journey began. I know he would have gotten a real kick out of holding my published book in his hands. This one's for you, Dad.

ABOUT THE AUTHOR

Diana Quincy is an award-winning television journalist who decided she'd rather make up stories where a happy ending is always guaranteed.

Growing up as a foreign service brat, Diana lived in many countries and is now settled in Virginia with her husband and two sons. When not bent over her laptop or trying to keep up with laundry, she enjoys reading, spending time with her family and dreams of traveling much more than her current schedule (and budget) allows.

Diana loves to hear from readers. You can follow her on Twitter @Diana_Quincy or visit her website at www.dianaquincy.com.

Other books by Diana Quincy
COMPROMISING WILLA
Book Three of the Accidental Peers Series

England 1805

Lady Wilhelmina Stanhope is ruined and everyone knows it. Back in Town for the first season since her downfall, Willa plans to remain firmly on the shelf, assuming only fortune hunters will want her now. Instead she focuses on her unique tea blends, secretly supporting a coffee house which employs poor women and children. If her clandestine involvement in trade is discovered, she'll be ruined. Again.

No one is more shocked by Willa's lack of quality suitors than the newly minted Duke of Hartwell. Having just returned from India, the dark duke is instantly attracted to the mysterious wallflower. His pursuit is hampered by the ruthless Earl of Bellingham, who once jilted Willa and is now determined to reclaim her.

Caught between the clash of two powerful men, a furious Willa refuses to concede her independence to save her reputation. But will she compromise her heart?

Made in the USA
Coppell, TX
11 April 2022

76384587R10144